Caryl Brahms (Doris Caroline Abrahams) was born in Surrey in 1901, into a colourful Sephardic Jewish family who had come from Turkey a generation earlier. She was educated privately before studying at the Royal Academy of Music. She began to write for the *Evening Standard*, then the *Daily Telegraph*, where she was ballet correspondent. Her first book, *Footnotes to Ballet*, appeared in 1936, and her long partnership with S. J. Simon, fellow lodger in London, started in 1937. After his death she continued to write and then, in the late 1950s, began a second remarkable partnership, with Ned Sherrin, who edited her memoirs, *Too Dirty for the Windmill*, published posthumously by Constable. A governor of the National Theatre, Caryl Brahms remained a forceful figure in the theatrical world until her death in 1982.

S. J. Simon (Seca Jascha Skidelsky) was born in 1904 in Harbin, Manchuria, into an equally idiosyncratic White Russian Jewish family. During his lifetime he was famous as a bridge player – representative of Great Britain in numerous championships, joint inventor of the Acol System, and author of the classic *Why You Lose at Bridge*. His wife, Carmel Withers, was also an international bridge player. He died in London in 1948.

Brahms and Simon published *A Bullet in the Ballet* in 1937 and followed this hit with *Casino for Sale* (1938). During the war they turned to 'backstairs history', producing hilarious versions of the past in books like *Don't, Mr Disraeli!* (1940) and *No Bed for Bacon* (1941). The close, if occasionally turbulent, partnership of these 'Lunatics of Genius', with their bubbling wit and fantastic invention, is unique in British comic writing.

ENVOY ON EXCURSION

Caryl Brahms
& S. J. Simon

New Introduction by
Ned Sherrin

THE HOGARTH PRESS
LONDON

To
ADELINE AND WALTER FORDE
whose optimism
we trust
will some day be rewarded

Published in 1988 by
The Hogarth Press
30 Bedford Square, London WC1B 3RP

First published in Great Britain by Michael Joseph Ltd 1940
Copyright © Caryl Brahms and S. J. Simon
Introduction copyright © Ned Sherrin 1988

All rights reserved. No part of this publication may be reproduced, stored in a retrieval system, or transmitted in any form, or by any means, electronic, mechanical, photocopying, recording or otherwise, without the prior permission of the publisher.

British Library Cataloguing in Publication Data

Brahms, Caryl
Envoy on excursion
Rn: Simon Jascha Skidelsky   I. Title
II. Simon, S.J.
823'.912[F]   PR6052.R264/

ISBN 0 7012 0794 9

Printed in Great Britain by
Cox & Wyman Ltd
Reading, Berkshire

INTRODUCTION

Envoy on Excursion dates from that extraordinary, uncertain period at the beginning of the Second World War. 'Fortunes of War' country, as farce. It was written in late 1939 when Caryl Brahms and S.J. Simon had already published three novels: the classic *A Bullet in the Ballet*, a sequel, *Casino for Sale*, and another joke on 'funny foreigners', *The Elephant is White* (later made into a movie simply because a film producer came upon his teenage daughter reading it and laughing aloud). Brahms and Simon thought of *Envoy* as part of their war effort. They felt they had a duty to make their apprehensive fellow countrymen laugh.

Brahms's ancestors, Sephardic Jews, had migrated centuries earlier from Spain to Constantinople and then, in the nineteenth century, to England; Simon was born in Harbin, Manchuria. Both had changed their names when they became writing collaborators. Caryl Brahms began life in Croydon as Doris Caroline Abrahams and S.J. Simon – whose nickname was 'Skid' – was orginally Seca Jascha Skidelsky. 'Brahms and Simon' had, by 1939, become a familiar partnership and a much more manageable title for British readers.

For all their alien backgrounds and boundless eccentricities both were fanatically devoted to the British way of life – though they did see it through their own highly individual eyes. Bridge and ballet, greyhound racing and show jumping, large hats and dark glasses (Brahms), and soup-stained, ash-bespattered ties (Simon) were their passions and their trademarks.

While they were writing *Envoy on Excursion* they were still hoping that a film would be made of their first success, *A Bullet in the Ballet*. In it the immortal Ballet Stroganoff had first burst onto the scene. In her memoir, *Too Dirty for the Windmill*, Caryl records:

One day, with the war looming nearer and nearer, we had a letter from a film producer, Walter Jarve. He wanted the rights in *Bullet* and offered us £100 for them. We knew that as an offer for a film this was a bad joke – worse than any we had perpetrated in our book. But we accepted it in the belief that it would at least serve to show us what a film script should look like. £50 each had to be better than seven ha'penny, ten shillings, three guineas, five guineas, or fifteen guineas, the individual earnings of our partnership to date, and our publisher seemed to share much the same view of our work. War clouds were gathering overhead – we ignored them. One at least had a silver lining in the shape of a trip to Paris to advise with our expertise on *Petroushka*, which was to be recreated in the film of *Bullet* by Nijinska, the sister of the great Nijinsky. We scampered round Paris for two carefree, luxurious days, during which time our counsel was sought once only.

'What's the difference between Russian and English music?' we were asked. There was only one answer.

'Russian's louder,' we said.

Their visit to Paris did not advance the movie, but rumours of a production continued to reach them. Perhaps it was in this spirit that they dedicated *Envoy* 'to Adeline and Walter Forde, whose optimism we trust will someday be rewarded.' In this case it was not – except in an advantageous sale of the rights to *Bullet* in which the creators did not share.

'Mad world, mad kings, mad composition.' Brahms and Simon quote before their story begins, a madly apposite line from *King John* (Act II Scene i). Only the first edition of *Envoy* carries a disclaimer which was dropped when the book was reprinted in 1954 and 1978: 'All the characters in this book are imaginary: particulary Herr Von Papen, whom the authors are convinced they have imagined.' Poor Von Papen, so potent a symbol of German diplomacy in 1939, so forgotten after a mere fifteen years that he no longer deserved to be a small joke in an apologia. He remains in the book as a running gag – a device to which Brahms and Simon were addicted – rather like their use of the famous Russian Diaghilev designer, Alexandre Benois, who never seems to arrive when Stroganoff expects him to appear at an important premier . . . 'Benois, if 'ee come.'

Benois certainly fails to arrive in Rumba-Rumba, the capital of Insomnia, the Ruritanian kingdom which is the scene of much of the action in *Envoy*, though Stroganoff and his ballet are there in all their competitive splendour, unfurling *fouettés* and failing to 'schange small scheques'. It was the last book in which the two authors double-mindedly chased funny names: Señor Centime, King Hannibal the Hothead, the Countess de Kashkavar, Stung and Bauldstok . . . Later they (or at least Caryl, I cannot speak for Simon, whom I never met) were embarrassed by this slapstick tendency; but they were both determined to make their fellow countrymen smile in the anxious days which led up to Dunkirk. They wrote quickly and topically. To anyone who dimly remembers that awkward period at the beginning of the war, the air of uncertainty is captured in exuberant fashion. Whitehall already has its 'Sir Humphrey' – he is at the Ministry of Elimination and the hectic plot starts with the murder of a foreign diplomat in his office. Detective Inspector Adam Quill of Scotland Yard – the sanity factor in *Bullet* and *Casino for Sale* – is in charge of the 'Department for the Protection of Neutrals', based in an oast house in Kent, and is given the job because, before the war, he had investigated the Ballet Stroganoff and therefore 'had experience of coping with the Foreign Mentality'. As Brahms and Simon say, 'One of the better jokes of the War'.

I shall not try to unravel the plot which takes Adam Quill to Insomnia; but look out for Canterbury Brindle, the wizard Foreign Correspondent, full of echoes of Sefton Delmer and Vernon Bartlett; the rift between Stung and Bauldstok and a country weekend wasted on beagling; a reunion with Madame Arenskaya and a reflection on Goebbels and Hitler. Señor Centime, a foreign journalist, is talking:

'At least when I was in Germany they gave me many stories to print. The good Doctor Goebbels wrote them himself. A charming man.' He sighed.

'Kind to children?' suggested Quill.

Señor Centime shook his head. 'No,' he said. 'That's Hitler.'

The year before Caryl Brahms had published an ironic poem in *Punch* which ended:

> It's peace! It's peace!
> We're going to use diplomacy
> For every strained relation.
> We're going to live on friendly terms
> With each and every nation.
> And we've just completed all our plans
>   for swift evacuation,
> It's peace! It's peace!

The international uncertainty was omnipresent. In her wartime diary, Caryl detailed the publication of *Envoy on Excursion*: 'It appeared on the day Hitler marched into Holland, so relegating the Maginot line to lavender and making *us* out of date before copies reached the shops.' Nearly fifty years on the book captures some of the hectic confusion of its provenance and it has a documentary recall which marches alongside its lunatic invention. Repeats of 'Spitting Image' in 2038 will be lucky if they can match its survival qualities. Caryl goes on in her diary to record one reaction to their book:

Harold Kahn, who was a very special influence on my life, had, while his regiment was at Lille, just received an early copy, and marched into Belgium with it. It kept right on retreating with him till the order came through to the BEF [British Expeditionary Force] to make for the coast. It looked as though Harold would be taken prisoner, together with the greater part of the BEF, and he didn't think a Brahms-Simon book would make the right impression on the Nazis. So, three-quarters through, he scuttled *Envoy*. He was furious at having to leave the tale unfinished and almost the first thing he asked when he arrived in England after twenty-four hours on the beaches at Dunkirk, was how *Envoy* ended. 'I had to get back to find out,' he told me.

The collaborators went on to publish eight more books before S.J. Simon's sudden death in 1948. Caryl Brahms completed their work in progress, *You Were There*, and went on to publish more novels, essays and criticism on her own and to write novels, plays, songs, radio and television scripts and musicals with me. She died in 1982, three days before her eighty-first birthday.

Ned Sherrin, London 1987

'Mad world, mad kings, mad composition.'
SHAKESPEARE

CHAPTER

1

RETURNING to his office, Sir Humphrey Spratt was annoyed to find his swivel chair occupied by a stranger. A bearded stranger. Wearing a suit much too narrow at the waist. To make it worse the johnny was dead. He had no right to be there in the first place.

It was five o'clock on a Thursday afternoon in the late autumn of '39.

At 4.30 p.m. the yellow light heralding the approach of enemy aircraft had shone in every room in the Ministry of Elimination. It had shone, too, in every room in the Ministry of Information, the Ministry of Distribution, the Ministries of Demand, Supply and Exchange, and in all the other Ministries in Whitehall. In a few minutes a red light would replace the yellow to show that the sirens were sounding all over London. Calmly the Departmental heads folded their portfolios. Coolly their staffs collected their gas masks. Quietly, without panic, they all went into the corridors and marched steadily down, pausing politely to wave on, and be waved forward by, any of the neutrals in their midst—all very, very British.

Efficiently they shepherded themselves into the cellars and looked round for chairs to offer old ladies. There were neither. Sir Humphrey scribbled a hasty memo to order half a dozen of both.

Thirty minutes later a green light shone through the Whitehall cellars. All clear. No sirens had sounded over London at all. It had been a false alarm.

Regretfully Sir Humphrey turned his back on the dart board. The staff hurried back to their rooms, jostling past the neutrals who couldn't find the way to the exits.

Back in his room, Sir Humphrey came to the conclusion that he was baffled. He rang a bell. Nothing happened. The efficient Miss Peacock was downstairs talking Hungarian to a Roumanian and was fully occupied.

Sir Humphrey rang twice. This should summon his private secretary, Joe what's-his-name, who could be relied on to bustle in briskly and completely misunderstand what was wanted of him.

The door opened. Joe bustled in briskly. Sternly Sir Humphrey pointed to the body.

'This johnny,' he said. 'How did he get here?'

Joe pondered.

'Don't know,' he decided. 'But I'll soon have him out.' He strode across purposefully.

'Stop,' shouted Sir Humphrey. 'He's dead.'

Joe looked at the body. Joe looked at Sir Humphrey. Joe clicked his tongue.

'I suppose,' he hazarded, 'it was absolutely necessary.'

'What do you mean?' said Sir Humphrey.

'I know,' said Joe. 'I quite understand. State secrets. A leakage. You had to kill him.'

Sir Humphrey glared.

'And now,' continued Joe, 'it's up to us to dispose of the body. Leave it to me.' He strode over.

'Drop it,' shouted Sir Humphrey. 'You must be mad. And that reminds me,' he snapped, 'was it you who put that rubber dart in my stack?'

Joe shifted his stance uneasily. 'Practical joke,' he muttered. 'Knew you'd see the funny side,' he said doubtfully.

Stymied, Sir Humphrey returned to the body.

'Stop fooling,' he said. 'Listen. I found this man dead in my chair. How did he get here?'

Joe looked blank.

'Where does he come from?'

Joe shook his head.

'Who is he?'

Joe gave it up.

'Tell you what,' said Sir Humphrey, inspired. 'Let's see if he's got a visiting card on him.'

Together they went over the body.

'No visiting cards,' said Sir Humphrey, emerging with a cigarette-lighter captured from the stranger's pocket. Joe what's-his-name took it from him and clicked it. It worked.

'Curious,' said Joe.

They bent over the body again.

A door shut with a snap behind them. They swung round. The Roumanian having given up in despair, the efficient Miss Peacock had returned. She took in the situation at a glance.

'I suppose,' she said, controlling herself superbly, 'it was absolutely necessary.'

They glared at her.

'State secrets,' said Miss Peacock. 'A leakage. I understand. And now I suppose we must get rid of the body.' She looked vaguely at an attaché case.

'Listen,' said Sir Humphrey. 'Get this clear.'

The phone bell rang.

It was the Ministry of Information wanting to know if there had been an air raid anywhere.

'No,' snapped Sir Humphrey.

'Bad luck,' said the Ministry of Information and hung up.

The efficient Miss Peacock had picked up the stranger's gas mask and was brooding over it.

'It's not a bit like mine,' she said.

'It's foreign,' said Joe. 'Wonder if the man is an alien.'

'Must be,' said Sir Humphrey. 'Look at the cut of his coat.'

They gazed at the waistline with disapproval.

There was a knock at the door.

'Quick,' hissed Sir Humphrey. 'The screen.'

The efficient Miss Peacock placed it round the desk.

'Come in,' said Sir Humphrey with perfect self-control.

A small man in spectacles ventured into the room.

'Ah, Señor Centime!' Sir Humphrey bounded across and shook him warmly by the hand. 'You've brought me a story to suppress—what?' He laughed heartily at his own joke.

Señor Centime did not laugh. London correspondents of important neutral papers such as the *Insomnian Daily Sentinel* had long ago stopped laughing at having their stories suppressed by the Ministry of Elimination.

'I hope not,' he said earnestly. 'I have only been allowed to send one story this week and that was broadcast in America three days before you released it.'

Sir Humphrey sighed. How difficult this johnny was being. The Ministry of Elimination had done its utmost to offer every facility to the neutral pressmen. They had set aside a special room for them, furnished lavishly with telephones, each connected to a censor who could cut them off if necessary, or even forget to switch them on. They had provided them with a squash court, which they seemed curiously reluctant to use, and they had put an interpreter, Miss Peacock, at their disposal. And still they grumbled. Would they never understand that this was war and that no news of any kind could be permitted in any country whatsoever?

He took a look at the manuscript.

'Impossible,' he said promptly. 'Where's my pencil?'

He stretched out a hand. The screen got in the way. Testily he pushed it. It rocked giddily. The efficient Miss Peacock arrived just too late to catch it.

The body was exposed to neutral eyes.

Señor Centime looked at it curiously.

'He is dead,' he said. 'Why,' he demanded, puzzled, 'did you kill him?'

Sir Humphrey closed the door. In a crisis he developed unexpected qualities.

'Señor Centime,' he said impressively. 'His Majesty's Government will take you into its confidence. We do not know who this man is.'

'You do not know?' said Señor Centime. He seemed amazed.

The telephone rang.

'I say,' said the Ministry of Information, 'have you chappies heard anything about a Señor Sardinko—a foreign johnny? The Cabinet has been waiting for him all afternoon.'

'No,' said Sir Humphrey testily, and hung up.

CHAPTER

2

DETECTIVE-INSPECTOR ADAM QUILL, back to the force for the duration, sat at his desk in his office at Scotland Yard. It was an oast-house. It was in the middle of Kent. It was sandbagged up to the eyebrows—no cow could hope to get near it. It was the Department for the Protection of Neutrals and was responsible for every neutral arriving, departing, and even remaining in this country. That it had been evacuated to a place where no neutral could hope to find it was perhaps an oversight.

To put Quill in charge of it on the grounds of his experience in coping with the foreign mentality (The Stroganoff Russian Ballet) was definitely one of the better jokes of the war. But Quill, gazing ruefully at the dictionaries on his desk, did not think it at all funny. Even now he was coping with a letter that began 'Distinguished Sir,' worked itself into a frenzy over a camera unkindly torn from it at Bow Street, a present, Quill was given to understand, from an honourable aunt, and containing nothing but some harmless pictures, of no interest except to the owner, of some so noble openings to underground aerodromes, and ended up with a flowery threat to bring the matter up before the League of Nations as soon as it could be persuaded to meet.

Quill sighed and reached for the printed answer that dealt with such letters.

The telephone rang. A snarl came across the wire.

'That you, Quill? Why didn't you answer before?'

Quill recognized the voice of his chief.

'We've lost a neutral,' said the Snarl.

'Careless,' said Quill.

'Shut up!' The Snarl became a bellow. 'He's a very important neutral. The whole Cabinet is waiting for him. Go and find him at once.'

'Where shall I look?' asked Quill.

The bellow became inarticulate. Between blasts Quill gathered that the important neutral was an envoy from the Central European Kingdom of Insomnia, that he was called Auguste Sardinko, that he had arrived at the Savoy Hotel last night, and that he had failed to turn up at Downing Street that afternoon. And now the entire Cabinet were waiting for him, Quill, to get going. So would he stop asking fatuous questions and snap into it.

Galvanized, Quill shot into the yard. A pretty girl was pressing the self-starter of a car.

'Hey,' shouted Quill. 'Stop.'

Belinda Briggs stopped. 'Just going to take mother shopping,' she said brightly.

'On Government petrol?' said Quill. 'Oh no you don't. You're taking me to London.'

'But it's four o'clock,' said Belinda. 'And I've got a date at six.'

'Break it,' said Quill. 'We're going to the 'Savoy.' '

'Darling,' said Belinda, and let in the clutch. 'Can we have oysters?' she asked hopefully.

'Now see here,' said Quill. 'Let's get this thing clear. There's a war on. Got that? You're my driver for the duration. Got that? It's your job to take me about on my police work. Got that? And I'm not a war-time substitute for a boy friend. Got that?'

'Easily,' said Belinda. She trod on the accelerator and missed a farm waggon by inches.

* * * * *

At half-past five Quill's car pulled up outside the Ministry of Elimination. Immediately a tin helmet bobbed out from behind a sandbag and ordered it to move on. The tin helmet was surmounting two knapsacks rampant on a pair of plus-fours. The whole formed a police officer of the War Reserve.

'Sorry, old man,' said the temporary police officer. (Eight-hour shifts—seven day week—£3 wage—if he could prove he needed it.) 'You'll have to move along.' He smiled radiantly.

Quill felt a little uncomfortable at so much misdirected charm until he realized it was trained on Belinda. He slipped quietly out of the car and left them to it.

The first thing to do was to find the entrance to the Ministry. Even for a detective this was no easy task. There are three schools of thought in the disposition of sandbags. School One bolsters up the portico, leaving the rest of the building to take care of itself. School Two spreads them on the pavements to trip up blacked-out pedestrians, while the third school—the artistic—is bent on making the most of their opportunity to black out as much of the architecture as possible. This last school, flushed with its successes in blacking out fire alarms and equestrian statues, had set itself to make a really good job of the Ministry of Elimination. A small part of the roof was still visible, but they were working on that now.

Quill nozed hopelessly through the masses of sandbags looking for an opening. Not until a bowler hat, peering through an aperture, whistled shrilly, did Quill discover the entrance to the maze. It was camouflaged by sacking. Pushing this aside, he groped his way to the entrance hall. The bowler hat came to meet him.

'Can't come in,' said the bowler hat importantly.

'Banner,' said Quill. 'What on earth are you doing in a bowler?'

'C.I.D.,' said Sergeant Banner proudly.

Quill looked at him. Gone was the tight blue stomach, the breathed-on buttons, the triumphant stripes. Sergeant Banner was attired in the full glories of 'civvies,' plus a bowler hat, the badge of the Sergeant of the C.I.D. Judging by the expectant look in his eye, Quill gathered it was only a matter of time before he got the promotion that would entitle him to an umbrella.

'What are you doing here?' he asked.

Sergeant Banner smirked. 'Guarding the neutrals in our midst. Very important.' He looked round apprehensively. 'Didn't ought to have told you that.'

'Quite,' said Quill severely. 'The information might be of value to the enemy.'

Sergeant Banner went dim.

'As you're guarding the neutrals,' said Quill, 'perhaps you can help me. I'm looking for one.'

'We've got plenty round here,' said Sergeant Banner spaciously. 'What sort would you like?'

'He doesn't work here,' said Quill. 'He's an Insomnian. The whole Cabinet have been waiting for him since three o'clock.'

'Cor,' said Sergeant Banner, impressed.

'I've traced him here,' said Quill a little wearily.

He had. Señor Sardinko had breakfasted at the Savoy at nine, gone to a cinema at ten, emerged at twelve, had an aperitif at the Café Royal. He had lunched at the Regent Palace and taken his coffee at the Trocadero. He had bought a book in Charing Cross Road, a pair of socks in Oxford Street, and a cigar at Marble Arch. He had boarded a bus for Whitehall, got off very angry at Swiss Cottage, and taken a taxi back to the Ministry of Elimination. Quill had been to all these places.

'He should have arrived at about half-past four,' said Quill.

Something about the time stirred a chord in Banner's breast.

'Ah, yes,' he said with relish. 'A sight for sore eyes, that was.'

Quill looked at him.

'That was the time Sir Humphrey got beaten up at darts,' explained the Sergeant. 'Someone put a rubber dart in his stack. I didn't half laugh.' He sat down, his shoulders heaving at the recollection. 'I bet it was Joe what's-his-name done it. Bright boy, Joe,' said Sergeant Banner admiringly.

'Darts,' said Quill disapprovingly. 'Is that the way they pass the time at the Ministry of Elimination?'

'Well, there was an air-raid warning,' said Sergeant Banner defensively. 'We were in the cellar.'

'There hasn't been an air raid,' said Quill, exasperated.

'I wouldn't know about that,' said Banner righteously. 'All I know is we got the warning.'

'So,' said Quill, 'you spend your time lurking in cellars, disloyally laughing at your chief, instead of looking after a very distinguished neutral trying to find his way in.'

Banner blushed. 'No one told me he was coming.'

'So you don't know whether he arrived or not?'

Banner considered. 'No,' he said frankly. 'I don't.'

'Take me to Sir Humphrey,' said Quill.

Together they tried to find a lift.

* * * * *

'But why,' Señor Centime was saying indignantly, 'do you not send for the police?'

Miss Peacock looked shocked. Joe what's-his-name clicked his tongue. Sir Humphrey explained kindly.

'There is a war,' he pointed out. 'The police are very busy enrolling new members. We must not disturb them unnecessarily.'

Señor Centime pondered this.

'Besides,' said Sir Humphrey, clinching the matter, 'this johnny has been found at the Ministry of Elimination. We cannot divulge the fact to anybody until we have discovered if it is important.'

There was a knock at the door.

'Quick,' hissed Sir Humphrey. 'The screen.'

Miss Peacock went smartly into action.

'I rely on your discretion, Señor,' said Sir Humphrey, lighting a nonchalant cigar. In an emergency he was superb.

'Come in,' he said.

Quill came in. So did Sergeant Banner.

'I'm Detective-Inspector Adam Quill from Scotland Yard,' Quill introduced himself.

'Good Gad,' said Sir Humphrey, stepping back.

The screen tottered. But this time Miss Peacock was ready for it.

'I have come,' said Quill, 'to enquire about the movements of a Señor Auguste Sardinko.'

'Never heard of him,' said Sir Humphrey, well pleased. 'Have a cigarette?'

Joe passed a case. Quill stretched out a hand. He drew, he pulled, he tugged. The cigarette stayed where it was.

'Sorry,' said Joe, abashed. 'Passed you the wrong case.'

'Glued on,' said Sergeant Banner gloating. 'We caught the P.M. with it last week.'

'Oh,' said Sir Humphrey. 'Did we? Is that why he behaved like a bear with a sore head?'

'Not at all,' said Miss Peacock loyally. 'The Prime Minister has a great sense of humour. He just wasn't feeling himself.'

'About Señor Sardinko,' essayed Quill.

'Try the Ministry of Information,' suggested Sir Humphrey. 'Oh, no,' he remembered. 'I believe they rang me up to ask about him. Try Scotland Yard.'

'They're trying me,' said Quill. 'I've traced the Señor here.'

'In that case,' said Sir Humphrey, 'the thing is simple. Ask Banner. He's sure to know. Miss Peacock, ring for Sergeant Banner.'

The efficient Miss Peacock rang.

'I'm here,' said Sergeant Banner apologetically.

'You've been quick,' said Sir Humphrey. 'Well done. Take the Inspector downstairs,' he said with meaning, 'and tell him all he wants to know. Good-bye. Glad I've been able to help you.'

He shook hands with Quill. The interview was at an end.

'I've asked Banner already,' said Quill, starting the interview all over again. 'He doesn't know.'

Sir Humphrey glared. 'How is that?'

'He was in the cellar,' said Quill amiably, 'watching a game of darts.'

Sir Humphrey winced.

'Have you,' asked Quill, 'any department that deals with the Kingdom of Insomnia?'

'Insomnia!' Señor Centime, who had been fidgeting on a chair, bobbed into the limelight. 'I am an Insomnian—I am at your service.'

Miss Peacock looked at him reproachfully. Señor Centime subsided. Quill nodded at him. 'Señor Sardinko,' he explained, 'is a delegate from the Insomnian Government.'

Señor Centime smiled. 'You tell me that!'

Sir Humphrey stroked his chin. 'I wonder,' he mused, 'if by any chance it's the dead johnny?'

'Dead!' said Quill.

'Dead!' said the apprehensive Banner.

'Dead,' said Sir Humphrey conclusively.

Banner, his umbrella vanishing into thin air, looked appealingly at Sir Humphrey. Sir Humphrey came to a decision.

'Found a dead johnny in my office this afternoon,' he explained lucidly, 'sitting at my desk. Don't know the fellow from Adam,' he observed peevishly. 'I suppose you want to have a look at him?'

'Please,' said Quill.

Sir Humphrey nodded to Miss Peacock. Miss Peacock removed the screen.

'There,' said Sir Humphrey, pointing.

They looked.

'Poor Sardinko,' said Señor Centime.

Quill turned. 'Sardinko!'

'But, yes,' said Señor Centime, 'I have been trying to tell them this for ten minutes.'

There was a silence.

'Well,' said Quill. 'I seem to have found him.'

'He is most dead,' said Señor Centime. 'Killed! A fellow countryman!' He sat down, overcome by the thought. The efficient Miss Peacock patted him on the shoulder. Absently he held her hand.

'I am sad at his death,' he said pathetically, 'even though I did not care much for his politics.'

'Communist—eh?' said Sir Humphrey keenly.

Señor Centime shook his head.

'No,' he said simply. 'He was pro-British.'

* * * * *

'Get me Whitehall 1212,' said Quill.

'That's Scotland Yard,' said an astonished voice cutting in.

'Who the hell are you?' snapped Quill.

'I'm the telephone censor,' said the voice. 'And what the hell do you mean by trying to telephone Scotland Yard without filling up a form?' In a burst of moral indignation he cut Quill off.

The efficient Miss Peacock appeared with the necessary form. Quill looked at it witheringly.

'Fill it up,' counselled Sergeant Banner. 'It's quicker.'

Quill looked at the form again. It read:

To Telephone any Department of His Majesty's Government, Army, Navy, R.A.F., A.R.P., and Police Force. . . .

There followed seventeen intimate enquiries.

'It'll be quicker to walk there,' said Quill in some disgust.

'Here's my pen,' offered Banner. 'It leaks,' he added apologetically.

The telephone rang.

'So sorry,' said the censor's voice. 'We've just found out you're a police officer. That's different. We'll put you through,' he said generously.

The line went dead. Quill swore. It was ten solid minutes since the identity of the body had been discovered and still he had not been able to contact Scotland Yard. Five of the precious minutes had been taken up by Sir Humphrey swearing everybody to secrecy before waddling off to Downing Street to inform the Cabinet they need wait no longer. (Quill had wondered at the time why he had not used the telephone, but no doubt this was because they would have wanted him to fill up a form.) Two minutes had been devoted to soothing Señor Centime and convincing him that the murder need not necessarily be a violation of the Neutrality Act. Another minute went in the Señor's broken peroration over the body, and thirty seconds for the click-over of the resourceful mind of Joe what's-his-name who led the Señor away to his quarters. Which left a minute for Sergeant Banner to observe that the whole business struck him as very queer.

The wire came to life. Several voices bubbled over it at once. Somehow Quill managed to wave them away, and after a further struggle got through to the Snarl's office.

'I've found your man,' he announced.

'Good,' said the Snarl, with satisfaction. 'You've been a long time about it,' it added back to normal.

'There's just one small snag,' said Quill apologetically.

'What's that?'

'He's dead,' said Quill.

'What's that?' shouted the Snarl.

'He's dead,' said Quill. 'Murdered. I found him in . . .'

Sir Humphrey came into the room, took in the situation at a glance, raced over to Quill, and clamped a hand over the receiver. He was superb in an emergency.

'Not a word, not a word,' he panted. 'Orders from Downing Street.'

'Say that again,' roared the Snarl.

In his agitation Sir Humphrey uncovered the receiver.

'Not a word,' he shrilled. 'Go away. Orders from Downing Street.'

'Quill—are you mad?' bellowed the Snarl.

'This isn't Quill,' said Sir Humphrey with dignity. 'This is Spratt of the Ministry of Elimination.'

'Get off the line,' shouted the Snarl furiously. 'I want to talk to our man Quill.'

'We cannot allow you to talk to anybody without filling up a form,' said the censor, cutting in. The line went dead.

'Phew,' said Sir Humphrey, relaxing into a chair. 'That was a narrow squeak.'

Quill looked at him.

'They tell me at Downing Street,' explained Sir Humphrey, 'that this dead johnny is a very important blighter. You will remember,' he pleaded, 'that I suspected it from the first.'

'Clearly,' said the efficient Miss Peacock.

Banner shot her a dirty look.

'Not a word of this unfortunate business must be allowed to leak out,' said Sir Humphrey. 'I have my orders. No, newspapers must not hear a word of this. It's a matter of national security.'

Quill got up. 'In that case I might as well go home.'

'Not at all,' said Sir Humphrey. 'Scotland Yard has got to clear this matter up. Discreetly, of course. Telephone them at once,' he ordered.

Quill sat down.

The telephone rang.

'I say,' said the Ministry of Information, 'have you heard anything about that johnny Sardinko yet?'

'Plenty,' said Quill, and hung up.

* * * * *

'Cor,' said Sergeant Banner, impressed. 'You throw a lovely dart. Why,' he suggested, 'don't you challenge Sir Humphrey?'

Quill smirked and threw another dart. It missed the board completely.

'Better not,' said Banner, changing his mind.

They were down in the cellar. It was the only place in the Ministry where Quill could isolate Banner long enough to ask a few questions with some hope of getting them answered.

It was almost seven. An hour had gone by since Sir Humphrey had ordered Quill to get in touch with Scotland Yard. A swarm of criminological experts had descended like groping locusts and filtered their way through the sandbags to the Ministry of Elimination. There they had got busy with routine, measuring, photographing, and finger-printing. It was left to Sir Humphrey to placate the Insomnian Consul, who had arrived post-haste and who everyone in turn had insisted on treating as a suspect. And all to supply Quill with what he could have found out in two minutes by himself: the fact that Señor Sardinko had been shot at close range by a service revolver which the assassin had thoughtfully dropped into the waste-paper basket. The history of the weapon was brief. The number was referred back to the Ministry of Munitions, who, on checking up, found that it had not yet been issued. That was all.

Pressed, Sergeant Banner admitted that quite a few of the staff had not been in the cellar during the black-out. Reluctantly he undertook to supply Quill with a list.

'Though it will probably cost me my job,' he said sourly, 'leaving the neutrals to look after themselves.'

'For the duration of the case you're hitched on to me,' said Quill. 'I'm used to you,' he explained.

Banner failed to brighten.

Joe what's-his-name bustled in.

'Having a confab?' he asked. 'Good. I'll join you.' He walked over to the stack of darts, picked out the rubber one, twisted it ecstatically, and put it carefully in his pocket.

'Might be useful again,' he said. 'Worked it on Sir Humphrey,' he told Quill.

'So I heard,' said Quill drily.

Joe brooded. 'I say,' he said, 'have you chaps got a sense of humour?'

Quill looked at him.

'No, I don't think I'd better tell you,' said Joe. He turned to leave. 'It's a pity, though,' he mused. 'It's awfully funny. You'd have loved it.' He shook his head regretfully. 'But perhaps I'd better not.'

'Quite,' said Quill, fully resigned to having to listen. But to his surprise Joe was not yet ready to unbosom.

'You know,' he said, 'a sense of humour is a funny thing. Most unexpected people have it. Last man I should have suspected.'

'Who?' said Quill. 'Me?'

'Never mind,' said Joe hastily, and went.

'He is a one,' said Banner, with relish. 'Why, only the other day he sent the Minister of Fisheries an india-rubber kipper for his tea. Laugh!' said Banner, suiting the action to the word. 'Did I ever tell you about the time when he . . .'

'Later,' said Quill, and got up.

In the passage they ran into Sir Humphrey.

'Ah, Quill,' said Sir Humphrey. 'Found the murderer yet?'

Quill winced. The joke, he felt, was due to be an old friend in less than no time.

'Remember,' said Sir Humphrey. 'Not a word to the Press.'

'Not a word,' promised Quill.

He groped his way towards the exit. Seven minutes' search with a pocket torch revealed his car. Belinda was in it. So was the police officer of the War Reserve.

'Sorry to disturb you,' said Quill, 'but it's time to go home.' The War Reserve, his blush hidden by the black-out, scrambled out.

'Don't be unkind to Archie,' said Belinda. 'Let him sit down while he's got the chance. How would you like to stand for eight hours,' she pursued relentlessly.

'We're going home,' said Quill, and got in.

'Good-bye, Archie,' said Belinda tenderly. 'Take care of yourself.'

Quill pressed the self-starter.

'When shall I see you again?' shouted Archie above the noise.

'To-morrow morning,' said Quill bitterly, 'as soon as the Ministry opens.'

'But I'm not on duty until four,' wailed the despairing Archie.

'Too bad,' said Quill.

The car crawled cautiously forward.

CHAPTER

3

THE Ministry of Elimination had leapt into existence almost overnight. All it took was the time necessary for the heads of departments to collect sundry second cousins due to be retired from the Services at the end of the year. Its duties were to supplement, counteract, and override the Ministry of Information.

For some time the Government had been feeling uneasy about the Ministry of Information. Fleet Street did not seem fond of it. Perhaps, felt the Government, it had been a mistake to include those forty-three journalists. They did not get on too well with the Historians.

Fortunately, the remedy was at hand. Following the traditional formula—if a measure is unpopular, double it (then, if necessary, you can take away the department you first thought of)—they had commandeered for the Ministry of Elimination the main branch of the only insurance company still doing any non-war risk business, ordered an enormous quantity of sandbags, summoned Sir Humphrey from the Balloon Barrage, and, long before they found time to inform the dailies, they were open.

In make-up the Ministry of Elimination was almost the exact replica of its brother, the Ministry of Information. Alike in kind, but different in degree. There was the same flight of infuriated foreign correspondents from both portals to seek news elsewhere. The same rigid censorship. The same departments for cultural relations and propaganda by film and radio. The same services for statistics, cordial relations with Neutrals, and coping with the Balkan States. Their functions clashed in every particular with the corresponding departments at the brother Ministry. It was precisely in this, as Sir Humphrey pointed out, that their value lay. A troublesome enquirer at either Ministry could now be pushed on to the other, who could, if necessary, push him back again. All on that delightful old principle of 'I'd do it with pleasure, old man, but my partner . . .'

A new departure, however, was the Department for Popularizing the Ministries. It was high time, Sir Humphrey had pointed out, that Ministers, who swayed the destiny of a nation, got at least as good a build up as footballers or film stars. To achieve this the Department had been put in charge of Al Schenk.

Al was an experienced business man. In his time he had been bankrupt in every capital in Europe—though not in London nor New York. That is where his business sense showed. He knew all about handling publicity, having in the past frequently paid large sums for having his own suppressed. Anything to do with suppression going big with the Government, he got the appointment without further query.

The Department had got off to a flying start with some fascinating copy of the favourite menus of our Cabinet Ministers. Published side by side with the rationing restrictions, they were just what the nation needed to make it realize there was a war on.

With so many departments to be co-ordinated, so many details to be obscured, and so many salaries to be raised, it was hardly a slur on the efficiency of the staff that a dead body should be able to sneak its way unobserved into the Chief's chair. In any case Sir Humphrey was not unduly depressed about this.

Humming, he alighted from his car, nodded affably at a sandbag, and made his way jauntily into the Ministry. It was the morning after the murder, and Sir Humphrey was feeling fine. The R.A.F. had dropped some more leaflets where picnickers in the Black Forest could hardly help finding them. The Siegfried Line had a dent in it. The shares that he had sold last week had dropped to zero. And by this time the efficient Miss Peacock had no doubt removed the dead johnny. Gad! It was good to be alive when one was sixty-nine and could settle down to a hard day's work without being actually called upon to do any of it.

Still humming, Sir Humphrey arrived at his office and glanced round approvingly. Not a dead man anywhere. Luxuriously he settled at his desk and started in on his morning's work.

This consisted of reading the morning papers. He skirmished through *The Times*, glanced at the *Telegraph*, and threw away the *Daily Express*. He purred over the *News Chronicle*, the *Mail*, and the *Mirror*. Not an item of news in any of them. Magnificent! Who said the Ministry of Elimination was inefficient!

And then he picked up the *Daily Shmooze*.

* * * * *

Quill, too, was reading the *Daily Shmooze*. The headlines ran:

MURDER AT THE MINISTRY

ENVOY SHOT WHILE CABINET WAITS

DEMARCHE EXPECTED FROM INSOMNIA

Quill read with interest of the discovery of the body in Sir Humphrey's office and his own efficiency in getting it identified. He learnt, too, that the Cabinet viewed the murder with some misgivings. They had spent the entire afternoon waiting for Señor Sardinko to show up, which went to emphasize the gravity of the situation. In some diplomatic quarters it was feared that the incident might imperil the cordial relations that had always existed between Great Britain and the Kingdom of Insomnia. No country likes seeing its envoy bumped off.

There was also an interesting article about Insomnia. It was famed, Quill learnt, for its vodtsch, a beverage half-way between vodka and kirsch, but stronger than either. It exported pin-machines, wood pulp, and picture postcards. Its lake contained eighty per cent of the world's supply of Gardenium, a mineral of which Quill had never heard. Insomnia was situated between the pincers of Nazi Germany and Soviet Russia, and maintained its independence not so much by its own efforts, as the reluctance of either of these powers to let the other have it. Its monarch was King Hannibal, the Hothead, a familiar figure in the night life of Paris.

'What is Gardenium?' Quill asked Belinda.

'My favourite perfume,' said Belinda, muddled.

* * * * *

'I say,' said the Ministry of Information. 'What is Gardenium?'

'Don't know.' Sir Humphrey, breathing heavily, hung up.

All his good humour had vanished. That article in the *Daily Shmooze!* How dared they! That detective johnny must have tipped them off. He glared at Joe what's-his-name who had come bustling in.

'I say,' said Joe. 'You might tell a johnny. What is Gardenium?'

'Don't know,' snapped Sir Humphrey.

Joe's attitude stiffened to one of alarm. 'Sit quite still,' he said, 'there's a spider crawling over you.'

Sir Humphrey sat still. Joe ran his hands over him and produced a billiard ball. He threw it on the ground. It bounced.

'Get out!' said Sir Humphrey, losing his temper.

There was a knock on the door. Quill came in.

'Morning,' he said cheerfully. 'Wonder if you could tell me. What is Gardenium?'

Sir Humphrey looked at him mournfully.

'You know,' he said, 'I'm disappointed in you. Really, I am.'

'But I just don't happen to know,' said Quill.

'I take you into my confidence,' said Sir Humphrey, more in sorrow than in anger, 'I show you the dead johnny. And what do you do? Rush straight off to the *Daily Shmooze*.'

'But I didn't,' said Quill.

Joe what's-his-name clicked his tongue reproachfully.

'Anyway, they had no right to print it without the official release stamp,' brooded Sir Humphrey. 'We'll fine them a packet,' he added, brightening.

Quill made a mental note to call round on the *Daily Shmooze* and find out how they got hold of the story. Meanwhile, there was Sir Humphrey to be placated.

While he was protesting his innocence, the telephone rang.

'I say,' said the Ministry of Information, 'the Cabinet's awfully upset. Something to do with that man you murdered. Very important johnny apparently. By the way,' it remembered, 'that was a topping story you released to the *Daily Shmooze*. Congratulations.'

Sir Humphrey rang up on them. He looked at Quill.

'Good-bye,' he said coldly.

The interview was at an end. But Quill reopened it.

'I'm sorry, but there are a few questions I must ask you.'

'Questions!' said Sir Humphrey, astonished. 'What on earth for?'

'They've put me in charge of this case,' said Quill. 'I've got to tackle it systematically.'

'System,' said Sir Humphrey approvingly. 'We're very keen on it here. Keep a check on everything.'

'Do you really?' said Quill.

'Absolutely,' Sir Humphrey was emphatic. 'Nothing,' he said, 'can happen in any of the Ministries without our knowing at once.'

'I suppose a dead body doesn't count?' said Quill.

For a moment Sir Humphrey was stymied.

'Well, I was the first person to know about it, wasn't I?' he retorted.

'You and one other,' said Quill.

'Who?' asked Sir Humphrey.

'The murderer,' said Quill.

'Got you there,' said Joe, chuckling.

Sir Humphrey looked at him.

The telephone rang.

'I say,' said the Ministry of Information. 'Munitions are simply livid with you. They say you've cost them a packet of Gardenium. In fact, you've practically lost the war.'

'Us,' said Sir Humphrey.

'You,' said the Ministry of Information, and hung up coldly.

Sir Humphrey looked puzzled.

'I say,' he asked Quill. 'What is Gardenium?'

* * * * *

Strictly speaking, it was not correct on the part of Munitions to suggest that in allowing a man to be murdered in his office Sir Humphrey had lost the war. All he had done was to come darn near it.

The news of Señor Sardinko's death had sent every diplomat in Europe into a frenzy of activity. They hopped into aeroplanes, buzzed round the Continent, and tried to dodge Herr von Ribbentrop. Rumours spread everywhere. What hand had struck down the unfortunate Señor Sardinko? U.S.A. suggested it was the OGPU. Paris hinted at the Gestapo. Goebbels said right out that it was Winston Churchill.

What was Insomnia going to do? Would she abandon her neutrality?

Would she join Germany? Would she join Russia? Would she just sulk and refuse to join anyone?

Señor Sardinko had come to England armed with full plenipotentiary powers to negotiate a treaty. It was a trade treaty. England was to supply Insomnia with practically everything (including a large loan), and accept payment in pin-tables, picture postcards, and Gardenium. Gardenium was the only one of these products in which the British Government was interested, though, for the sake of form, they were prepared to spend several days haggling over the exact number of pins to be supplied with each table.

For they had had it on expert authority that the country that controlled Gardenium would win the war.

It was odd that they had only just found this out, for Señor Sardinko had spent the last five years hawking his Gardenium hopelessly to every government in Europe. At one time he had even offered to swop it for the Eiffel Tower, arguing eloquently that Paris must surely be tired of it by now.

But that was before the experts had got busy and endowed Gardenium with just those qualities that make an armament manufacturer's mouth water.

From that moment Insomnia had become a centre of diplomatic activity. Never had King Hannibal the Hothead held so many official receptions. Never had the President of the Board of Trade been given so many free lunches. And never had Señor Sardinko found so many people to laugh at his jokes. Powers vied with each other, wheedling, bribing, and threatening. And still Insomnia refused to commit herself.

'Take it easy, gentlemen,' that shrewd monarch, Hannibal the Hothead, advised his Cabinet. 'Refuse nobody—but sign nothing. The longer we can keep them haggling the better the price we'll get. We might even get enough to let me live in Paris all the year round,' he added wistfully.

At one time it looked as if Germany, in spite of having sent Herr von Papen, was going to pull off the Insomnian Treaty. But at the critical moment that unfortunate diplomat, having once again lost his dispatch case, had been forced to rely on his memory and had returned to his gloating Government laden with pin-machines. They sent him to Turkey.

At this point England stepped in. After some hush-hush negotiations it was agreed that Señor Sardinko should come to London (fares paid). Not a word of his mission was to leak out in case some other power should try a wheedle on the way. So well had the secret been kept that no one met him at the station in London.

'This,' said the Prime Minister, as the Cabinet, armed with Insomnian dictionaries, gathered together at Downing Street on that fateful afternoon, 'will be hailed as a diplomatic triumph in the U.S.A.'

He was still saying it a trifle wanly at seven when the news of the murder came through.

'Can we go home now?' asked the First Lord of the Admiralty restlessly.

* * * * *

But to Quill all this was just another murder case.

CHAPTER

4

'THIS,' said Joe proudly, 'is my new baby. The Alibi Department.'

He flung open the door.

Quill walked in and gazed at an array of empty desks.

'They're all at lunch,' said Joe, disappointed.

But he was wrong. Stretched luxuriously on a sofa was a gaunt figure. Unbrushed black hair flopped over an intellectual forehead. A slender delicate hand held in its repose a still-smouldering cigarette.

'There's your man,' said Joe, pointing.

Quill consulted his list. 'Misha Podushkin,' he said. 'He looks just like Mischa Auer.'

At that moment the still-smouldering cigarette produced a spurt and burnt the delicate finger. With a yell, Misha Podushkin woke up.

Joe roared with laughter. Misha looked at him reproachfully.

'It is not funny this,' he said reprovingly. He stubbed out his cigarette, leant back, and closed his eyes.

Quill crossed over and shook him. Misha opened an incurious eye.

'Who are you?' he said. 'Go away.' He closed it again.

'Detective-Inspector Adam Quill, Scotland Yard,' said Quill impressively.

The eyes remained closed. Quill took a step forward.

'Don't irritate him,' said Joe. 'Valuable man.'

'Valuable?' said Quill doubtfully.

'Practically neutral,' said Joe. 'Born Russian,' he explained.

'What's he doing here?' asked Quill, puzzled.

'But it is simple,' said Misha, suddenly coming to life. 'The others are at lunch. For the first time all day the sofa is empty and I can sleep in peace. Good-bye.' He lay down again.

'I mean,' said Quill, 'what are you doing working in the Ministry?'

'But that is simple, too,' said Misha, not bothering to sit up this time. 'I love my Russia. Also long ago I became naturalized British. Above everything I am a patriot.'

'Quite,' said Quill, 'but whose side are you on?'

'On the side of my country,' said Misha, and closed his eyes again.

'England or Russia?' persevered Quill.

'But both,' said Misha. He sat up. 'It was like this,' he explained. 'For many years now I have lived in Paris. I love France,' he sighed.

'Quite,' said Quill.

'Then one morning in the spring I pick up a paper and what do I see? England and Russia are talking about a pact. Then I am very happy. I will, I say to myself, serve both my countries. Only,' he pointed out, 'England is nearer. So I borrow the fare and I come here. And then,' Misha sighed heavily, 'I pick up another paper and I see that it is Germany that has signed the pact with Russia. Then,' said Misha, 'I am in despair, but it is too late, for already they have made me censor and I am reading many letters every day. You have no idea,' he told Quill, 'how stupid these letters can be. If it were not for the postal orders that I find in them from time to time . . .'

'Misha!' said Joe, horrified.

'I only took the small ones,' pleaded Misha, 'and always I was careful to cross out heavily in blue pencil all that spoke of money in the letter. Never can it be reproached me that I have disappointed anyone.'

'Just as well I transferred you,' said Joe palely. He turned to Quill. 'You won't let this get any further, will you, old man? It might give the Ministry a bad name.'

'I promise,' said Quill.

'I am not certain,' said Misha, brooding, 'that I am going to like my new job. To invent excuses for the English it is not easy. The Frenchman can always plead that it was romance. The German that he was encircled. And the Russian that he did not remember. But here in England you pride yourselves on your calm, your common sense, and your organization. With what is there left to make the alibi?' He shrugged despairingly. 'Already this morning . . .'

'What?' said Quill.

'I am asked to explain why we did not allow the Press to print a speech by Daladier until three days after it was broadcast to Germany.

Actually this was because Miss Peacock had put it in the pigeon-hole marked "Goebbels," but how can we tell them this? It was a bad speech,' he added dispassionately. 'No jokes. . . .' He closed his eyes.

Quill brought up the object of his visit.

'I am told that you did not go down to the cellar during the air-raid warning yesterday.'

'But naturally,' said Misha, 'I am a fatalist. If a bomb is on its way it is useless to move. Not only,' he pointed out logically, 'might one move to where the next will fall, but one has to use up energy to get there. Me, I prefer to stay where I am. Also,' he admitted, 'I was asleep and did not see the signal.'

Quill made a note. 'Did you,' he asked, 'see Señor Sardinko?'

Misha looked interested. 'Sardinko? He is in England—the old *macreau?*'

Quill pounced. 'You knew him.'

'A little.' Misha nodded. 'I met him when I was on the parapet of my bridge in Paris.'

'Parapet!' said Quill, startled.

'It was the period of my life when I was committing suicide,' explained Misha.

'Period?' said Quill.

'Every night for two years I committed suicide from the *Pont des Cent Bougis*,' said Misha. 'Very exhausting,' he said pathetically.

Quill thought it out. 'I get it. You let people snatch you from the parapet in what they imagined was the nick of time and then worked on their feelings to give you money.'

'Misha,' said Joe, 'I am ashamed of you.'

'But why?' said Misha blankly. 'They would not have given me money if it had not made them feel good to do it. Besides,' he added, 'sometimes they gave me only food. That,' he remembered, 'is how I met Sardinko. He offers me a meal so I take him to our restaurant, *Chez Petroushka*, and we run him up a bill of eight hundred francs. He was very cross.' Misha laughed heartily.

'Your restaurant?' said Quill.

'But, yes,' said Misha. 'We run a restaurant to catch the suckers. The food is bad and the prices phenomenal, but we play Otchi Tchernia and we shade the lights, and they think they have been Bohemian. . . .'

'And this,' said Joe sorrowfully, 'is the johnny I put up for my club. You'll have to resign,' he told Misha.

'Do not upset yourself,' said Misha, 'I have done this already. They try to make me play a game called "Squash," ' he told Quill. 'Me! An Elephant!'

'Elephant?' said Quill.

'Certainly,' said Misha proudly, 'a White Elephant. It is a society pledged to do no useful work,' he explained.

Quill nodded. 'That's why you got yourself a job here, I suppose.'

'We understand each other perfectly,' said Misha cordially.

'I think we do,' said Quill. 'You are a filcher of postal orders, a professional suicide, a blackmailer, and a restaurant profiteer.'

Misha bowed and leant back on his sofa.

'And how,' asked Quill sweetly, 'do you manage to pick up a living?'

But Misha Podushkin was already asleep.

*   *   *   *   *

The Department for the Defence of Propagation had collared the largest room in the building. At first sight it looked like a pornographic bookshop. At second sight it did as well.

The walls were decorated with snappy anatomical charts demonstrating the attainment of strength through joy, and joy through strength. The shelves were crammed with obscure medical treatises with the more illuminating pages meanly written in Latin. Havelock Ellis, Kraft-Ehbbing, Bertrand Russell, and Thorne Smith nestled cosily between Latin dictionaries. There was also a paper-covered volume called *Seventy-seven Nights in Paris*.

At a desk littered with pamphlets on hygiene and piled high with dictionaries sat Brigadier-General Tunnyfish. He was reading Dr Marie Stopes and blushing slightly.

'Nonsense,' he kept muttering to himself. 'Nonsense.'

But he read steadily on.

Just as he was beginning to feel that it was in some ways perhaps a pity he had evacuated his wife, he was interrupted.

Joe what's-his-name came into the room. Instinctively the General ducked.

Joe made the necessary introductions. The General looked at Quill warily. Any friend of Joe's . . .

The General was an embittered man. Ever since the Boer War, when he had doggedly marched three battalions half-way across Africa to relieve a small village no one else had noticed, let alone attacked, they had kept him out of active service. In 1914 they had sent him to Brighton, and in this war of specialization ('Follow your trade in the army'), when he had every right to expect to be sent at least to Holland to help them flood it, they had put him in charge of 'Propagation.' He had only ever had one child, and he was horribly doubtful even about that—though, of course, the girl at the tobacco kiosk had pleaded most eloquently that there was no one else.

He glared at Quill.

It was established almost at once that the General knew nothing and remembered less. He had spent the entire air-raid warning at his desk—he could not remember what he was doing.

Joe pointed suggestively to *Seventy-seven Nights in Paris*. The General blushed.

'Did you,' asked Quill, 'ever know a Señor Sardinko?'

'Never heard of him,' said the General promptly.

Quill made a note.

But something was stirring in that massive mind.

'What was the name?'

'Sardinko,' supplied Quill. 'Auguste Sardinko.'

The General went purple in the face.

'How dare you speak of that man to me?' he bellowed.

Quill backed.

'Swindler,' said the General, puffing. 'Scoundrel. Nothing against you personally, sir,' he told Quill, 'but I don't like your friends.'

Quill smiled. 'He isn't my friend. In fact, he's dead.'

'Good job, too,' said the General. 'Who did it?'

'Oh!' said Quill, 'you knew it was murder?'

'Guessed it,' said the General proudly. 'Johnny like that bound to be murdered. Inevitable!'

'You didn't like the dead man?' asked Quill.

'Like him,' said the General explosively, 'after what he did to me!'

'Tell me about it,' said Quill.

The General settled down. He lit a cigar and even passed the box to Quill. Joe made hurriedly for the door. 'I'll see you in the canteen,' he told Quill.

'It just shows you,' began the General, 'that you can never trust a foreigner. I remember back in the 'nineties . . .'

'Señor Sardinko,' reminded Quill.

'I'm coming to that,' said the General testily, 'don't be in such a hurry. There's plenty of time. It was back in 1891,' he resumed firmly, 'that the pater brought an Argentinian johnny back to tiffin. The mater was horrified. But the pater would have it that the johnny was a sahib. Played polo. What happened?' He stopped.

The suspense was awful. 'What?' asked Quill.

'He sold the guv'nor a gold mine.'

'Ah,' said Quill.

'There was no gold in it,' explained the General.

'Tough,' said Quill, not altogether surprised.

'Left us penniless,' said the General. 'Stared ruin in the face. If I hadn't been able to pass on the mine to Cousin Amelia's husband in Poona,' he added, 'don't know what we'd have done.'

'Slick,' said Quill.

The General frowned. 'You'd have thought,' he resumed, 'that a thing like that would have been a lesson to me. And so it was. Never trusted a foreigner again. Not even a Frenchman. That is,' said the General, 'until this Sardinko blighter.'

He settled himself more comfortably and plunged into the story.

It seemed to Quill almost identical with his father's experience excepting that the General felt it more keenly. He had met Sardinko at Cousin Amelia's ('ought to be ashamed of herself at her age') and found him very civil. Acting on his advice he had purchased a packet of shares in a company called 'Insomnia Inc.' only to find that he was practically the owner of a near-derelict pin-machine company.

'Lost a packet,' he announced. 'Stared ruin in the face. Useless shares. Even Cousin Amelia wouldn't touch 'em.'

'Tough,' said Quill.

The General searched in vain for Sardinko. He searched for months. Then came the day when he found him. He found him on his front-door step. In point of fact Sardinko was calling on him.

'Told him what I thought of him,' puffed the General, 'and believe it or not, he apologized. Said it was all a mistake. Even offered to take the shares back at the full price I had paid for them. Jumped at it. Shook his hand. Brought him in to tiffin. The wife was horrified. I pointed out the Johnny was a sahib. Played solo. And when he left I actually asked him to call again. But he never had the nerve to show up,' said the General grimly, 'so now you understand why I don't like him.'

'No,' said Quill.

'Of course,' said the General, 'forgot to tell you. Read in paper next day that the pin factory had signed a big contract with Germany. Shares worth a fortune. And I'd sold them all back,' he finished, a broken man.

'Too bad,' said Quill.

'To make it worse,' said the General savagely, 'the cheque he gave me bounced.'

* * * * *

Quill was thoughtful as he walked along the corridors towards the canteen. It was curious the way the dead bodies he worked on developed personalities. Only yesterday Auguste Sardinko had been a dead man with a beard, an envoy from a country he had barely heard of, and a line in the Cabinet's appointment diary. And to-day he had become a striving little man, clever, not too scrupulous and obviously energetic. A commercial rather than a political adventurer, one would have said, and yet he had met his death while representing his country on an important mission.

Engrossed in his thoughts Quill walked right past the canteen. But Joe what's-his-name, looking up from his table, saw him and beckoned him in.

'Cup of tea,' offered Joe hospitably, 'all ready for you.'

Quill accepted gratefully. He took a sip and sneezed.

'Pepper!' explained Joe, laughing uproariously.

Quill picked up the milk jug and poured it over Joe's head.

'Just my fun,' he told the startled waitress amiably.

In reproachful silence Joe dried himself

'Okay,' grinned Quill, 'where do we go from here?'

Joe looked at Quill, decided to forgive him and smiled.

'Ministerial Publicity,' he said. 'You'll like Al Schenk.'

'Al Schenk,' said Quill as they walked off together, 'sounds like an American.'

'Near enough,' said Joe. 'Naturalized, I think. Anyway, he's a great chap. Queer sense of humour. And doing a wonderful job of work.'

'What's that?' asked Quill.

'Endearing the Ministries to the public,' explained Joe. 'Making them fond of us.'

'What, all of you?'

'Why—yes,' said Joe. 'We don't want the public to think of the Ministries as so many pigeon-holes. We want them to think of us as pulsating, alive, alert. . . .'

'Alert!' said Quill.

'Why not,' said Joe. 'And every time we make a mistake we don't grovel about it. We get Al to explain it away. For instance, the last time the War Office left its lights on in the black-out we didn't deny it. We admitted it cheerfully. Al simply explained that the Minister was absent-minded like all great men.'

'And did the public appreciate that?' asked Quill.

'Well no,' said Joe, 'but it went big with the dons.'

They entered the outer office. The efficient Miss Peacock had borrowed it to interview a tied-in-the-knot neutral.

'Do you speak Armenian?' she turned to Quill helplessly.

'Ah,' said the neutral, relieved, 'why you not tell me that you speak the English. Now we get on like the mansions on fire.'

Quill left them to it and knocked on a door marked: 'Keep Out.' Somebody grunted. Quill went in.

Seated at a desk, efficiently bawling down the telephone, was Al Schenk. He was a little bald, a little fat, a little short-sighted, and very noisy. He wore tortoiseshell glasses and was in a bad temper.

'Who are you?' he snapped.

Quill passed his card. Al Schenk read it keenly.

'Pleased to have you meet me,' he said glibly. 'It's about the awkward business of Sardinko, I suppose.'

'Well—yes,' said Quill.

'Glad to help you all I can,' said Al, 'though candidly I've had a belly-full of this murder already. Been sweating out a popular angle on a body in a Ministry. Taken me all morning.'

'You've got a nerve,' said Quill. 'It will most likely take me all of a month.'

'That's your job,' said Al without sympathy.

Quill opened his note-book.

'You were not in the cellar during the air-raid warning yesterday.'

'I stayed right here in my office.'

'Claustrophobia?' asked Quill.

Al shook a forceful head. 'Nope. I was on my way down. Even collected my gas mask. And then I got an idea for explaining why the Ministry of Transport had ordered the suppression of all bus stops.'

'Difficult,' said Quill. 'After the public had been kept sprinting for forty-eight hours.'

'Anyway,' said Al, 'I thought of an angle to make the whole thing seem sensible. So I jotted it down before I should forget it.'

Quill was interested. 'What was it?'

'Simple,' said Al proudly. 'National Fitness Campaign.'

'Great work,' said Joe admiringly.

Al picked up a cigar and chewed it peevishly.

'What's the use,' he said, 'it's like trying to stem an ocean with a match-stick. You just can't keep up with the chucks. The waste, the overlapping, the inefficiency and the sheer idiocy that goes on in the Ministries—it's enough to make a business man weep. The whole outfit needs to be reorganized from top to bottom. I could run this place more efficiently with a staff of two. Me and my brother.'

Joe roared with laughter. 'Told you he had a great sense of humour.'

Al looked at him.

'He loves a joke,' said Joe. 'Don't you, Al? Shall I tell him about...'

Al waved away the babble, snapped out his watch, and looked at it.

'I can spare you exactly ten minutes,' he announced, every inch the business man. 'Shoot.'

The door burst open. An agitated Sir Humphrey burst into the room.

'I'm in a spot,' he announced. 'Got to get me out of it, Schenk.'

'Put it in writing,' said Al coolly. 'I'll attend to it when I'm through with the Fisheries.'

'But look here, old man,' said Sir Humphrey, 'this is urgent. The P.M. has been giving me hell.'

Al relented. 'Okay, I'll listen. Shoot.'

Sir Humphrey pondered on the best way of presenting his dilemma. 'The *Daily Shmooze*,' he said, 'they gave our body away.'

Al nodded. 'I read it. You sure handed them a swell story.'

'I didn't hand it to them,' snapped Sir Humphrey. 'They sneaked it. And because I can't find who sent it the P.M. is holding me responsible.'

'So you haven't found out,' said Quill.

Sir Humphrey shrugged a beaten shoulder. 'Searched high and low. Had every censor on the mat. All innocent.'

'Have you been on to the *Daily Shmooze?*' asked Quill.

'Gosh,' said Sir Humphrey, 'never thought of it.' He reached for the telephone.

'I'll attend to it,' said Al.

'Right,' said Sir Humphrey. 'Let me know what they say. But what I really came to you for, old man, was some good excuse to give to the P.M.'

Al nodded.

'Otherwise,' said Sir Humphrey, 'he might think we were inefficient.'

One of the telephones rang. Al picked up the receiver. He listened.

'The P.M. is asking for you,' he told Sir Humphrey. 'Sounds a bit grim. I'd take the call in your own room if I were you,' he advised.

'By gad,' said Sir Humphrey and rushed whitely away.

Al looked at his watch. 'I can now spare you exactly two minutes.'

'Right,' said Quill. 'Did you know Auguste Sardinko?'

'Oh, yes, I knew him,' said Al. 'At one time I knew him quite well. Did a spot of business together.'

'Was Sardinko a business man?' asked Quill.

'Well not exactly. But he never missed a rake-off.'

'When did this business take place?'

Al reflected. 'It was just after I had gone bankrupt in Prague,' he remembered. 'Just over a year ago. Put me right on my feet again.'

'Had this business by any chance anything to do with pin machines?' asked Quill.

Al looked surprised. 'How did you know?'

Quill managed to look enigmatic.

'Matter of fact, it was,' said Al. 'Wangled a big deal with Germany. Must say Sardinko put across a grand job of work. I found the capital.'

'Capital!' said Quill. 'I thought you said you were bankrupt.'

'Technically,' said Al, 'I was. But fortunately at the time I happened to be business adviser to an Armenian trust fund. You know how these things are.' He spread his hands expressively.

'I know,' said Quill. 'And how did you find Sardinko as a business associate?'

'Promising,' said Al. 'A certain amount of low cunning and no scruples whatever. Only somehow,' he ended, 'one never quite felt one could trust him.'

Quill closed his book.

'Still, I'm sorry he's dead,' said Al. 'There's plenty of margins for a good rake-off in this war.'

In the outer office the neutral was taking a cordial farewell of the exhausted Miss Peacock.

'Why,' he demanded amiably, 'is Oxford Circus?'

Miss Peacock was baffled.

'He means "where,"' said Quill helpfully and made his way out.

* * * * *

So far—not so good. Quill decided his next call would be on Señor Centime, the foreign correspondent of the *Insomnian Sentinel*.

Joe what's-his-name escorted him to the door of the Neutrals Room.

'Be seeing you,' he said and turned curtly on his heel.

Quill turned him back again. 'Aren't you coming in?'

'Not on your life,' said Joe. 'Every time they see me they pester me for news.'

'But isn't that what you're there to give them?'

Joe looked really shocked.

'Oh, no, old man, the Germans do that. Our job is to contradict them three days later.'

Quill gave it up. 'Where shall I find you?'

'In the cellar,' said Joe. 'Got a new idea I want to try out.' He disappeared.

'Pick you up in half an hour,' said Quill and walked in.

The room was seething with activity. Foreign correspondents of various shapes and sizes were busily pounding out stories with an enthusiasm entirely unimpaired by the sure knowledge that they would never be allowed to send them. Foreign newspapers, innocent of any stories of their writing, littered desks and floors. Those reporters who were not writing were talking politics and not agreeing any too well.

In the centre of this pressmen's hell, a monument of calm, sat Sergeant Banner. He was reading *Tit-Bits*. He looked up as Quill entered and jerked his thumb to a corner where Señor Centime was wrestling with a telephone.

'It is terrible, this service,' complained Señor Centime. 'The telegram girls are good, but the censors—*Mon Dieu!* They cannot spell at all.'

'Funny,' said Quill. 'They're all dons.'

'*Ach*,' said Señor Centime disgusted. All at once he remembered his manners, bowed, and clicked his heels. 'What can I do for you, Inspector?' he enquired.

'Just a few routine questions,' said Quill.

'Ah,' said Señor Centime interested. 'It concerns, no doubt, my fellow-countryman—Auguste Sardinko.'

Quill nodded.

Señor Centime sighed. 'It makes the best newspaper story Insomnia has had since the day that Herr von Papen fell in the lake.'

'Did he fall or was he pushed?' asked Banner fascinated.

'That was the big mystery,' explained Señor Centime, with delight. 'It was curious that our King Hannibal the Hothead was standing just behind him, but of course one does not suspect a monarch.'

Quill suppressed a smile.

'This,' said Señor Centime, 'will be an even bigger sensation.'

'Not on the Wilhelmstrasse,' suggested Quill.

But Señor Centime had seen the light. 'A four-column spread,' he said wraptly. 'A moving portrait of the man painted in words, a lucid summary of his mission, a masterly analysis of the crime, and then the dramatic moment when the criminal is arrested. Ah—what a story!' he gloated.

'Will they ever allow you to send it?' asked Quill.

Señor Centime sagged. 'No,' he said in a small flat voice. 'It would not be to the taste of Sir Humphrey.'

'Too bad,' Quill sympathized. 'Do all the stories go through him?'

'Impossible to tell you,' said Señor Centime. 'The system it changes all the time. Sometimes a story comes back with five okays, sometimes only with one. We neutrals,' he explained, 'have developed our own technique to get the quick okays. We take it ourselves to the one we think it will displease least.'

'Ah!' said Quill. 'And now perhaps you will tell me all you know about the dead man.'

Señor Centime bowed. 'But certainly.' He picked up *Who's Who in Insomnia.* 'Auguste Sardinko,' he began chattily, 'was born in Palookistan in 1886.' He paused to make a marginal note. 'Died November '39.'

'Palookistan?' said Quill.

'Our *plage*,' said Señor Centime. 'Like your Deauville.' He pulled a parchment out of his pocket, unfolded it, and spread it on the floor. It was a map of Insomnia.

'This,' said Señor Centime, pointing proudly to a blue circle spreading itself luxuriously almost over the entire map, 'is our lake.'

'Pretty,' said Quill.

'It produces eighty per cent of the world's Gardenium,' said Señor Centime proudly.

'I'd heard about that,' said Quill.

'Soon you will hear more,' boasted Señor Centime. 'Now this,' he pushed the Sergeant's thumb out of the way, 'is our capital, Rumba-Rumba. It is a model town,' he said with pride. 'Also,' he boasted, 'we have a radio hook-up. Two stations. Have you ever listened in to our broadcasts?' he asked.

Quill shook his head.

'A pity,' said Señor Centime. 'Our Band Waggon was very popular. But now, alas, we have sold all our air space to another country, and all that one hears is praise of Russia in a German accent. *C'est pas gai!*' he sighed.

'Too bad,' said Quill.

'In our Main Street,' resumed Señor Centime, shaking off his momentary depression, 'we have an ice-cream parlour. There are fifty-seven varieties of ice-cream soda. Though, personally,' he added, 'I prefer black coffee and a cigarette.'

Quill passed him one.

'What was Auguste Sardinko's political position?' he asked.

'Sardinko,' said Señor Centime, consulting his records, 'entered politics late in life. First he was a Captain of Industry, but after he had gone bankrupt he stood for Parliament.' He laid his book aside. 'In England,' he said disparagingly, 'you do not elect an undischarged bankrupt to your House of Commons, but we in Insomnia are more practical. How else,' he appealed to Quill, 'could we collect our Cabinet? In this way, too, we make certain that we are represented by a body of men who are used to facing crises. Thàt, in Europe to-day, is not without value.'

'Quite,' said Quill.

Señor Centime bowed and resumed his story.

'After his election it did not take Sardinko long to become President of the Board of Trade.'

'I see,' said Banner. 'Local lad makes good.'

'He was very successful,' said Señor Centime. 'Never have we signed so many treaties by barter. At one time you could not buy a picture postcard in the whole of Insomnia. All, all were used for export—principally to Paris.'

'Well, well,' said Quill.

'But what has really balanced our Budget,' said Señor Centime, 'is our phenomenal export of pin-tables. And it was Sardinko who accomplished it.'

'I heard something about that,' said Quill. 'Floated a company, didn't he?'

'It had been in existence for some years,' said Señor Centime, 'but the shares were of no great value until after Sardinko had bought out the concession.' He shook his head. 'He might have been a rich man to-day if he had not revisited Palookistan. Our Casino,' he added, explaining all.

'Ar,' said Sergeant Banner.

'On top of this,' said Señor Centime, 'he has to send his son to Cambridge. It was a mistake this.'

'Why?' asked Quill.

'When he came back,' said Señor Centime sadly, 'he was pro-English.' He pursed his lips. 'I do not care for the English.'

'Ah,' said Quill.

'They are snobbish, treacherous, and they have no sense of humour,' announced Señor Centime. 'Herr von Ribbentrop himself told me this.'

'Did he also tell you we wouldn't fight?' asked Quill.

'Anyone can make the mistake,' said Señor Centime, broad-mindedly. 'And at least when I was in Germany they gave me many stories to print. The good Doctor Goebbels wrote them himself. A charming man.' He sighed.

'Kind to children?' suggested Quill.

Señor Centime shook his head. 'No,' he said. 'That's Hitler.'

CHAPTER

5

SIR HUMPHREY's door was ajar. Passing it, Quill looked in.

A wasp-waisted little man leapt three feet into the half-light.

'Sorry,' said Quill as the little man came down. 'I wanted Sir Humphrey.'

'The office is closed,' said the little man. He bowed, 'Good-bye.'

Quill examined the startled doe in the well-creased suit.

He looked again.

He peered.

He crossed the room and switched on the lights.

'My God,' he said. 'Kurt!'

'*Mon Dieu!*' said the little man. 'M'sieu Quill!' He rushed forward and embraced him. 'But I am delighted to see you.'

Quill, too, was delighted to renew his acquaintance with Kurt. He had grown quite fond of the little crook since the day the latter had tried to sell him a gold brick on the Riviera. But that was a wax impression he was trying to stow away in his handkerchief! Quill stepped forward and salvaged it.

'I can explain,' said Kurt quickly. He sat down and pondered.

To help the process Quill passed his card. Kurt started.

'Scotland Yard,' he said unhappily. 'Do not tell me, my friend, you have become honest.'

Quill grinned. 'Only for the duration,' he promised.

'Me too,' said Kurt. 'I am now Kurt Carruthers. I am English since seven months,' he said with pride. 'I work here in the censorship.'

'You're getting on,' said Quill approvingly. 'When last I knew you you were a confidence trickster—rather a bad confidence trickster.'

Kurt looked hurt. 'I was magnificent,' he said. 'You joke—no?'

'I joke,' agreed Quill solemnly.

Kurt laughed merrily. 'I was stupid to think you were serious. Did you not always admire my technique?'

'Always,' said Quill.

Kurt beamed. 'But now,' he said, 'I am the confidence man no more. I have promoted myself.' He paused for the effect. 'I am now a spy.'

'Good God!' said Quill.

'I work here,' said Kurt, 'in the employment of a foreign Government. They are very generous. Maybe,' he offered, 'I can get you a job too.'

'Kind of you,' said Quill.

'You will find the work interesting,' promised Kurt. 'And my Government will pay you well.'

'Ah,' said Quill.

'It is fascinating, this espionage,' mused Kurt. 'Always I had imagined there was nothing in life to compare to the moment when one sold a gold-mine to a sucker, but, my friend, I was wrong.'

'Ah,' said Quill.

'It does not compare with the selling of the secrets of one Government to another. There is little doubt,' Kurt boasted, 'that I shall finish as the most successful spy in history. I have for espionage a natural talent. But that is not all. I am also thorough. I study my subject. I have exhausted all the available literature on it in the public libraries. Have you,' he demanded, 'read *Fifty Years a Beautiful Spy?*'

'No,' said Quill.

'It is my favourite,' said Kurt. 'Also I have seen it on the pictures. Aubrey Smith.' He sighed. 'A magnificent performance.'

'Sorry, I missed it,' said Quill.

'It is showing at the Elephant and Castle,' said Kurt. 'If you like we will see together.'

'Some other time,' pleaded Quill.

'As you wish,' said Kurt, disappointed. 'But it contains many lessons not without value in our profession. To succeed as a spy,' said Kurt earnestly, 'one must have courage.'

'Undoubtedly,' said Quill.

'Only yesterday,' boasted Kurt, 'while the others shivered in the air-raid shelter I was up here alone.'

'Oh, were you,' said Quill.

'It is not often,' said Kurt, 'that the ordnance-room is left open and I can examine the blue-prints at leisure.'

'I should jolly well hope not,' said Quill.

Kurt lit a cigar and passed across the case. Quill examined it.

'*Ersatz?*' he asked.

'Why not?' said Kurt. 'My Government gave it to me.'

'For services rendered?' asked Quill.

Kurt bowed. 'You are marvelling, no doubt,' he said, 'that I am so ready to entrust you with my secrets. But I am a man of great decisions.'

'Like the Fuehrer?' suggested Quill.

'A little, perhaps,' said Kurt, well pleased. 'I have decided that I can trust you. There is,' he admitted frankly, 'nothing else I can do. Also,' he threatened, 'should you betray me, our Gestapo will be quick to avenge.'

'You frighten me,' said Quill.

'There is no occasion for alarm while you obey my orders,' said Kurt kindly.

'Ah,' said Quill.

Kurt leant back in his chair and puffed a ring of smoke into the air. How simple these Englishmen were, he reflected. Really there was no excuse for Ribbentrop for not getting on with them.

'What do you know about Auguste Sardinko?' asked Quill, breaking into this bubble.

Kurt looked haughty. 'Sardinko,' he said, 'was an enemy of my country. I need say no more.'

'Oh, yes, you need,' said Quill. 'A lot more.'

'I weep no tears that he is dead,' announced Kurt. 'Gladly I would have killed him myself had I known he was here. Only my Government did not let me know.'

'Unaccountable,' said Quill.

'Sardinko,' said Kurt, 'was a menace to the Reich. He was going to send to England the Gardenium that my Government needs. Now that he is dead there is a chance for other Powers to negotiate for the Gardenium.'

'So?' said Quill.

'This time there will be no mistake,' said Kurt. 'We shall not send Von Papen again,' he promised darkly. 'He misses too many trains, that one.'

Sir Humphrey burst into the room.

'Good afternoon,' he boomed cordially at Kurt.

'Good afternoon, Sir Humphrey,' said Kurt, and scuttled off.

Sir Humphrey hung up his gas mask. 'That,' he told Quill, 'was Kurt Carruthers. Nice johnny.'

Quill hated to give away an old friend, but after all there was a war on.

'That nice johnny,' he said drily, 'was making a wax impression of the lock in your desk.'

'Good,' said Sir Humphrey. 'Excellent.'

Quill looked at him. 'I caught him in the act,' he said urgently.

Sir Humphrey looked alarmed. 'Good gad,' he said. 'Hope you didn't scare him.'

Quill went back to the beginning. 'You don't seem to understand,' he said. 'This man is in the pay of a foreign Government.'

'Known it for ages,' said Sir Humphrey happily. 'He's our favourite spy.'

Quill looked at him.

'Wouldn't have him alarmed for worlds,' said Sir Humphrey. 'Invaluable johnny. Guaranteed to find out everything we want him to.'

'But a spy,' said Quill.

'I know,' said Sir Humphrey soothingly. 'Felt a little like that myself when I first heard of it. But Al Schenk pointed out just how valuable he could be to us selling his Government dud secrets. Clever man, Al.'

'Very,' said Quill.

'Besides,' said Sir Humphrey, 'if we arrest him they might send someone to take his place who was really good at it. As it is everybody's happy. There's only one small snag.'

'Yes,' said Quill.

'We're worried stiff the johnny might get the sack from Germany. So we have to keep on thinking up secrets for him to find out.'

'If you keep on leaving the ordnance doors open during air raids,' said Quill, 'you won't have to worry about that.'

'Good gad,' said Sir Humphrey, shaken. 'Did we do that?'

The phone bell rang.

'I say,' said the Ministry of Information. 'Is there any news?'

'I'll see,' said Sir Humphrey.

He switched on the radio.

'Englishmen, snug in your beds, you do not know how your Government is deceiving you,' said the radio unexpectedly. 'The Fuehrer loves you all. That ship we sank yesterday was a mistake.'

Sir Humphrey blinked.

'What's this?' he asked.

'Hamburg,' said Quill.

'Ah,' said Sir Humphrey profoundly.

The somewhat guttural Oxford accent cleared its throat.

'Your Government has not dared to tell you the truth about the murder of the Insomnian emissary. Do you know what Sardinko stood for? No! Do you know why he came to England? No! Do you know the truth behind the murder?'

'No,' said Quill.

'We will tell you.'

Quill settled down to listen. He might as well get the low-down on his case without sweating for it.

'Sardinko,' said the Oxford accent, 'was due to sign a treaty that would give to England the sole concession of Insomnia's wealth of Gardenium. The ogre Churchill, with his leather-lunged panoply of false benevolence, lured the unsuspecting delegate Sardinko . . .'

'Good gad,' said Sir Humphrey whitely. 'It's treason. We can't listen to this.' He switched off.

'Oh, yes, we can,' said Quill. He switched on again.

'This murder has shocked the world,' the Oxford accent was gloating. 'And what is the British Government doing to reassure Insomnian public opinion that the outrage will be avenged? They have put in charge of the case a man from Scotland Yard whose sole claim to fame lies in his habit of arresting the wrong people. . . .'

'That's you,' said Sir Humphrey accusingly.

'. . . And left him to plod his weary way round the Ballyhoo factory run by the biggest noodle in Whitehall.'

'That's you,' said Quill.

'Listeners in Great Britain,' the Oxford accent took on a sinister note. 'It may interest you to hear that a German mission is now on its way to Insomnia.'

Quill and Sir Humphrey looked at one another.

'Herr von Papen is in charge.'

'Better,' said Quill, relieved.

'With public opinion running high against England, Insomnia will prefer to do business with a country she can trust. The success of the German mission is assured. Insomnia's Gardenium is virtually on its way to Germany.'

'Listeners in England.' The Oxford accent disappeared in a bellow. 'Soon you will be free. You have lost the war. Heil!'

It stopped.

'We will now,' said a new voice in German, 'play you the Marseillaise.'

Sir Humphrey stood to attention.

'Not a word of this,' he hissed urgently to Quill.

The telephone rang.

'Hallo,' said Sir Humphrey. He listened. He choked.

'It's scandalous,' he exploded. 'A blot on the services. How do you expect us to get our work done if you send us down to the cellars every five minutes.' He hung up.

'Just letting the Air Ministry know what I think of them for giving us that false alarm yesterday,' he told Quill.

'Splendid,' said Quill.

'Do you know,' said Sir Humphrey, indignation boiling over, 'that they've just had the nerve to enquire why we didn't deliver the R.A.F. pamphlets on schedule. Impatient johnnies! Sent the planes without them.'

'Ah,' said Quill. 'A reconnaisance flight.'

Sir Humphrey turned on him—a stag at bay. 'Well, the pamphlets were only put in hand three weeks ago.'

'So you've blamed it on the air-raid warning,' said Quill.

'And why not?' said Sir Humphrey. 'Delayed us at least an hour.'

The telephone rang.

'Hallo,' roared Sir Humphrey. He listened. He deflated. His face fell. 'Oh,' he said, 'that's different.' He put the receiver back almost gently.

'Curious thing,' he told Quill, 'they say the air-raid warning yesterday started here.'

'What's that?' said Quill quickly.

'That air-raid warning,' bleated Sir Humphrey. 'They say we

started it. Incredible. Must ask Miss Peacock.' He rang a bell. Nothing happened. The efficient Miss Peacock was at that moment explaining to baffled 'Pliss?' the exact difference between A.R.P. and A.F.S., and exactly how he should go about joining both.

'It's beyond me,' Sir Humphrey was bleating.

But it was easy to Quill. Ever since he had started on the case his subconscious had been nagging him over the coincidence of an air-raid alarm that had so obligingly cleared the stage for the murder.

'How exactly does the air-raid alarm system function here?' he asked.

'Dashed if I know,' said Sir Humphrey. 'All the Ministries are on a circuit. Everyone telephones everyone else. Colossal organization,' said Sir Humphrey. 'Joe will explain it to you.'

'Would you mind if I had a word with the Control Room?'

'Impossible,' said Sir Humphrey from force of habit. He reflected. 'Yes, that's all right, old man. You'll find it somewhere about the building.'

The door opened. A young man wearing a dazzling pullover, and carrying an enormous portfolio, strode in.

'Afternoon, Sir Humphrey,' he said brightly.

'Good afternoon,' said Sir Humphrey.

'Just looked in to tell you I'm back.'

'Fine,' said Sir Humphrey.

'So long,' said the young man and strode out.

'Who was that?' asked Quill.

'No idea,' said Sir Humphrey.

* * * * *

In the vestibule Quill located a commissionaire and asked his way to the Control Room.

The commissionaire thought it over.

The commissionaire got into his verbal stride.

He pushed Quill along a winding corridor, propelled him through a swing door, hoisted him up a staircase, allowed him to admire himself in a mirror, and talked him into a room marked No. 7.

'Thanks,' said Quill. He was just plodding off when the commissionaire called him back.

'Sorry,' he said. 'I made a mistake. Number Seven is the Department for the Illuminated Leaflets.'

'Illuminated?' asked Quill.

'They're not allowed to pick them up in Germany,' explained the commissionaire. 'It was Sir Humphrey's idea,' he added with pride.

'Oh,' said Quill.

'Control,' said the commissionaire, 'is in the basement. You take . . .'

But Quill had gone.

The corridor downstairs was deserted. Quill looked vaguely at various doors and tried one of them.

Two pairs of legs were propped on the mantelpiece. One pair inevitably belonged to Misha Podushkin. Neither stirred at Quill's entrance.

'Transferred?' Quill asked Misha.

'Temporarily,' said Misha. 'You see,' he explained, 'the lift was non-stop. But it does not matter,' he added broad-mindedly, 'for it is comfortable here, and Sandy,' he pointed to the other pair of legs, 'is my good friend. We do not agree about anything, and that makes for conversation.'

Sandy took his legs off the mantelpiece.

'Sit down,' he said. 'Make yourself comfortable. Have a War Communiqué.' He picked up a sheaf of papers and passed them over to Quill.

Quill glanced at the first. It read:

'There was reduced activity during the night.'

'Lucid,' said Quill.

Sandy sighed. 'He's a wonderful general,' he said, 'but as a journalist he wouldna last two minutes—not even on *The Times*.'

'Who?' asked Quill.

'Gamelin,' said Sandy.

Misha laughed. 'Poor Sandy. All day he sits here and reads the literature of our good General. It is not very gay. But he does not turn aside from his duty even when there is an air raid.'

Quill looked up. 'Didn't you go into the shelter yesterday?'

'Me,' said Sandy resentfully. 'I'm a journalist.'

'I have often reflected,' said Misha, 'how curious it is that I have never been a journalist. I have all the qualifications. I am curious, I am thirsty, and I have no ambition.'

'Quite,' said Quill drily.

'One day,' said Misha, warming to this reception, 'I will write a novel. It will be a very fine novel. It has been in my mind for many years, but somehow there has never been time.'

'Me too,' said Sandy. 'Mon, I've got a grand novel in my head. All about my childhood in Aberdeen.'

'Stark,' suggested Quill.

'Grim,' said Sandy, with satisfaction.

'My novel,' said Misha, 'will be gay but underneath will be the despair of every Russian.'

'Mine,' said Sandy, 'will be grim.'

'Poor Sandy,' said Misha, 'everything to him it is the grim. I have been trying to cheer him with the news of a club that I will organize soon, but he is a sceptic.'

'Huh,' said Sandy.

'It is,' explained Misha, 'a club for the absent-minded. It will be decorated with unburnable fabrics, asbestos furniture, and spare pairs of spectacles. The carpet will be an ash-tray.'

'Can I join?' asked Quill.

'*Enchanté*,' said Misha. 'You will like it. Every month the club will meet for dinner.'

'Anyone who remembers to turn up will have to resign,' suggested Sandy.

'But of course,' Misha made a note. 'My brother will approve of that.'

'Your brother!' said Quill.

'My brother,' said Misha, well pleased. 'The club was his idea, though it might easily have been mine. We are very much alike,' he boasted. 'He is a parachute-jumper.'

'Parachute?' said Sandy.

'But yes,' said Misha. 'He finds it restful.'

'Restful?' said Quill.

'Certainly,' said Misha. 'They take him up and they float him down. He hardly deranges himself at all. It is a good life this.'

'Ah,' said Quill.

'But about the club,' said Misha. 'The subscription is five guineas. Maybe,' he asked Quill hopefully, 'you like to pay me now?'

'Sorry,' said Quill. 'I've come out without my wallet. You see,' he explained, 'I'm absent-minded.'

* * * * *

The Control Room gave out an aura of intense concentration. The colossal switchboard was manned to a woman, all of them reading novels.

An efficient young woman in spectacles rose to greet Quill.

Quill introduced himself. The young woman nodded.

'You've come here to ask questions about the Ministry murder. Okay. I'll tell you all about this department.'

She began to talk. Quill gathered that the safety of the whole of London hung on her shoulders. They were decorative but not very broad.

'Did you do all this in the air-raid warning yesterday?' he asked in awe.

'I wasn't on duty,' said the young woman smugly.

Quill patted her on the head and passed on. He questioned his way down the switchboard. In the far corner sat a man. In private life he assembled delicate mechanisms of microscopic wrist-watches. Quill enquired into the affair of the false alarm.

'Don't blame me,' said the watchmaker. 'I wasn't on duty.' He turned abruptly and plugged a line into a socket.

'Blast,' he said, unplugging it hurriedly. 'Hope I haven't woken up Sir Humphrey.'

'So you weren't on duty?' asked Quill.

'Well, I was and I wasn't,' said the watchmaker. 'As a matter of fact, I obliged someone by going on a message.'

'Who took your place at the switchboard?'

'The fellow who sent me,' said the watchmaker. 'You know. Joe thingmebob.'

'So Joe was at the switchboard when the alarm came through?'

The watchmaker shrugged. 'I suppose so.'

CHAPTER

6

QUILL felt the need for a cigarette and a think. He found his way to street level, leant against the nearest sandbag, and studied the sky. The balloons, fat, inactive dolphins floated unconcernedly above his head. Theirs was a simple job, thought Quill. All they had to do was to stay blown up while a group of men pulled them up or hauled them down. They did not have their peaceful repose in a Kentish oast-house interrupted by ubiquitous corpses in a Ministry. They did not have to rush around asking fool questions of people trained not to answer them. They did not have to report to a Snarl waiting to find out how little one had found out. And if an aeroplane hit them —well, the aeroplane got badly the worst of it.

Joe what's-his-name had got the worst of it this afternoon with the milk jug. Quill's chuckle stopped abruptly. Joe what's-his-name was no longer particularly funny. He never had been, thought Quill savagely, and the discovery that he was responsible for the air-raid warning brought him well into the radius of the murderer. The air-raid warning was essential to the execution of the crime. Of course, bumping off the Cabinet's pet delegate might be Joe's idea of a funny joke. And yet . . . Quill threw away his cigarette. It hit a War Reserve.

'Sorry,' said Quill.

'Quite all right, old man,' said the War Reserve, examining his uniform. 'Don't do it again.'

Somehow Quill could not see Joe in the role of murderer. It seemed outside the scope of his practical jokes. Palming a rubber dart off on Sir Humphrey, putting ink in Banner's beer, or immobilizing a Ministry with a false air-raid alarm . . . these required a different technique. Anyone wanting to achieve any of these would call in Joe at once. That was it! Someone had called in Joe!

In his excitement Quill threw away his second cigarette. It hit the War Reserve.

'Now look here,' said the War Reserve, examining his uniform. 'Nobody can say I haven't got a sense of humour, but . . .'

'Sorry,' said Quill.

He resumed his pacing. The murderer had needed a clear field. Supposing he had suggested to Joe that a false air-raid alarm would be a damn good joke. Joe would be certain to agree with him. Quill could almost see Joe jumping at the idea.

But wouldn't the murderer be taking a chance, employing the expansive Joe as his assistant? He must have realized that Joe was incapable of keeping such a gorgeous joke to himself for long. Sooner or later he would be bound to babble about it to someone. Come to think of it, he had almost babbled it last night in the cellar. When he had announced that unexpected people could be found to have a sense of humour he had been talking about the murderer. Now who, in this Ministry, had an unexpected sense of humour? At any rate, thought Quill, it should be easy to get a confession out of Joe.

If he were still there to give it!

This was a workman-like murder, carefully planned, timed, and carried out. A murderer of this calibre would never leave a Joe carelessly lying about to babble vital clues. He would remove him. He would remove him at the first opportunity.

By God!

Quill threw away his cigarette.

'Hey,' said the War Reserve, hurt, 'you've missed me.'

But Quill was racing down the corridor.

* * * * *

The air struck cold as Quill raced into the dark stone cellar, raid-shelter to the Ministry, to keep his date with Joe what's-his-name.

Quill groped about the wall for some switch to turn on light and, groping, shivered.

There was something menacing about the stillness inside these stone walls—some lack of warmth from the living world, which pervaded the air like a spoken threat.

Unable to locate the switch, Quill snapped on his service torch and shone it over the walls. They were bland and, save for Sir Humphrey's dart-board hanging on its familiar hook, and the regulation fire-buckets filled with water and sand, they were empty.

The beam travelled to the floor. Then over to the far corner, where it discovered a long wooden stand, from the hooks of which the gas-proof coats and snoods and the tin shrapnel-hats of the A.R.P. wardens were hanging. Quill crossed to the stand and gingerly peered into the garments. If Joe boos out on me now, he thought, I shall let out a yell and run for it.

But the rows of oilskin garments concealed no lurking joker.

Reassured, Quill raked the ceiling with his torch. Suddenly the light halted.

From the beam in the centre someone had suspended a gas proof garment, snood and all, high and limp, and unmoving. Below the folds of the oilskin a pair of patent shoes were dangling. Quill had no need to search the face in the snood to learn who it was who was hanging by the neck in the air-raid shelter.

Joe what's-his-name was due to play his next annoying, senseless, yet somehow endearing joke on St Peter.

Quill shook his head. Somehow he felt quite sorry he had poured that milk over Joe.

As he turned away in search of a knife to hack the body down, Quill stumbled over an object on the floor in the dark.

Lying at Joe's lifeless feet was a grinning face carved out of wood. Red cheeks and a gaping scarlet mouth had been painted on the object. A woolly fuzz of hair had been gummed beneath a revolting pink cotton mob-cap. The whole was attached to a wire frame, from which hung a 'dress' of the same bright pink cotton material. In the gaping wooden mouth there was the broken stem of a clay pipe. An Aunt Sally socket, prepared for the flying missives aimed to break the pipe that now had fallen from its mouth.

CHAPTER
7

'How on earth did the murderer persuade him to put his head in the noose?' asked Quill.

'Poor old Joe,' sighed Banner. 'It had to be him. I shall miss him.' He looked at Quill reproachfully.

'Dash it all,' said Quill savagely. 'Was it my fault the murderer had a grudge against him?'

Quill had had a trying afternoon. Unravelling a murder—probably political—with the entire Cabinet looking on was enough to make any policeman temperamental. And then to stumble across a second body in the middle of it. . . .

But this was uneasy ground. If only he had arrived at his conclusions quicker he might have reached the cellar in time to save an amiable bloke a nasty death, catch his man, grab Belinda, and be back at his oast-house for dinner. For it was now a certainty that whoever had murdered Joe had also murdered Sardinko. If only he had got to that cellar earlier.

And now there would be a Snarl to carp and grumble at him, endless interviews, and a barely concealed atmosphere of reproach to work in. Already Sir Humphrey had practically accused him of carelessness, Miss Peacock of callousness, and Misha Podushkin of crassness. ('The English are childish—it is well known.')

The afternoon had been full of effort to no end. Time spent in getting the Yard to the cellar. Time spent in detaching them from a spell of practice on Sir Humphrey's dart-board. Time spent in explaining to Belinda just why he couldn't put her War Reserve (an evident admirer of Poirot) in charge of the case. Time doubly wasted because Archie had still persisted in hanging around and being helpful. No lunch. Warding off a host of dons each with theory. And all to an accompaniment of commands, bleats, and entreaties from Sir Humphrey that not one word of this must leak out to the papers. Finally a desperate Quill had sought out Sergeant Banner, detached him from his neutrals, and taken him to a tea-shop to discuss the case.

So far Banner had not proved very helpful. He mourned for Joe and would not be comforted.

'He was a nice bloke,' he said regretfully. 'Put a bit of life into the place. I shall never forget the day when the Prime Minister . . .'

'Oh, shut up,' said Quill, 'and let's get down to it.'

With a visible effort Banner controlled his emotion and concentrated on duty. He produced a bulky note-pad, turned to a virgin sheet, pulled out a stump of pencil, licked it, and looked at Quill expectantly.

'For God's sake put that away,' said Quill. 'Listen to me. Two men have been murdered in this Ministry within twenty-four hours. The two murders are so closely connected that if the same hand did not kill them both then the same brain must have directed them.'

'A gang?' asked Banner interested.

'I think not,' said Quill. 'There's something cosy—almost home-made—about these murders. A gang would have been quicker on the trigger. They would never have left Joe alive for so long after he had given the false air-raid alarm.'

'False alarm?' said Banner. 'You mean the one yesterday?'

'One of Joe's jokes,' said Quill briefly.

Banner thought it over. The yellow light. All the Ministries rushing to cover. Sir Humphrey reaching for his gas mask. . . .

He shook his head regretfully and spoke Joe's epitaph.

'He was a one,' he said.

'But it wasn't his idea,' said Quill. 'I'm pretty certain someone put him up to it.'

'Who?' said Banner unconvinced.

'The murderer,' said Quill.

Banner thought it out. He had not been promoted to the C.I.D. for nothing. He got there.

'Our man wanted the coast clear—eh?' he mused. 'And then Joe, simple like, cleared it for him.'

'Yes,' said Quill.

'And then he ups and bumps off our Joe before he could give him away?'

'That's about it.'

'Clever,' said Sergeant Banner impartially. 'Still he oughtn't to have done Joe in. Not our Joe.' He pondered and came to a resolution. 'Tell you what—I'll help you catch him. I'll hand over my neutrals to Archie for a day or so.'

'Wish to God you would,' said Quill. 'That will keep everyone busy.'

But Banner was off on another angle.

'Who do you think done it?' he asked.

'No idea,' said Quill.

'No clues?' asked Banner disappointed.

Quill shook his head.

Silence descended upon them. Both were thinking.

Suddenly Sergeant Banner wriggled.

'I got an idea,' he said diffidently.

'Yes?' said Quill.

'Remember last night in the cellar?'

Quill did vividly.

'Joe said something funny.'

'Never!' said Quill.

'Something queer,' explained Banner. 'He says out of the blue like that some quite unexpected blokes had a sense of humour.'

'Yes?' said Quill.

'I bin thinking,' said Banner. 'Maybe he meant our man.'

Quill passed him his packet of cigarettes.

'You've got something there,' he said.

Banner looked elated.

'But how does it help?'

Banner went dim.

'I've got it,' said Quill. 'We can now safely assume that the murderer was a man who never appreciated Joe's jokes.'

Banner nodded. 'No sense of humour,' he said severely.

'That is why,' pointed out Quill, 'Joe was so surprised when the murderer suggested to him that a false air-raid alarm would be a bright idea.'

Banner nodded again. 'Just the way I see it,' he said with considerable satisfaction.

'Obviously,' continued Quill, 'he was not the type of man from whom Joe would expect such a suggestion.'

'Ar,' said Sergeant Banner.

'Now,' said Quill, 'what we've got to do is to find that man. All we know about him is that he didn't like practical jokes. It isn't much,' he admitted ruefully, 'but it's something.'

Banner sat up. 'And what do we do about it?' he asked eagerly.

'I'll tell you,' said Quill. 'We know that the murderer was a man with whom Joe was in contact. It is to be supposed he worked in the Ministry. We know that none of these seven names,' Quill tapped his list with an emphatic pencil, 'took refuge in the cellar during the warning. All that remains to be done,' he added optimistically, 'is to find out which one of them doesn't like practical jokes.'

'How?' asked Banner.

'Play them,' said Quill.

'Ar,' said Banner. The theory appealed to him. 'Who will you start with?'

'I'll be busy,' said Quill. 'But you can begin with Sir Humphrey.'

'Me!' Banner started.

'You'll be all right,' said Quill encouragingly. 'Pull his chair away, or something.'

'Me!' said Banner in despair.

Quill passed him a cigarette.

* * * * *

In the street a newsboy was giving tongue.

'Murder in the Ministry special,' he gloated. ''Orrible sensation,' he added with relish.

He was doing a brisk business. Beside him an older, colder vendor sat hunched over his routine placard. All it said was: 'Another Leaflet Raid on Germany.'

Quill patronized the younger generation. It turned out to be the *Evening Kibbitzer*, sister paper to the *Daily Shmooze*. The headline ran:

ANOTHER MURDER IN WHITEHALL

CHAPTER

8

QUILL sat in his oast-house smoking 'pool' tobacco and gazed with loathing on a drawing of Sherlock Holmes that a bright Belinda had positively glued on the wall.

The stern echoes of international repercussions exploding out of his case were getting Quill down. He just wasn't used to having the fate of the Empire dependent on his efforts. It made him nervous. A bearded body, all by itself, is usually considered ample for a young detective to tackle. To embroider it with eighty per cent of the world's Gardenium, a Cabinet, egged on by an impatient First Lord of the Admiralty, and then to throw in another body, was definitely unethical. If it wasn't that he had practically solved the damned thing Quill would have thrown a bout of temperament and resigned from the case.

He had been following the process, strongly recommended in the *Detective's Handbook*, of putting himself in the murderer's place. Deciding to assassinate a political envoy, he had met him at Dover as he disembarked, followed him into an empty railway compartment, and pushed him into a convenient tunnel. Now why hadn't the murderer done this? Why all this complicated business with a Ministry, false alarms, and an accomplice who, it must have been obvious even to the dullest murderer, would have to be bumped off immediately afterwards. There must be a reason, thought Quill. There was nothing *extempore* about this murder. Almost it might have been planned by a Press agent.

Of course that was it. Quill felt himself blushing under the disapproving eye of Mr Holmes. Shoving a body into a tunnel where it might lie unnoticed for days was, though lethal enough, a very homemade method. Obviously, when you worked on an international body, publicity was what you were after.

The chief value of murdering Sardinko lay not in preventing him from signing the treaty, but in raising such a barrage of anti-British feeling in Insomnia that no treaty could be negotiated between the two countries. From this angle choosing the Ministry of Elimination as a depository was a stroke of genius. A murdered envoy is hard enough to explain away to his surprised Government in any case, but murder him in your own Ministry, in the heart of Whitehall, and you will never convince that Government that you did not do it on purpose.

If this murder had received international publicity thought Quill, it was because it had been planned to receive it. The leakage of news to the *Daily Shmooze* was not the work of an energetic reporter trying to bring off a solitary scoop. It had been issued by the murderer himself.

The *Daily Shmooze* had confirmed this. Calling on the editor, a busy man, Quill had been informed that the copy had been turned in with the official O.K. It was unsigned, but the editor was in no mood to ask questions and give the Ministry a chance to change its mind and ban it.

A visit to the munition depot that had lost the fatal gun before issuing it gave Quill his final link.

Who, in the Ministry of Elimination, knew Sardinko well enough to invite him to call without arousing suspicion?

Who, in his official capacity, could send out a story uncensored by anyone except himself?

Who could come and go to any Government depot without question?

Who was the last man on earth Joe what's-his-name would have expected to instigate practical jokes?

The telephone rang.

'How are you doing?' asked Al Schenk chattily.

Quill started. It is always embarrassing to be rung up by a man who, on paper, you have just decided is a murderer.

'Narrowing it down?' pursued Al.

'Well—yes,' said Quill.

'Ruled out Sir Humphrey?'

'Perhaps.'

'And now everything is beginning to point to me?'

Quill pulled at his collar. 'Well . . .'

'Quit stalling,' said Al. 'I haven't much time. You know darn well I did it. And if you haven't proved it yet you soon will.'

'Ah,' said Quill.

'As a matter of fact,' said Al frankly, 'I've been careless. Left clues about. That revolver, for instance. I suppose you're on to that?'

'I am,' said Quill.

'And the Aunt Sally's head?'

'Well, that was a bit more difficult.'

'Sure,' said Al. 'Mind you, it was quite easy to persuade Joe that a hanging baby would give you a nasty turn, but it took all my genius to auto-suggest to Joe that it would be a good joke to put his own head in the noose and frighten me. Then I pulled the noose.'

'For a murderer,' said Quill, 'you're unusually candid.'

'As a spy,' said Al, 'I'm unusually ruthless. So don't go getting the idea I phoned you to save you trouble. This is a warning.'

'Warning?' said Quill.

'Call it friendly advice,' said Al. 'You are about to receive a summons from the Foreign Office. They will tell you to proceed to Insomnia. You will refuse.'

'Oh, will I?' said Quill.

'It would be wise,' said Al. 'You'll save your neck and you'll save me a hell of a lot of trouble.'

'Well, that I can follow,' said Quill.

'Now listen,' said Al. 'I'm not in this spy racket for my health. I like you, Quill. I liked Joe what's-his-name too, but that didn't keep me from killing him when he stood in the way of my deal.'

'Deal?'

'Strictly business,' said Al. 'My job is to see to it that Germany gets the Gardenium. So stay out of Insomnia, sonny. Save your neck. Land of Hope and Glory,' said Al, 'may be all very good for the soul, but it won't line your pockets.'

'Where are you speaking from?' said Quill desperately.

Al chuckled. 'I'll tell you. Save you the trouble of tracing it. My 'plane leaves for Holland in one minute.'

'Blast,' said Quill.

'Good-bye, sonny' said Al. 'Hope I shan't be seeing you.' He hung up.

Quill flashed the receiver. 'Croydon Aerodrome,' he snapped.

'Gone to Glamorgan,' said the Exchange brightly. 'Will you take an incoming call?'

'No,' said Quill.

'Oh, yes, you will,' bellowed a voice from the other end. It was the Snarl. 'You're to report to the Foreign Office at once. Room 37h.'

'Right now?' asked Quill.

'Now,' said the Snarl. 'And, Quill, pack a bag and take your passport.'

'Fine,' said Quill.

'By the way,' said the Snarl as an afterthought. 'Have you got a visa for Insomnia?'

* * * * *

. . . Throwing three shirts and four collars into a bag. Bracing himself to wake up Belinda. A stroke of luck in finding her alone. Coaxing the car to start on 'Pool' petrol. Triumph! Crawling flinchingly to London, every locomotive whistle an air-raid siren. Stopping for a red light that was tired and refused to move. Chancing it. The reproachful War Reserve stationed on the other side. Impact with a shadow that turned out to be a street refuge. A lucky taxi. A lucky air-raid warden to take care of Belinda. Arrival at the Foreign Office. Asking the way to Room 37h. . . .

'Go up to the second floor,' said the commissionaire, 'turn left, go down the corridor, turn right. . . .'

'Take me there,' said Quill firmly.

A little man in a bowler hat who had been sitting in a resigned manner in a corner of the hall got up and ran after them.

'Look here,' he pleaded, clutching the commissionaire's sleeve with a desperate hand. 'I simply must see him.'

'Yes, yes,' said the commissionaire soothingly. 'Presently.'

'But it's frightfully important,' said the little man. 'Urgent. A matter of national importance.'

'I know, I know,' said the commissionaire. 'Now just you go and sit down and I'll attend to it presently.'

'You promise?' said the little man.

'Trust me,' said the commissionaire.

He led Quill away. The little man looked uncertainly after them, sighed, and went back to his seat.

'A crank,' explained the commissionaire. 'Been here every night this week.' He paused doubtfully. 'We've come the wrong way,' he said and turned back. 'Down here,' he said confidently. . . .

Eventually by the simple process of trying the one corridor the commissionaire was certain did not contain Room 37h, Quill found it. He knocked and entered.

'You've been a hell of a time,' said the Snarl. 'The P.M. couldn't wait.'

He had made himself at home at a desk, usurping the rightful position of a Bland Manner, now seated on his right, and crowding an apprehensive pair of pince-nez on his left.

'Sorry,' said Quill.

The Snarl muttered introductions. They were quite inaudible.

'And this is Quill,' he said distastefully.

The pince-nez was charmed. But the Bland Manner opined that Quill seemed a little young for so responsible a task.

'We are rushing a delegate to Insomnia,' said the Snarl. 'His job is to sign the Gardenium treaty. Your job, Quill, is to go with him.'

'Ah,' said Quill.

'Further,' said the Bland Manner, feeling it was time it asserted itself, 'should they send another envoy over here it will be your responsibility to escort him back to England.'

'And see that he doesn't get murdered on the way,' said the Snarl.

Quill remembered something.

'By the way,' he said. 'It seems a bit irrelevant now, but I know who murdered Sardinko.'

'What's that?' The Snarl was alert.

'At the moment,' said Quill regretfully, 'he is on his way to Holland.'

The door burst open. The little man in the bowler hat burst into the room.

'You've simply got to listen to me,' he told the Bland Manner despairingly.

'Surely, surely,' said the Bland Manner. 'Write to me about it,' he suggested.

The pince-nez, for once confident in its ability to cope with the situation, got to its feet, collected the little man and led him protesting away.

'A crank,' explained the Bland Manner. 'Been trying to see me every day this week. Probably another invention to win the war,' he opined, dismissing the subject.

'We're wasting time,' said the Snarl. 'Quill, a car is waiting to take you to the aerodrome. Get going.'

'Right,' said Quill. A thought struck him. 'By the way,' he enquired. 'Who are we sending?'

'Stung,' said the Bland Manner with deep satisfaction. 'Mr Stung.'

CHAPTER 9

THERE is a growing school of thought which holds that it is less trouble to fight a war than to remain neutral in the midst of it. On the whole, the authors of this book are inclined to agree with it. In earlier wars perhaps it was different. Neutrals in Europe, you perched cosily on your commercial fence and exported happily to both belligerents, and even if you did not know what to do with the accumulated gold afterwards—well, that was a matter for the economists. But to-day the fence has developed a wobble. On one side you can trade with a belligerent who can't afford to pay, even if you do manage to deliver the goods, but who will certainly invade you if you don't. While, on the other side of the fence, lurks a benevolent Power, surrounded by a mine-field, who'll pay cash—but you've got to go and get it. You can, of course, trade with one another, but who wants to do business with the family?

Quite apart from this there is the National Debt. Oh, yes—you're going to have a National Debt quite soon. What with increasing the army, rebuilding the navy, flooding your arable lands, and reorganizing the fire brigade, the cost of neutrality is rapidly becoming prohibitive. Even the electricity saved during the week-end crisis blackouts has to be written off against the cost of ammunition hopefully hurled at belligerent planes taking a short cut across your territory to bomb one another.

Don't take this thing too personally, Holland. You're not the only one. Consider, for instance, Insomnia.

Already, to preserve her neutrality, Insomnia has been forced to sign a non-aggression pact with Ribbentrop, hand over a naval base to Stalin, lend a tactical prop to Mussolini's well-known Mediterranean *status quo*, and swop a bewildered minority with Jugo-Slavia. In addition they had an uneasy feeling that the Allies were trying to put one across them too. 'When Winston Churchill in two successive broadcasts calls you "That Great Little Country that has never taken up arms against Us," ' said King Hannibal the Hothead in one of his moments of acumen, 'then for God's sake look out!'

The *Insomnia National Echo* has been saying much the same thing in powerful leaders throughout the autumn of 1939.

'Insomnians—remember you are Neutrals!'

Insomnians had little chance to forget it. Half the national boy friends were in the army, while the other half were being called away from important business deals to blow up the Balloon Barrage. The Casino at Palookistan was requisitioned by the Government and, what was worse, left empty. Gas-masks were fitted, but not issued. And a state of emergency declared every Saturday night. There was a National Savings drive, a no-treating order, and no civilian was allowed to run a car. All this was very annoying—another twist in the taut state of neutrality—but the limit was reached when Insomnians were enjoined to 'Dig for Neutrality—dig impartially—but anyway dig,' and King Hannibal himself, after an all night wrangle with the Cabinet, gave in and appeared in the Bond Street of Rumba-Rumba carrying a spade and wiping some carefully placed mud off his trousers.

And just in case anybody should try to get away from the war for a bit there was café conversation. Regretfully it has to be announced that Insomnian opinion, at no time pro-British (they thought we started the war by not giving in to Hitler), has, since the murder of Sardinko, become definitely antagonistic to the Allied cause. While not entirely in agreement with the Goebbels theory that Winston Churchill had done-in Sardinko in his lunch hour, they felt that the British Government had been distinctly careless, and the Man in the Street hoped devoutly that the Gardenium Treaty would now go to Germany. After all, he argued, the Fuehrer is unlikely to attack us until after we have delivered the goods. And with our rolling-stock ...

In the Palace the Cabinet was making much the same points to King Hannibal.

Bauldstok, the Prime Minister, an honest crook, who had projected himself into popularity by posing as a typical blunt Insomnian, and never allowing a photograph or caricature of himself without a hookah (the national pipe) and flagon of vodscht (the national beverage), was most emphatic.

'I am a blunt man,' he pointed out again, 'and what I think is . . .'

'Quite,' said King Hannibal, 'but England will pay cash.'

'Germany,' said the Chancellor of the Exchequer, 'will pay us after she has won the war. I have the Fuehrer's promise for that.'

'You've got yourself muddled,' said King Hannibal crossly. 'You're thinking of his last territorial demand.'

But the Cabinet, bought to a man, refused to laugh. Only last night the local Gauleiter had guaranteed them an invitation to the garden party which the Fuehrer, with a fine disregard for the climate, was going to hold at Buckingham Palace next Christmas, and they rather fancied themselves with swords. 'But,' warned the Gauleiter darkly, 'should England get the Gardenium the Fuehrer will invite you to Berchtesgarten.'

'I'm a blunt man,' said the Prime Minister. 'And what I say is when the German mission arrives—sign!'

There was a murmur of approval.

'We can't do that,' said King Hannibal, shocked. 'A British mission is on its way, too. It would be discourteous to settle anything before it arrives. Great Britain will be offended.'

'So what?' said the Minister of Fine Arts, an uncouth man.

'When Great Britain is offended,' said King Hannibal, 'she sends a warship.'

'Ah,' said the Minister of Fine Arts.

* * * * *

'So,' said Mr Stung, 'we sent a warship.'

'Ah,' said Quill.

They had been in the plane for four hours, and now dawn was breaking over Eastern Europe. They could not see it, for the aeroplane was blacked-out.

During the journey Mr Stung had beguiled Quill with his reminiscences. According to Stung diplomacy was easy—for an Englishman. It was much more difficult for foreigners on account of those warships we kept on sending. He himself had always been against disarmament. If only, he said, we had sent a warship to Russia, or even a destroyer. . . .

As for his present mission, Quill gathered this was going to be chicken feed. Quill had his doubts about this. Al Schenk, though one of the nicest murderers Quill had ever known, was a man of strong determination, and he seemed to have set his face against this deal. He was probably waiting to meet them in Insomnia right now.

'Wonder if they'll meet us with military honours?' mused Mr Stung.

Quill thought this quite likely, particularly if the military included Al behind a Bren gun.

'You look worried,' said Mr Stung kindly. 'There's nothing to worry about. Trade treaties are child's play. We're twice as rich as any other European country, so of course they're all anxious to sign up with us. You'll see,' he prophesied.

Quill, remembering Señor Centime's attitude towards the English, and the Hamburg radio threat of the German mission on its way, hoped to God he would.

'Foreigners,' said Mr Stung, 'are like children. Treat them like grown-ups and they're delighted.'

'So you don't expect any difficulty,' said Quill.

'Difficulty,' said Mr Stung. 'Good Lord—no! Why, old Bauldstok, that's the Prime Minister, and I are like that.' He put his fingers together.

'Better,' said Quill, relieved.

'Had him up to my place for the week-end once,' said Mr Stung. 'Gave him a grand time.'

'Oh,' said Quill.

* * * * *

'Stung,' said Bauldstok, purple in the face. 'They've sent Stung!'

'Why not?' said King Hannibal. 'Don't you like him?'

'Like him?' said Bauldstok. 'I spent a week-end with him.'

King Hannibal raised an eyebrow.

'He took me beagling,' said Bauldstok.

'Ah,' said King Hannibal.

The Cabinet relaxed. They had been arguing with the King for a long time, and for the moment both sides had lost.

'Well, gentlemen,' said King Hannibal, 'I won't insist now. We can postpone our decision. But in the meantime we must make the thing look good. Have you arranged a reception for Stung at the aerodrome?'

'We've arranged it,' said the Minister of Fine Arts, with considerable satisfaction.

There was a sound of thin cheering below. King Hannibal and the Cabinet rushed to the window.

'The German mission,' breathed the Chancellor of the Exchequer.

A procession was turning into the courtyard. It was led by the local Gauleiter, mounted none too securely on a white horse. Behind, heiling furiously, marched the local storm troopers. The eldest was fifteen. Behind them, in a bullet-proof car covered with swastikas, came the mission. They looked a little sheepish.

'I don't see Papen,' said King Hannibal, peering.

Again the thin cheers rang out.

The Gauleiter looked round peevishly.

'Blast,' said the Minister of Fine Arts. 'They've forgotten to put on the cheer records Goebbels sent us.'

The Chancellor of the Exchequer opened a drawer, produced a swastika flag, and draped it artistically over the King's chair. Absently, the King went and sat somewhere else.

The door was flung open. The deputation filed through, advanced, and waited.

'Heil Hitler,' said the Minister of Fine Arts with great presence of mind.

'Greetings from the Fuehrer,' said a spokesman, trying to make them sound cordial.

'Quite,' said King Hannibal.

They looked at one another. The deputation shuffled uneasily.

'And Herr von Papen?' enquired King Hannibal graciously. 'I trust he is well?'

The spokesman blushed.

'Franzi,' he said, 'is in the best of health. Unfortunately he is in Budapest.'

'Budapest,' said King Hannibal enviously.

'No doubt he will arrive to-morrow,' said the Nazi spokesman. 'For the moment he has missed his train.'

'Splendid,' said King Hannibal.

*   *   *   *   *

A big black bird bore down on the aerodrome at Rumba-Rumba.

Mr Poparescu braced himself. His big moment was upon him.

Mr Poparescu had been sent to welcome the English mission. It was easily his most important assignment since he had joined the Insomnian diplomatic service. In point of fact, the Cabinet had selected him as an appropriate sneer at Mr Stung.

The black bird grew bigger. Mr Poparescu went into action.

'Hoist the Union Jack,' he commanded. 'Bring up the red carpet. And for God's sake line up your guard of honour,' he snapped at an exasperated captain.

The black bird came bumping over the airfield, coming to a stop in the opposite corner from the red carpet. Hurriedly they moved the carpet over.

With perfect poise Mr Stung bent double and scooped himself out of the plane.

Mr Poparescu leapt to attention.

'Welcome to Insomnia,' he intoned.

'How do you do?' said Mr Stung.

Mr Poparescu made a signal to the band. They burst triumphantly into *Deutschland Über Alles*.

Mr Stung, who was stone deaf, stood rigidly to attention.

'It's the wrong tune,' hissed Quill, equally rigid, but a bit bewildered.

A series of frantic sshshes were signalled by the despairing Mr Poparescu.

'They make a mistake,' he explained. 'They think you are Von Papen.'

Mr Stung looked incredulous.

As though to atone for its error, the band burst into God Save the King—all three verses.

Mr Poparescu showed his innate love of England by singing the third. He only got it slightly wrong.

Mr Stung relaxed.

'We are not yet finished,' said Mr Poparescu hurriedly.

The band burst into the Insomnian National anthem. All seven verses.

Mr Stung stood to attention.

The anthem came to a close. Mr Stung, taking no more chances, remained at attention.

'It is finish,' said Mr Poparescu, and bowed.

There was a surge of pressmen across the field. They surrounded Stung and fired a salvo of questions.

'Why did you kill Sardinko?'

'Why have you not caught the assassin?'

Quill blushed.

'Why do you try to take our Gardenium from us?'

'Why do you not accept Hitler's peace offer?'

'Which offer?' asked Mr Stung cautiously.

'All of them,' said the pressmen, and returned to the attack.

'Why do you let Mr Churchill sink our ships?'

'How is Mr Chamberlain's gout?'

'Hostile,' hissed Stung as they climbed into the car that was to take them to their hotel. 'Definitely hostile.'

'I can explain that.' A fat man, smoking a cigar, followed them in and settled himself comfortably in a corner. Mr Poparescu, after a despairing look round, climbed in beside the chauffeur. The car started off.

'Who are you?' said Mr Stung, startled.

The fat man removed his cigar. 'I'm Canterbury Brindle,' he said and put it back.

Clearly this should have been enough. But Mr Stung's 'ah' seemed a little forced.

Quill took a chance. 'How's your book selling?'

'Twenty-third edition,' said Canterbury Brindle complacently. 'And it's going into the Penguins next month.'

'Detective story?' enquired Mr Stung.

Canterbury Brindle looked hurt. *Lunatic Asylum*, his brilliant survey of post-war Europe, had been read by every guaranteed subscriber in England, but apparently it had not yet reached the Foreign Office.

Quill changed the subject. 'What brings you to Insomnia?'

'News,' said Canterbury Brindle smugly. 'Where there's news there's Brindle.' He frowned. 'They ought to print that over my column in the *Daily Shmooze*. But they won't. No vision. Half a mind to resign.'

'Try *The Times*,' suggested Quill.

Brindle grinned. 'Anyway, I'm always on the spot. I was in Vienna when Hitler marched into it. I was at Munich when Chamberlain flew out of it. I was in Prague in the spring. And now I'm in Rumba-Rumba.' He paused to let the awful portent sink in. 'Came here the moment Sardinko left for England.'

Quill sat up. 'Did you know he was going to be murdered?'

'Expected it,' said Brindle. 'So I came here to be on the spot.'

'Surely,' said Quill, 'the spot would be the Ministry of Elimination?'

'Not altogether,' said Brindle. 'That's only where the stone dropped. But the ripples have widened and it interests me. It interests me very much.' He turned to Stung. 'What, Sir, do you consider your chances of pulling off this treaty?'

'Excellent,' said Mr Stung curtly. He was just beginning to decide that he did not care for Canterbury Brindle. No reticence.

'I don't agree,' said Brindle.

That settled it. Definitely he did not care for him.

'Insomnia,' explained Brindle, 'is in a peculiar frame of mind. They're propaganda-pumped.'

'German propaganda?' asked Quill.

'Sure,' said Brindle. 'And Russian and Italian and Japanese and all sorts of others. You see,' he explained, 'we in Western Europe are cinema-conscious. Anything we see on the silver screen looks good to us. But here in Insomnia they get their philosophy from their radio sets. Were you aware,' he asked Mr Stung, 'that the average Insomnian can speak five languages?'

Mr Stung loathed him.

'It's in my book,' said Brindle happily. 'Anyway,' he resumed, 'for years now Insomnia has been a hot-bed for radio oratory. And it isn't only politics. They do their morning physical jerks to Hamburg. Tokio talks to them on etiquette, with a little ju-jitzu thrown in for luck. Milan sends them Rossini, and they know the repertory of the Moscow Arts Theatre by heart.'

'And what does England do?' asked Quill.

'So far,' said Brindle, 'we've sent them the Folk Dancers.'

A group of youths standing on a street corner shook their fists at the Union Jack draped over the car. The short-sighted Mr Stung bowed to them.

'Insomnia,' said Brindle, 'while not yet actively pro-German, is definitely anti-British.'

'Well, why not?' said Quill affably. 'After all, England has never had much objection to being disliked passively. Ireland doesn't like us. India doesn't love us. And I've heard that the Scots don't think too much of us at that.'

'Gosh,' said Brindle, impressed. 'That's an angle.' He scribbled. 'Mind if I use it?' he enquired with the innate courtesy of the journalist.

'Help yourself,' said Quill.

'Thanks,' said Brindle. He tapped Mr Stung on the knee. Mr Stung withdrew to the furthest corner.

'Take my tip,' said Brindle. 'And concentrate on King Hannibal.'

'Indeed,' said Mr Stung coldly.

'Buy him a couple of years in Paris,' urged Brindle. 'It's your only hope, Laddie.'

Mr Stung felt it was time to put this detective writer johnny in his place.

'His Majesty's Government,' he said icily, 'has its own plans of diplomatic procedure.'

'I know,' said Brindle. 'You're relying on Bauldstok.'

Mr Stung retired into dignified silence.

'Is that the man who eats out of your hand?' asked Quill.

'We are on excellent terms,' said Mr Stung stiffly.

'Just so,' said Brindle. 'All the same, it's a pity you didn't send a car to meet him at the station when he spent that week-end with you.'

'What's that,' said Mr Stung, alarmed.

'It's in my book,' said Brindle. 'He trudged five miles through the rain.'

'Good Lord,' said Mr Stung, really shaken. 'Is that why his shoes were muddy?'

*　　*　　*　　*　　*

Quill stood on the balcony of his room at the Hôtel des Ambassadeurs and gazed into the Main Street of Rumba-Rumba. It was a fascinating spectacle. There was a traffic light. One bicycle stamped impatiently in front of it. There was a Radio parlour. It resembled the Chinese Theatre in Hollywood. Several sacred footsteps of favourite announcers were corded off from vulgar tread. There was the Café Adolph, with excitable Insomnians gesticulating to each other from every table. There was a newspaper kiosk. It was selling this morning's *National Zeitung*, yesterday's *Izvestia*, and last month's *Times*. Ominous black shutters shortly to be closed for the week-end black-out festooned the shop windows. Gaily painted sandbags propped up the Insomnian National Bank, while a large red arrow pointed invitingly to the Rumba-Rumba air-raid shelter (room for

250). One fat balloon hung lazily in the sky. When the second arrived they would have a barrage. And Insomnian maidens, carrying their gas-masks, whisked tantalizingly along the pavements.

It was a pity, thought Quill, that he had not time to go out and investigate. But he was due to collect Stung in the lounge forthwith and deliver him, still alive, to the Insomnian Cabinet in twenty minutes.

Quill hoped that Stung would be in a better temper by now. A large dose of Canterbury Brindle followed by the polite but implacable refusal of the management of the Hôtel des Ambassadeurs to give him the Royal Suite for which he had cabled, on the grounds that it was reserved for Von Papen, had left the British envoy distinctly morose. He had gone to the bar to cheer himself up. Quill had warned him against vodscht (the national beverage—two parts vodka—two parts kirsch, and stronger than both), but even that had not been thought funny.

They were proud of their bar at the Hôtel des Ambassadeurs. The counter was the real thing—straight from a café in Paris. At a table by the window, talking to a deferential back, was Mr Stung. He appeared to be in a better humour.

'Ah, Quill,' he greeted him. 'Meet M. Dupont.'

'*Enchanté*,' said the deferential back and scuttled away without turning.

Quill gazed after it. There was something familiar about M. Dupont's back.

'Singular,' said Mr Stung. 'And I was just thinking what good manners he had for a foreigner.'

'Who is he?' Quill asked sharply.

'Just a johnny,' said Stung vaguely. 'Charming fellow. Pro-British. Sees our point of view. And paid for his round of drinks like an Englishman.' He yawned.

'What's yours?' asked Quill jerked to his senses.

'Vodscht,' said Stung. 'Excellent stuff. Half something and half something else, but stronger than both.' He yawned again.

Quill looked at him.

'Tired,' said Stung pathetically. 'The journey. But this'll wake me up.' He reached for his glass.

'Stop!' shouted Quill jumping to it.

But he was too late. The last of the vodscht had already been swallowed.

Mr Stung looked at him, tried to focus, failed, and rubbed his eyes.

'Tired,' he announced. 'Ver' tired boy. Wanta sleep.'

He cradled his head in his arms. He slept.

Quill picked up the empty glass. He sniffed. He reeled. He came back to Stung and shook him.

'You waste your time,' said a voice cheerfully. 'He will sleep for many hours, your Mr Stung.'

Quill turned. M. Dupont had come back. He was Kurt Carruthers.

'You!' said Quill.

Kurt beamed. 'None other,' he agreed happily. 'It is only an hour since I arrive at the aerodrome and already my task it is accomplished.'

'So I see,' said Quill sadly. 'And it will probably cost me my job.'

'I am sorry,' said Kurt simply. He hung his head. 'It was for my Government,' he added, brightening a little.

'Well, they'll surely be pleased with you about this,' said Quill.

'It was easy,' said Kurt modestly. 'Your Mr Stung—pah!' He produced a bundle of Bank of England notes and gloated over them. 'To buy a gold-mine from a stranger is perhaps understandable, but to drink with him is just silly. You will not find our Fuehrer doing that.'

'A pity,' agreed Quill with regret. 'Is there anything I can do to revive Stung?'

'Impossible,' said Kurt, shaking a sage head. 'Your Mr Stung will sleep for many hours and wake up with a headache. It will get bigger,' he said, 'when he learns that Papen has by this time caught another train and the Gardenium goes to Germany.'

'Von Papen will be late again,' said Quill without much hope.

'Not this time,' crowed Kurt. 'Himmler himself is seeing him off. He has also promised to meet him on his return.'

A waiter ambled into the room, glanced at the group and, unimpressed, went on his way. Quill took it that drugged diplomats were an everyday occurrence at the Hôtel des Ambassadeurs.

'And now,' said Kurt, 'I must hurry to telephone the good news to my Government. Good-bye.' He scuttled off.

Mr Stung slept on.

From a phone box emerged Canterbury Brindle. He walked unhurriedly across and sank into the chair next to Mr Stung.

'Just phoned the news to my paper,' he told Quill. 'Wonderful story.'

Quill looked at him. 'How did you know?'

'Anticipation,' said Brindle. 'The moment I saw Stung drinking to that German spy I guessed what was going to happen.'

'Why didn't you stop him?' said Quill furious.

'Me,' said Brindle astonished. 'And what would happen to my reputation for impartiality.'

'Damn your reputation,' said Quill. He stopped. 'What do you mean, "impartiality?"'

'Haven't you heard?' said Brindle. 'I'm impartial. My impartiality is a byword. In the Spanish War,' he announced, 'I was so impartial that I got condemned to death by both sides.'

'Ah,' said Quill.

'So you see,' said Brindle, 'I couldn't possibly interfere. And anyway there was only just time to get my story through before Hamburg broadcasts it.'

'Have they got it already,' said Quill dismayed.

'They're getting it now,' said Brindle. He puffed complacently at his cigar.

Quill lost his temper.

'Don't sit there puffing,' he snapped. 'Tell me what I'm to do now?'

Brindle shrugged a shoulder. 'Only one thing to do,' he said. 'Go and see the Cabinet yourself.'

'Me,' said Quill.

'Certainly,' said Brindle. 'Go and explain what has happened to Stung before Hamburg does it.'

'But dash it all,' protested Quill. 'I'm not a diplomat.'

'Neither is Stung,' said Brindle inexorably. 'So on your way! Apologize. Grovel. And promise to bring them a wide-awake Stung to-morrow morning.'

'Will they listen to me?' asked Quill.

'King Hannibal will,' said Brindle.

Quill crossed to the counter.

'Vodscht,' he said.

* * * * *

'You've changed a lot,' said Bauldstok looking at Quill with disapproval.

Quill swallowed. The vodscht had been all that Insomnia claimed for it and even more. It had carried him blithely through the streets. Sustained him on his march past the guard of honour (one drum). Ebbed a little in the pillared corridor. But now, when he needed it most, it had vanished altogether. What on earth was the protocol for informing a foreign Government that you weren't the man they were expecting. The *Detective's Handbook*, though eloquent on the proprieties in establishing Means, Motive and Opportunity, was dumb on this point.

'Sit down,' said King Hannibal hospitably. 'Have a drink.'

It was vodscht. Quill gulped gratefully. The lights went brighter. King Hannibal was a damn good sort for a foreign monarch and the

Cabinet was as attractive a gang of cut-throats as ever he had met.

'Skol,' he said and drank again.

'Skol,' said King Hannibal, surprised but willing.

After all, thought Quill, many people would envy him. Here he was, a simple policeman, hobnobbing with kings and handling a delicate diplomatic situation with flair. He chuckled.

The Minister of Fine Arts looked reproachful.

'You've changed,' said Bauldstok brooding. 'Never would have thought you were the same man.'

'That's where I've got you all,' said Quill in high good humour. 'I'm not.' He slapped what he took to be his own knee. It was King Hannibal's.

An awkward pause fell on the Cabinet. There was nothing in Protocol to cover a drunk detective.

'We don't want to seem inquisitive,' said King Hannibal, 'but who are you?'

Automatically Quill produced his card. The effect was not as good as usual.

'I'm here to look after the safety of Mr Stung,' he explained.

'And where is Mr Stung?' enquired Bauldstok drily.

'He's drugged,' said Quill and giggled.

A shocked murmur went through the Cabinet.

'Drugged!' said the Minister of Fine Arts.

'Drugged!' said King Hannibal.

'Drugged,' said Quill with great satisfaction. 'Sleeping like a baby.'

'Then he won't be here this afternoon?' demanded Bauldstok.

'Not a chance,' said Quill happily. He reached for the bottle of vodscht, filled up, drank it at a gulp, and broke the glass over his shoulder.

'Skol,' he said.

The Cabinet looked at each other.

The Cabinet saw their chance.

The Cabinet made no bones about it.

'Majesty,' said the Prime Minister. 'Great Britain is guilty of a diplomatic discourtesy. This is the gravest insult in the history of Protocol.'

'Nerts,' said Quill.

King Hannibal shushed him. After all, Great Britain could buy him two years in Paris.

The Prime Minister waxed eloquent. It appeared that Insomnian dignity was a mockery if the whole Cabinet was expected to wait while an English diplomat finished his afternoon nap. Quill decided that he did not like his tone.

'Any why not?' he demanded. 'Didn't our Cabinet wait all afternoon for your Sardinko?'

'That's different,' said the Minister of Fine Arts with dignity. 'Sardinko was murdered.'

'So he was,' said Quill abashed.

'But dash it all,' said King Hannibal, stepping into the breach, 'if Mr Stung is drugged it isn't his fault he isn't here.'

'That is not our concern,' said Bauldstok promptly. 'It is up to the British Government to deliver their envoys in good time.'

'Absolutely,' said Quill.

'We cannot keep the German mission hanging about,' pointed out the Chancellor of the Exchequer, a punctual man.

'Why not?' said King Hannibal with relish. 'Papen isn't here either?'

The Cabinet went dim. They cursed Von Papen under their breath. If only that tactful diplomat would buy himself a wrist-watch, they felt, they might have been in a position to clinch the issue on the spot.

'Tell you what, old man,' said King Hannibal to Quill. 'It'll be all right if you leave us now.'

'It's early yet,' said Quill.

'Yes, yes,' said King Hannibal. 'But you've got a job to do. Bring Mr Stung here to-morrow morning at ten-thirty and we'll adjourn till then.'

'And don't be late,' said the Chancellor of the Exchequer severely.

Quill looked at him owlishly.

'I'll drink to that,' he decided.

'I say, old man,' said King Hannibal, taking him by the arm. 'You'd better come along with me and have some black coffee.'

CHAPTER

10

MORNING dawned reluctantly over Rumba-Rumba. The sun, heavy-eyed from lack of sleep, owing to the Insomnian system of a staggered summer time, stumbled into the heavens, and with a heavy sigh set about its duties. It directed a cautious ray on *rue Lord Haw-Haw* where a carpet-slippered Madame Dupont was shaking a morning mat, shone feebly on the postman, hid distastefully behind a cloud on sighting a morning bather breaking the ice in the Insomnian Serpentine, noted Mr Pinsk leaving Berchtes Villa clad in a heavy overcoat and a muffler, brightened considerably, made a bet with itself that it would have that muffler off long before Mr Pinsk reached his office, and concentrated. It won easily.

Encouraged by this success the sun gazed ruminatively at the Hôtel des Ambassadeurs. For years now the place had been giving it a pain in the neck. Why should the tourists be allowed to sleep so late while he, the alleged ruler of the heavens, was expected to be up at the crack of dawn to gladden all the mat-shaking Madame Duponts in Insomnia. Even the sight of the German mission, dressed to a man, still awaiting the arrival of Von Papen, failed to cheer it noticeably. For there, a little higher up, more heavily curtained than any, was a window that made its rays boil. Fuming, the sun switched round (leaving the tropics to cope with an Arctic winter) and brought into play its secret weapon. Mr Pinsk took off his overcoat. But the sun could no longer be bothered with him. It was concentrating all its energy on the offending window.

Inside, the figure on the crumpled bed stirred uneasily and pulled the eiderdown over its head.

A bewildered appeal from the Sahara, hopelessly grappling with a snow-storm, brought the sun suddenly to its senses. Conscience-stricken it returned to normal. Mr Pinsk turned up the collar of his overcoat.

But one fascinated beam crept in through the curtains of the Hôtel des Ambassadeurs for a solo effort. It was too late. A hand was already shaking the figure on the bed.

It was not the hand of the detective waking his charge to deliver him safely to the Cabinet that morning. It was the hand of the charge waking the detective.

Mr Stung had slept all yesterday afternoon. But Quill, in spite of King Hannibal's coffee, had slept heavily from the moment he had got back to the hotel. Vodscht is like that.

'Ten o'clock,' said Mr Stung. ''Pon my soul, we'll be late.'

Quill came reluctantly to life. He looked at Mr Stung and realized he had a headache.

'Drink this,' said Mr Stung, handing him a glass.

Unquestioningly Quill gulped it down. It was vodscht. Galvanized, he leapt out of bed and made for the shower.

'Seen the papers?' asked Stung, sheltering to avoid the spray.

'My God—no!' said Quill transfixed.

'Discreet!' said Stung approvingly.

Quill emerged from the shower and snatched a headline:

ANGLO-INSOMNIAN TALKS TAKE PLACE IN FRIENDLY ATMOSPHERE

'Nice chap King Hannibal,' said Quill reminiscently.

Mr Stung nodded. 'I hear you made an excellent impression,' he said approvingly.

Quill blushed and changed the subject. 'What's the time?' he asked.

'We've got half an hour,' said Stung.

Quill applied his hair-brushes.

'You know,' said Stung, 'this mission is going to be more ticklish than I thought. Got enemies,' he explained.

'Really?' said Quill.

'Must be on guard all the time,' said Stung. 'Alert,' he explained vividly. 'Drugging me is only the beginning.'

'Sure,' said Quill.

'They'll try again,' said Stung. 'But this time I'll be ready for them.'

The door burst open. Stung pulled out his revolver.

But it was the impartial Canterbury Brindle.

'Morning, Stung,' he said cheerfully. 'How're you feeling, sonny?' he asked Quill.

'Lousy,' said Quill.

'Congratulations,' said Brindle. 'You did a grand job of work on King Hannibal. He thinks you're the nicest Englishman he's ever met. Almost human, he called you.'

'Did he, by gad,' said Mr Stung.

'He's made a wonderful start for you, Stung,' said Brindle. 'So don't you go and muck it up to-day.'

If a ram-rod can be said to stiffen, Mr Stung did.

'I trust,' he said, 'that I can be relied upon to behave in accordance with the Protocol.'

'That's just it,' said Brindle. 'A little less Protocol and a little more getting together and we might have signed that pact with Russia.'

'Russia!' said Mr Stung. The way he said it was almost a *casus belli*.

'Let it go,' said Brindle wearily. 'Only if you think you are going to get anywhere with Bauldstok . . .'

'He eats out of Mr Stung's hand,' said Quill, rallying to his charge.

'I know,' said Brindle. 'That week-end. It's a pity though,' he told Stung, 'that you didn't have a fire in his bedroom.'

'Good gad,' said Stung appalled. 'Is that why he got pneumonia?'

* * * * *

Mr Stung opened the door and peered cautiously into the corridor.

'All clear?' he announced surprised.

'Get going,' said Brindle.

They got.

Quill rang for the lift.

'No,' said Mr Stung. 'I read a story once where a diplomat stepped into a lift that descended into a cellar which flooded at high tide.'

'Really?' said Brindle.

'It was,' said Mr Stung poignantly, 'high tide at the time.' He made firmly for the staircase.

Save for the waiter, clearing up after the German mission, hopefully gone to meet another train, the lounge was empty. Mr Stung hid behind a pillar and eyed the waiter narrowly.

'I think he's all right,' he decided and stepped out into the open. The waiter never turned a hair.

They walked across the lounge.

'Good morning, Herr Stung,' said the reception clerk.

'Good morning,' said Mr Stung cautiously.

The swing doors revolved. Mr Stung dodged behind an aspidistra.

It was a false alarm. Bored, the commissionaire was passing the time.

'Come along,' said Brindle, an impatient man. 'You'll never get there at this rate.'

They emerged into the street. A taxi on the other side of the road sprang to life and came whizzing over.

Mr Stung eyed it approvingly.

'Safe at last,' he announced and climbed happily in.

A hand swept Quill aside. The taxi door slammed in his face. The taxi made off.

'Kidnapped,' said the impartial Brindle with keen satisfaction.

* * * * *

It took five minutes for Quill to persuade Canterbury Brindle that he would not be violating his impartiality by coping with the kidnappery. ('You speak the lingo.') This accomplished, he waved aside another and perfectly innocent taxi and set out leaden-footed for the Palace.

What on earth was he going to say to King Hannibal?

The sentry outside the Palace gates clicked his heels, started a salute, recognized an Englishman, and stopped half-way. Quill cut him dead.

How dingy the Palace looked! Why on earth did they not sweep that red carpet? The frescoed ceiling, bright and high when viewed in the afterglow of vodscht, now looked gaudy and low. And it was too bad that 'Insomnia,' clad only in a national flag and ruling the lake with a trident in the very centre of the ceiling, had run to Rubens.

Quill sighed. How lovely it had been to be a simple policeman with nothing to worry him except two bodies and a Snarl permanently yammering on the other end of the line. Quill felt quite homesick for Sir Humphrey.

Instead he came face to face with King Hannibal. The monarch, in the very best Lubitsch tradition, was genial.

'Great news,' he said, rubbing his hands. 'Great! Franzi Papen has gone back to Berlin for his fountain-pen.'

'Great,' said Quill without much enthusiasm.

King Hannibal slapped him on the back. 'You realize what this means?'

'Not altogether,' said Quill uncertainly.

'But don't you see,' said King Hannibal. 'All you've got to do now is to produce your man and a bottle of ink and we'll have the treaty signed in a jiffy.'

'Ah,' said Quill, more depressed than ever.

'Don't you see,' said King Hannibal. 'I've got the Cabinet in a cleft-stick. I've only got to reproduce the comments they made about Stung yesterday on Papen to-day. . . . Diplomatic discourtesy! Unforgivable slight on the Protocol! *Lèse-majesté* and *Crachement sur le Roi!*' he gloated. 'Have I got them or have I got them.'

'Well,' said Quill, 'since you ask me—no.'

'Huh,' said King Hannibal. 'So you don't think I can do it, Laddie? Okay. Bring in your Stung and I'll show you.'

'That's just it,' said Quill miserably. 'I can't.'

King Hannibal dropped his eyeglass. 'What's that!'

'He's been kidnapped,' said Quill, treading on it.

King Hannibal put on a pair of spectacles. They made him look like Herbert Marshall concentrating.

'You know,' he complained, 'you're making this thing awfully difficult for me.' He sat down on the stairs and twiddled with Psyche preparing for her bath at the bottom of the banisters.

'My ministers,' he said, 'don't want this treaty. My people don't want this treaty. Even my moneylender is in two minds about it. But I'll let you into a secret, old man. I'm determined to pull it off.'

'Thanks,' said Quill, dazed.

'But,' said King Hannibal, smacking Psyche on her marble rump, 'I must have co-operation. I can't sign this treaty without a British representative. Don't you see that?' said the monarch reasonably.

'Sure,' said Quill, 'but . . .'

'Tell you what,' said King Hannibal. 'I'll throw one of my well-known fits of temperament. Throw things about.'

Quill looked at him.

'Absolutely unapproachable while it lasts,' said King Hannibal with pride. 'Why do you suppose they call me the Hothead?'

'But how will it help?' asked Quill.

'Leave it to me,' said King Hannibal confidently. 'Just give me three minutes and then knock at that door.' He gave Psyche a parting pat and paced the corridor three times, getting up momentum. Then, white heat achieved, he burst into the council chamber, slamming the door behind him.

'We're off,' said Quill to himself.

A babble of voices penetrated the heavy oak door. The babble swelled to a din. There was the sound of breaking china and several heavy thuds.

A surge of worried officials came sprinting down the corridors and stood shivering outside the council room. King Hannibal was shouting.

The three minutes were up. Quill knocked on the door. He knocked louder. He thumped.

It opened cautiously. Prime Minister Bauldstok, his hair decorated with china, motioned Quill away.

'*Ce n'est pas le moment*,' he hissed urgently. 'Go away. Far away. And do not bring your Mr Stung back till this afternoon.'

'I won't,' said Quill gratefully.

'If King Hannibal sees Stung now he will hit him, and then Great Britain will surely send a warship. Otherwise,' said Bauldstok, 'I would like it well enough. When I stayed the week-end with him he put me on a horse.'

'Ah,' said Quill.

A vase whizzed past them.

'*Pardon*,' said Bauldstok, and shut the door quickly.

* * * * *

Chuckling to himself, Quill made his way down the Palace steps and ran into a battery of cameras. This belated recognition of his importance pleased him. He posed.

There were no 'hold it's,' no clicks, no 'thank you's.'

'They are waiting for Von Papen,' said a voice at Quill's elbow.

Quill swung round. It was Señor Centime.

'Good God,' said Quill.

'Hold it!' The cameras were focused on them.

Quill posed again.

'It is not for you,' said Señor Centime. 'It is for me—Noted Son Returns to Insomnia.'

Quill felt neglected. But the sight of a little man twiddling a crayon a few paces away consoled him no end. At least some paper thought it worth while to carry a caricature of all that was left of the British mission.

The artist came up and thrust his caricature under Quill's nose.

'Big likeness,' he pointed out. 'One English ten-shilling. You buy,' he suggested hopefully.

'This,' said Señor Centime with unaccountable pride, 'is my half-brother, Señor Kopeck.'

'Kopeck?' said Quill.

'He changed his name when he got naturalized,' explained Señor Centime.

'Ah,' said Quill. 'And before that I suppose it was Pfennig.'

'No,' said the half-brother regretfully. 'It was Rabinovitch.'

'My brother,' boasted Señor Centime, 'is the leading cartoonist in Insomnia.'

Quill looked surprised.

'He has the angle of a Low without his political bias, and the politics of a Strube without his angle,' said Señor Centime. 'But at the moment he is sack.'

'I make the cartoon of Hitler,' said Señor Kopeck. 'It was the big mistake,' he added regretfully.

Señor Centime changed the subject. 'And how is the estimable Mr Stung?' he jeered.

'He slept well,' said Quill non-committally.

But Señor Centime was no longer listening. He was gazing with hero-worship at the approaching Canterbury Brindle. He rushed forward and embraced him.

'Brindle,' he breathed. '*Mon vieux Copain.*' He turned to Quill ecstatically. 'This is the biggest foreign correspondent in the world.'

Gazing at Brindle's fifteen stone, Quill saw no reason to doubt the accuracy of this statement.

Brindle patted his disciple on the back. 'Busy right now, Sonny,' he said. 'Let us have lunch together some time.'

'*Enchanté,*' said Señor Centime. 'I will go at once and study the menu.' He raced away happily. Señor Kopeck thought it over and followed.

Quill turned to Brindle. 'Where's Stung?'

Brindle chuckled. 'Sleeping the chloroform off.'

'Where?'

'In his hotel room,' said Brindle. 'Didn't want him on their hands. Their orders were merely to get him out of the way for a few hours while Von Papen signed the treaty. The whole plot,' expounded Brindle, 'would have succeeded perfectly if only Von Papen were here to sign.'

'But as Von Papen isn't here,' said Quill, still trying to work it out, 'why didn't they hold him?'

'Bad staff work,' said the impartial Brindle disapprovingly. 'No one let them know Franzi hadn't arrived.'

Quill began to chuckle. But the chuckle died on him.

'Good God,' he said. 'They'll kidnap him again.'

Brindle shook his head. 'Unlikely,' he opined. 'I've left a good man on guard.'

'Thanks,' said Quill.

'Don't mention it,' said Brindle. 'Charged it down to the office.'

Quill grinned.

'How was King Hannibal doing when you left?' asked Brindle. 'Reached the smashing stage yet?'

This man knew everything. 'In comfort,' said Quill.

'Did you see it?' asked Brindle with interest.

Quill shook a regretful head. 'But I heard most of it.'

'Funny thing about Hannibal's rages,' said Brindle. 'Everybody knows they're phony. It's in my book—page 437.'

'And yet they work,' said Quill.

'They work,' agreed Brindle. 'You can't throw a vase at a monarch.'

*　　*　　*　　*　　*

In his room at the Hôtel des Ambassadeurs Mr Stung slept soundly. Beside him a pair of long legs propped up the mantelpiece.

Quill, entering, surveyed them without astonishment. He was getting quite used to seeing his old friends from the Ministry of Elimination bobbing up in Insomnia.

'Hallo, Misha,' he said, and slapped him boisterously on the shoulders.

A reproachful head turned to look at him. The legs stayed where they were.

'Not Misha,' said the semi-recumbent form, 'Sasha.'

The same gaunt features, the same reclining stance, and apparently the same habits. It must run in the family, thought Quill. He said so.

'But, of course,' said Sasha, 'you cannot mistake a Podushkin. Should you meet my father you would know him at once.'

'I'll be careful not to wake him,' promised Quill.

'You would hardly succeed if you tried,' said Sasha. 'He sleeps well, the Pappa.'

'And your grandfather?' asked Quill, fascinated.

'He is in Russia, that one,' said Sasha. 'In 1917 they woke him to flee the country, but he argued that he had only just gone to bed. So he stayed where he was, and they built a prison camp round him.'

'Ah,' said Quill.

'I was very young in 1917,' mused Sasha. 'I remember in the train to Belgrade I even looked out of the window.' He blushed.

Quill gazed at him in some admiration. 'You're exactly like your brother.'

'Not at all,' said Sasha coldly. 'Misha is energetic. It is well known. He suicides himself.'

'Not any more,' said Quill. 'He is at the Ministry of Elimination in London.'

'*Tiens*,' said Sasha. 'A careerist!'

'Didn't he write and tell you?'

'Write!' said Sasha in horror. 'The Podushkins never write to each other. It is a tradition.'

'But how do you keep in touch?'

'There is always some fool who comes to bring us news,' said Sasha placidly.

'Thanks,' said Quill.

He turned to look at Mr Stung. It occurred to him that he might have done this earlier. Mr Stung was sleeping well. Quill prodded him. Nothing happened.

'He is still drugged,' said Sasha. 'He will sleep for many hours yet. It is curious,' he mused, 'that some people should need a drug to make them sleep.' He reached out a long hand, snaffled Stung's eiderdown, tucked it round himself, and closed his eyes.

'I say,' protested Quill. . . .

But it was too late. Sasha Podushkin was already asleep.

CHAPTER

11

At the Restaurant des Gourmets Señor Kopeck was sketching vigorously. Quill walked stealthily past him. He had had enough company for one morning and wanted to lunch alone. He spotted an empty table and made towards it. But he did not get that far.

'Hey, Sonny!' The impartial Brindle was beckoning to him. 'Come and lunch with us.'

'*Enchanté*,' agreed Señor Centime, his companion, without much enthusiasm.

A waiter flicked a napkin. The *Couvert* (one English threepence) was now prepared.

The change of air had put an edge on Quill's appetite. He scanned the menu for rump steak.

'Useless to look at the meat,' said the waiter triumphantly. 'There is none.'

'Meatless day,' said Canterbury Brindle.

This man knew everything.

'Rations?' asked Quill in surprise.

'*Du tout*,' said the waiter hotly. 'We cannot get any meat owing to the blockade.'

Quill looked again.

'The trout is very good here,' said Brindle. 'They breed it in the lake.'

'No more,' said the waiter. 'Now that the lake is given over to the Gardenium process. . . .' He spread apologetic hands.

The *plat du jour* caught Quill's eye. 'Goose Goering.'

'*Impossible*,' said the waiter well pleased. 'Señor Centime is eating the last portion now.'

Between mouthfuls Señor Centime brightened.

'Delicious,' he said and smacked his lips.

Quill looked at Brindle's plate. 'What are you eating?'

'Vegetable stew,' said Brindle. 'Lousy.'

'Vegetable stew,' said the waiter following the conversation. 'I bring her at once.' He shot off.

Señor Centime reached for the carafe of vodscht and filled Quill's glass.

'Drink this, my friend, and console yourself.'

'Nice of you,' said Quill touched. 'But really it doesn't matter. I can put up with a vegetarian meal for once.'

'I did not mean this,' said Señor Centime testily. 'I speak of the failure of your mission. Even at this moment the German delegation is at the station awaiting the arrival of Franzi Papen.'

'What again?' said Quill.

'But this time,' said Señor Centime, 'he will come. You will see. And he will sign the treaty.'

The door revolved. The German delegation filed lugubriously in. One glance showed Quill that Franzi Papen was not with them.

'Excuse me,' said Señor Centime. He hurried across..

A small boy hurtled into the restaurant and handed Brindle an envelope. Brindle ripped it open. 'Ah,' he said impartially. 'Franzi's been delayed.'

This man did know everything.

'Himmler is throwing him a farewell party.'

'It is not true,' said the returning Señor Centime hotly, 'that this is before he sends him to a concentration camp. Franzi arrives here to-night.'

'Will that delegation be at the station to meet him?' asked Quill.

'Certainly,' said Señor Centime grandly. 'You do not understand. A taxi fare to them it is the nothing.'

The waiter came skating back with the vegetable stew. It consisted entirely of swedes.

'Native vegetable,' said the waiter. 'Not very bad. Butter sauce?' he suggested helpfully. He whipped out a container, breathed into it and poured the contents over the swedes.

'*Ersatz*,' he announced proudly. 'Made with Chinese soap. It tastes just like butter, only different.'

A beaming chef appeared through the service door in person and made his way towards the German deputation. He was bearing a silver platter laden with an enormous turkey stuffed with sausages and chestnuts.

'*Ach!*' said the German delegation rubbing their hands.

A frantic little man sprang from the cash desk, pounced on the chef, seized him by the coat-tails, and dragged him protesting away.

The German delegation stopped rubbing.

'The chef,' explained the impartial Brindle, 'is pro-German. But the proprietor's name is Abramovitch.'

A newsboy came in. Quill beckoned him over and bought a paper. (Five hundred Insomnian peccoes.) He gave him one English penny. The newsboy dissolved into tears of gratitude, laid his entire stock on the table, and wept his way out.

Brindle picked up a copy and looked for the front-page story.

KING HANNIBAL IN A RAGE. VALUABLE VASE ALLEGED BROKEN

In smaller type, underneath it, said:

> Anglo-Insomnian Talks proceed in Friendly
> Atmosphere

'Good God,' said Quill slightly dazed.

* * * * *

There was a commotion at the cash desk.

It was Señor Kopeck offering to pay for his lunch with a caricature of A. Abramovitch.

* * * * *

An antique shop, the *Galleries-Tel-a-viv* (proprietor, B. Abramovitch—son-in-law), was proud of its window display. The proprietor himself dressed it every other Thursday. This was the other Thursday. In fact, the dressing was taking place as Quill emerged from the restaurant.

Reflcting that he could never face Belinda unless he brought her back some present, Quill crossed over.

Two baize-aproned men were lowering a large Ming vase into the very centre of the window. On the pavement, jumping up and down in agony, was the proprietor.

'Gently, gently,' he was urging. 'Treat it as though it were genu-ine.'

Quill caught sight of the letters-patent imposingly placed above the doorway.

By Appointment to H.M. King Hannibal

Perhaps this place was too expensive for him. He turned.

'Excuse me,' said B. Abramovitch, politely stepping into his path. 'Where are you going from?'

Quill blinked.

'You wish to look at our window. But you are welcome. Fill your eyes. No one will press you to buy. Now this,' he said, taking Quill by the arm and pointing to a green jade figure of a very large man threatening a bewildered and very square duck, which, on closer inspection, turned out to be a dove, 'is a wonderful piece of work.'

'Ah,' said Quill.

'It is called "Peace," ' said B. Abramovitch enthusiastically. 'Symbolic,' he explained. 'I would not part with it for a fortune.'

'Then that's all right,' said Quill, relieved. The thought of a dazed Customs Officer finding 'Peace' among his socks had been haunting him.

'But as I see you've taken a fancy to it,' said B. Abramovitch, 'I'll tell you what I'll consider. Say five hundred English pounds.'

Quill raised an eyebrow.

'Maybe you're right,' said B. Abramovitch. 'I, too, do not care much for modern art. Come inside and see the storehouse of the centuries. Have no fear,' he urged. 'No one will suggest you buy anything.'

He tripped over the doorstep in his eagerness to get this rather lanky fly inside.

'Now this,' he said untruthfully, 'is by Velasquez.'

Quill walked hurriedly to the other end of the shop.

'What I really want,' he said, 'is a modest gift for a girl friend.'

'I have the very thing,' said B. Abramovitch instantly. He rubbed his chin and pondered.

'I got it,' he said, and propelled Quill over to a dinner service.

'A beautiful piece,' he said admiringly.

'Forty-eight beautiful pieces,' said Quill, counting them.

'Forty-seven,' corrected B. Abramovitch. 'The ladle is extra.' He picked up a soup plate. 'Is it not beautiful?' he crooned. 'Such a quality! Such a glaze! And does it break easily? My!' he gloated.

'Is that an advantage?' asked Quill, surprised.

'For King Hannibal,' said B. Abramovitch, 'it is essential. And for his Court it is even more essential for so it does not hurt much. For years,' boasted B. Abramovitch, 'King Hannibal has been my best customer. Crockery, vases, chandeliers—everything I supply.'

'You ought to be getting another order at any moment,' said Quill.

The telephone rang.

It was the Palace. It appeared that King Hannibal was running out of ammunition.

'But, of course,' said B. Abramovitch, bowing into the receiver. 'Four dozen. I will send at once.'

He turned round to sell Quill the remnants of a Roman bath. Was he unlucky? The client had gone!

CHAPTER

12

'YOU'RE very late.'

Quill came to a stop. He had entered what he took to be his empty bedroom and there was Al Schenk playing patience at his writing-table.

'Come in,' said Al cordially. 'Sit down. I'll be with you in a minute.' He turned over a card, didn't like it, put it at the bottom of the pack, and selected another.

'You're cheating,' accused Quill.

'Only enough to make it come out,' pleaded Al. 'Seven of diamonds —no good.'

'It goes on the eight of spades,' Quill pointed out.

'Thanks,' said Al. 'And how is your Mr Stung? Sleeping well?'

'So you know about that?'

'Know about it,' said Al, 'I organized it!'

'You surprise me,' said Quill. 'It had all the air of a happy impromptu.'

Al flicked over a card. 'You know,' he said chattily, 'when we heard that you were sending Mr Stung you could have knocked us down with a feather.'

'Us?' said Quill.

'The Reich,' said Al.

'Then the news shook you?' Quill smirked.

'Shook us,' said Al. 'It convulsed us. And did they celebrate on Wilhelmstrasse! Boy—even Hitler had a ginger beer.'

'And what happened to his taster?' asked Quill.

'Ten of diamonds,' said Al. 'Where's that Knave?' He found it. 'Stung,' he resumed, 'was a penny from heaven, but you—you're a pain in the neck.'

'Glad to hear it,' said Quill.

'Knew you would be,' said Al moodily, tucking the two of diamonds under what otherwise would have been a sequence.

Quill pulled it out.

'Never had much hope you'd stay away,' said Al. 'The fact that I've already removed two obstacles that stood in my path doesn't seem to interest you at all.'

'On the contrary,' said Quill. 'It interests me a great deal.'

'The wrong way,' sighed Al. 'The wrong way. You've got no common sense—that's your trouble. When your profession interferes with your future health—take a holiday.'

'Al,' said Quill. 'You disappoint me. I thought you were a business man.'

'So I am,' said Al. 'That's why I'm here.'

'Is that it,' said Quill. 'I was just beginning to think you'd come in to borrow a table for your patience.'

Al swept the cards together peevishly. 'Darn thing won't come out, anyway.' He got up. 'Now listen. Let's get together on this. I'll put my cards on the table.'

'You've just thrown them in,' said Quill.

Al glared. 'Control your sense of humour, sonny, listen to facts. I'm in this Gardenium business up to my neck.'

'Neck is the right word,' said Quill.

Al ignored him. 'I did not kill two men for the pleasure of seeing you drinking with King Hannibal.'

'So you've heard about that,' said Quill uneasily.

'I hear about everything,' said Al. 'It's tough,' he complained. 'After all that preliminary work and with Stung thrown in, we had every right to expect an easy passage.'

'Even though Papen hasn't arrived.'

'That wouldn't have mattered a yard,' said Al. 'If only you hadn't made such a hit with Hannibal.'

'Sorry about that,' said Quill.

'I don't like the way things are,' said Al. 'I don't like them at all. Now you're a man of the world . . .'

Quill stiffened. In all his experience no one had yet called him a man of the world without trying to put something across him immediately afterwards.

'How much will you take to go straight back to England?'

'Eighty per cent of the world's Gardenium,' said Quill.

'There,' said Al. 'That's exactly what I mean. Obstinate. No common sense. Don't you realize that one way or another we're going to get that Gardenium. So you might as well give us a break and co-operate. That way at least you'll show a profit. Don't you see that?' he pleaded.

Quill glanced at his watch. Once again, in half an hour, he was due to deliver Mr Stung to the Cabinet. There was just time to say a few words himself.

'What I see,' said Quill, 'is that I'm a diplomat by chance and a policeman by profession. And while I'm at it, I might as well see both jobs through. I'm going to take Mr Stung to the Palace. I'm going to get the Gardenium treaty signed. And I'm going to get a warrant for your extradition.'

'Sonny,' said Al, unperturbed, 'you're wrong three times!'

* * * * *

Quill made his way to Mr Stung's room. The charge, awake, was sitting up in his bed looking incredulously at the guard, asleep.

'Who is this johnny?' he asked Quill.

'Your bodyguard,' said Quill apologetically.

Mr Stung looked indignant. 'Don't need a bodyguard,' he said sharply. 'Can look after myself.' He remembered and blushed.

Some noise must have penetrated the guard's ears. He stirred a little, buried his ear in the eiderdown, and slept on like a child.

They left him there and went into the corridor.

'Not the lift!' said Mr Stung, remembering.

On the entresol there was a settee. Mr Stung subsided on it.

'My head!' he moaned. 'Bursting,' he explained.

'Never mind,' said Quill, 'it's for England.'

Mr Stung pulled himself together and reached the vestibule. Exhausted, he sank down again.

He really did look a little green.

'Coffee?' suggested a waiter solicitously.

'Black,' said Mr Stung gratefully.

'Oh no you don't,' said Quill, yanking him up. 'Not a drop to drink till after you've met the Cabinet.' Sternly he marched him through the swing doors and into the bright street.

A taxi detached itself from the other side and came whizzing across. Mr Stung stepped forward.

'We'll walk,' said Quill firmly, and trundled him off.

At the corner of Platz Blitzkrieg they reached a café.

'Coffee,' pleaded Mr Stung pathetically.

Quill relented. 'All right, but only one cup, and I must taste it first. Waiter!' he beckoned.

'You're treating me like a child,' said Mr Stung crossly.

'Well, look what happened when I didn't,' said Quill reasonably enough.

'Different,' said Mr Stung. 'Now I'm on my guard. Waiter,' he snapped. 'Get me some aspirin.'

The waiter brightened. '*Toute de suite*,' he said, and scuttled merrily away.

'Now then,' said Quill. 'Try and get this straight. The Press is against us. The Cabinet is against us . . .'

'Good gad,' said Stung. 'Ought we to cable for a warship?'

Quill dismissed this as the effort of a drowsy liver.

'The only person on our side is King Hannibal. He's trying to push through this treaty single-handed. So concentrate on him. Be human. Have a drink. Tell him a funny story . . .'

'It's not in accordance with protocol,' said Mr Stung stiffly.

'Damn protocol,' said Quill. 'Forget protocol.'

Mr Stung stared.

'Got your fountain pen?'

'Certainly,' said Mr Stung.

'Well, that's one up on Franzi Papen, anyway,' said Quill.

'Given to me by Bauldstok himself as a souvenir of his week-end,' said Mr Stung, wiping his fingers genteelly underneath the edges of the tablecloth.

The waiter came back, deposited two glasses on the table, and fountained black liquid into them from a large urn.

'Not a drop is spilt,' he said with pride.

'Neat work,' approved Quill.

'I practise for many weeks,' said the waiter, 'but now I am perfect.

It was not so always,' he remembered. 'The first week I am nearly sack.'

Quill took a sip. 'O.K.,' he said to Mr Stung, 'but it's awfully bad coffee.'

'*Ersatz*,' said the waiter. 'The Blockade,' he shrugged.

'Of course,' said Mr Stung, proud of it.

The waiter deposited two white pellets on the table.

'Your aspirin,' he announced, and sped away.

'Curious-looking aspirin,' said Mr Stung, picking them up.

'Gimme,' said Quill sharply.

But he was too late. Mr Stung had already swallowed.

'Well, well,' said the impartial Brindle materializing from nowhere. 'Drugged again!'

Quill looked at his sleeping charge with despair.

'Run along to the Palace, sonny, and do what you can,' said Brindle. 'I'll take care of Stung.'

'Drown him,' said Quill, and went.

* * * * *

A tired but triumphant King Hannibal signified that he was ready to receive the British Mission.

'Good luck,' said the major-domo to the unfortunate Quill bracing himself outside. 'Never say die,' he slapped him on the back.

Quill thumped him back. It was not in accordance with protocol, but it did relieve his feelings.

A concealed gramophone record burst into the British National Anthem.

Horribly embarrassed, Quill stood to attention and watched the Cabinet passing from the clouds of resigned despair into the sunshine of a foe at its mercy. King Hannibal made the transit in the opposite direction.

The room had changed since Quill had seen it last. The antique china wore a distinctly new look. There was a huge ink-stain across the table which the small Union Jack they had spread upon it was unable to conceal. The Throne appeared to have lost one of its legs and was propped up with three volumes of *Mein Kampf* (signed). There was still some china in Prime Minister Bauldstok's hair.

'Have some lemonade,' said King Hannibal, a shade coldly. Thirteen years a king! Was it for this that he had thrown the rage of his reign?

Quill swallowed. 'Gentlemen,' he said. 'I am sorry to report that the British Envoy is indisposed.'

The Cabinet looked delighted.

'This,' said Bauldstok, beaming, 'is an insufferable affront.'

'Insufferable,' agreed the Cabinet, nodding mandarins of delight.

'Well, it does seem a bit rude,' said King Hannibal.

'Sire,' said Quill. 'That I have caused your Majesty inconvenience I regret profoundly . . .'

'*Tiens*,' said the Minister of Fine Arts in grudging admiration. 'He speaks well, that one!'

'But,' said Quill, ignoring him, 'I wish to register a protest. There is a conspiracy to prevent the emissary of Great Britain from reaching this Palace awake. Ever since he set foot in Insomnia,' said Quill bitterly, 'Mr Stung has done nothing but sleep.'

'When I spent a week-end with him,' said Bauldstok grimly, 'I did nothing but keep awake. Ghosts,' he explained.

A sympathetic murmur went round the Cabinet.

'In forty-eight hours,' said Quill, 'Mr Stung has been doped, kidnapped, and drugged. In these circumstances to accuse him of discourtesy,' said Quill, 'seems to me to be a little . . .' His fine language ratted on him; 'tough,' he finished lamely.

'Do you infer,' said Bauldstok, determined to show that he, too, was a master of English, 'that King Hannibal's Cabinet is in any way to blame for Mr Stung's—ah—miscalculations?'

'I do,' said Quill.

The Cabinet looked shocked.

'I warn you,' said Quill, 'that I know all the essentials of the situation. I know who murdered your emissary Sardinko and why. I know where that man is. And I shall be very surprised if you don't know as well.'

The Cabinet shuffled guiltily.

'Take note,' said Quill, 'that I intend formally to apply for a warrant for the extradition of Al Schenk.'

'Never heard of him,' said the Cabinet as one man.

Even King Hannibal shook a bland head and fixed his eyes on the portrait of his grandmother, Queen Brigitta the Beddable.

Quill sighed. Al had been right three times. He had not got Stung to the Palace, he had not got the treaty signed, and there wasn't a hope in hell of getting an extradition warrant. He lost his temper.

'What are you,' he demanded, thumping the table with both fists. 'A neutral Cabinet or a pack of bought thugs?'

Bauldstok sprang to his feet. 'Gentlemen,' he demanded, thumping the table, 'are we to stand here and be insulted by an Englishman?'

'By the head of King Philip the Fornicator—no!' cried the Minister of Fine Arts, thumping the mantelpiece.

'Hey,' said King Hannibal, 'if there's any more thumping to be done, I'm better qualified than any of you.'

The chandelier rocked.

'You flatter yourself,' said Quill, still thumping.

'Oh, do I?' said King Hannibal.

The chandelier crashed to the floor.

Clearly B. Abramovitch was in for a good day.

Shamefaced, the Cabinet came to their senses. But Quill was even more shamefaced.

'Perhaps I'd better go,' he said. 'I'm afraid I lost my temper.'

'I'm afraid you did,' said King Hannibal amiably. 'First time I knew an Englishman could lose his temper. Most interesting.' He shook his head. 'But hardly Protocol.' The Cabinet blushed.

'So shake hands all round,' said King Hannibal, 'and phone up Abramovitch.'

A little shamefaced, Bauldstok held out a pudgy hand.

'I'm sorry,' he said, 'you must understand that we have nothing against you personally. It's the policy you stand for.'

'Me, too,' said Quill. He shook hands warmly with the entire Cabinet. Really, except for losing his temper he was becoming quite a diplomat.

He completed the circle and returned to Bauldstok. They shook hands again.

'Perhaps,' Quill suggested, 'when the war is over. . . .'

Bauldstok backed. 'Not the week-end,' he pleaded. 'The half holiday.'

* * * * *

'Skol,' said King Hannibal.

'Skol,' said Quill cheerfully.

They drank.

'Tell me something,' said King Hannibal. 'Between ourselves—is Great Britain really trying to get our Gardenium.'

They were sitting in King Hannibal's den, a cosy room furnished mainly with a large day-bed and a painting of the King's great-grandmother, Queen Nana the Nymphomaniac, since whose reign the Royal Genealogical tree had never quite managed to straighten its branches.

King Hannibal was glum. Pending a secret session with his Cabinet, he had left Bauldstok to cope with the Press ('Anglo-Insomnian talks proceed in friendly atmosphere'), and retired to his den to console himself with Quill. There was also vodscht. Up to date neither appeared to have done their work.

'Gosh,' said King Hannibal. 'If only you could keep your man awake!' he sighed.

'Well,' said Quill defensively. 'Even Himmler doesn't seem able to get Papen here.'

'Neither he can,' said Hannibal brightening. 'By jove, laddie, I think you've put your finger on it.' He paced up and down the room. 'Yes, I think I can see my way.'

'Better,' said Quill.

'Not very much,' said King Hannibal. 'There is still this evening to be steered through. Very delicate,' he explained.

Quill looked at him.

'To-night,' said King Hannibal, 'is the official entertainment of the two rival missions. Rumba-Rumba,' he said apologetically, 'has only one Opera House. So I had to persuade the Cabinet to toss for it, and the German Mission goes to the Cinema.'

'What's on?' asked Quill.

'No idea,' said King Hannibal with Royal indifference. 'So get your man into a boiled shirt and bring him to the Opera in time for the overture.'

'What's on?' asked Quill again.

'*Les Sylphides*,' said King Hannibal unexpectedly. '*Coq D'Or* and the first performance in Europe of a new ballet, *Mélange Maginot*.'

'Ballet,' said Quill, startled.

'The Ballet Stroganoff,' said King Hannibal luxuriously.

'Good God,' said Quill.

* * * * *

The secret session was in full swing. It was being held in the Tibetan room, behind stuffed keyholes, while a strong detachment of Insomnian troops guarded the ingress to the secret passages with Bren guns. Not a pressman could get within a quarter of a mile of the precincts.

How Canterbury Brindle, comfortably installed inside the chubby Buddha, was going to get out, he had not yet decided.

'Gentlemen,' said King Hannibal, 'I have come to a decision.'

The Cabinet looked unhappy.

'As neither Great Britain nor yet the Third Reich seem able to get their envoys to us, we are going to send our envoys to them. Beginning,' said King Hannibal meaningly, 'with Great Britain.'

'But,' pointed out the Minister of Fine Arts, 'we've sent Great Britain one already, and we all know what happened to him.'

'Sardinko,' said King Hannibal severely, 'was unlucky. Gentlemen,' he pleaded, 'I know you are against me in this. I know you would prefer to sell our Gardenium to Germany. But I urge you to remember one thing. How is Germany going to pay us?'

'God knows,' said the Chancellor of the Exchequer, a just man.

'Precisely,' said King Hannibal. 'But Great Britain will pay in gold. What we want is a man to bring it back. Someone energetic,' said King Hannibal. 'Courageous. Resourceful. . . .'

'I know the very man,' said Buddha unexpectedly.

CHAPTER

13

AT the Opera House the Ballet Stroganoff had taken possession. They had removed the pictures of frenzied prima donnas in *Aida*, insultingly left in the foyer, and replaced them with photographs of ballerinas doing their best to look like film stars balanced on pinpoints. They had inspected the dressing-rooms, pronounced them uninhabitable, and then quarrelled fiercely over who should have which. They had offended the stage-doorkeeper, estranged the head electrician, and exasperated the business manager by demanding a large share of the seats for their mothers. Now they were running all over the stage, each one practising difficult bits of different ballets, while the orchestra played the brassy parts of *Prince Igor*, not due to be performed till Budapest. To-night they were to give a gala performance before His Majesty King Hannibal the Hothead.

It was an evening that would live in History, prophesied impresario Vladimir Stroganoff confidently. After they had enchanted Insomnia they might even have enough money to get them to the next country.

This was the dress-rehearsal. Only naturally the dresses had not arrived.

Judging by the commotion it had caused one might have supposed that such a delay were something unusual in ballet life. Two ballerinas had walked out and only come back because de Basil was in Australia and Massine nowhere at hand. A mother was declaring with all the breath at her command that she would never allow her Nina to dance before a crowned monarch in white cotton tights. Not even, she added bitterly, in the second row of the *corps de ballet*. Two dancers had chosen this moment to clamour for an increase in salary, and seventeen for back pay. On the floor Arenskaya, *Maîtresse de Ballet*, ageing, but full of vigour, was having hysterics.

'*Soyez calme*,' pleaded Stroganoff, his bald dome bobbing beseechingly at everyone in sight. 'The dresses they come soon. Have in me the confidence.'

The conductor rapped his baton on the desk. The orchestra projected themselves into the last act of *Coq d'Or*. The entire Stroganoff company rushed to take up their places in the processional. The straggle of supers co-opted for the occasion marched jauntily across the stage trailing the triumphant chariot of King Dodon.

In the chariot, neither smiling nor bowing, sat Quill and Canterbury Brindle.

They had settled in it while awaiting a favourable opportunity to approach Stroganoff. After which the march of events had proved too swift for them.

'Philistines!' screamed Arenskaya. 'You have ruin my *grand entrée*, and now we have to go on back to the beginning. Right back!' A miniature virago of venom, she advanced towards them.

Quill and Brindle struggled to their feet, only to be pushed firmly down again by a terrified super and trundled off.

In the wings the supers stopped, turned, and marched firmly on again. The lurching chariot went with them.

'Aie,' screamed Arenskaya. 'You are still with us. It is too much.' She advanced on Canterbury Brindle and boxed his ears with considerable vigour.

'Bet you don't put that in your book,' said Quill, delighted.

'*Et vous, M'sieur*,' Arenskaya bore down on Quill. But even as Quill ducked, the menace changed to a squeal of delight.

'But it is M'sieur Quill,' she announced. 'What make you here?' She embraced him warmly.

'He is persistent, that one,' she confided to the rubbing Canterbury Brindle. 'First in London, then on the Riviera, and now he has follow me to Insomnia. Almost,' she said coyly, 'I am tempted to yield.'

Quill crossed his fingers.

'But first,' said Arenskaya, 'you introduce me to your so sympathetic friend.'

'I thought you'd met,' said Quill. 'You seemed to know him pretty well.'

'*Ah ça!*' said Arenskaya, remembering her greeting. 'That was the mistake. You must understand that for the moment I am excite. The *grand entrée* we already do it three times.' She surveyed the vast expanse of Brindle with unconcealed admiration. 'But I do not bear the malice,' she announced, 'and to prove it I permit that you take me out to the supper.'

Canterbury Brindle eyed her dubiously. 'Don't know that I can manage it to-night,' he said in a strangled voice.

'But enough of the *chi-chi*,' said Arenskaya. 'There is much work to be done. Vladimir,' she shrilled at the bald dome of Stroganoff bobbing about amid the crowd. 'Come quick and see who is asking for you.'

'If it is the man from the wigs,' shouted Stroganoff, 'tell him we pay to-morrow.' He emerged from the rabble and caught sight of Quill.

'But it is M'sieur Quill,' he embraced him warmly. '*Tiens!*' he looked at Brindle. 'He has brought his brother with him.'

'He's not my brother,' said Quill.

But Stroganoff was not listening.

'This,' he was declaring to the world at large, 'is the gesture of a prince. To follow the Ballet Stroganoff to Insomnia when you might have followed Massine to the Metropolitan or Basil to the bush, it is the compliment overwhelming. But that it is deserved,' he preened himself, 'I do not attempt to deny.'

'Simple one,' said Arenskaya indulgently. 'He has follow me.'

'*Du tout*,' said Stroganoff snubbingly. 'I see it all. Our M'sieur Quill is the *vrai balletomane*. London without the ballet it is to him a desert with only the Sadler Well. So he and his brother they have come like Mahomet to the true mountain.'

'I'm not his brother,' said Canterbury Brindle.

'I recognize you at once,' said Stroganoff, well pleased. 'The resemblance it is marked. I am delighted,' he stretched out his hands, 'to welcome you both. Only,' he snatched them away again, 'you must leave immediate.'

Quill looked at him.

'You do me this small favour,' said Stroganoff pleadingly. He turned to Brindle. 'Whenever your brother he come to the ballet—poof!—there are the dead bodies. But this time,' said Stroganoff, 'you will understand that there is no dancer I can well spare.'

'The war,' said Canterbury Brindle.

Stroganoff nodded admiringly. 'He is quick your brother,' he told Quill. 'He makes the good detective.'

'I'm not a detective,' said Brindle.

'You persevere and soon you succeed,' put in Arenskaya soothingly. 'It cannot be difficult,' she added, looking at Quill.

'War,' put in Stroganoff solemnly, 'is a serious thing. Already my Fritzl, who jump higher than Idzikovsky . . .'

'Or nearly as high,' corrected Arenskaya.

'Already,' said Stroganoff, disregarding her, 'my Fritzl has been call back to his Fuehrer—no doubt to dance at the Kroll Opera House.'

'That's where the Reichstag meets,' said Brindle, asserting himself.

'It is curious this,' mused Stroganoff, not listening. 'To think that *au fond* our Hitler should turn out the true Balletomane.'

'You mix him up with Haskell,' said Arenskaya, crossly.

Stroganoff considered this.

'*Non*,' he decided.

It was time, thought Quill, to bring up the object of his visit.

'Stroggy,' he said. 'I'd like a word with you.'

Stroganoff looked at him understandingly and shook a regretful head.

'Alas, my friend,' he said. 'I, too, am the broke.'

Quill smiled.

'It is only for the moment, you understand,' explained Stroganoff to the embarrassed Canterbury Brindle. 'To-night we make the smash hit historic, we sign the contract lucrative and once again we are the rich. Then,' he promised Quill generously, 'I lend you what you ask me and do not press you to pay back.'

'Thanks,' said Quill. 'But I really want to discuss the arrangements for the safety of the British Mission.'

'*Ah ça!*' said Stroganoff shrugging. '*Bon.*' He took Quill by the arm. 'This we discuss as we watch the rehearsal of *Aurore* from my box. Come.' He beamed at Brindle. 'Your brother, the detective, he come too.'

'Oh, hell,' said the anonymous Canterbury Brindle.

* * * * *

'You must understand,' said Stroganoff, 'that since the war we have had the time terrible.'

On the stage seven princes were doing their best to ensure that their ballerinas should finish their turns facing the audience. Arenskaya had changed the lighting three times, the conductor had resigned once, and so far Quill had not been able to get in a word about the safety of Mr Stung. Canterbury Brindle had long since abandoned as hopeless any attempt to establish his identity and retired, still Quill's brother, to the role of listener.

'We are in London when the war it begin,' Stroganoff was babbling. 'The theatre it closes, the backer he bankrupt on me—he has no consideration that one—and for three days Arenskaya she refuse to come out of the air-raid shelter. *C'était bien compliqué,*' he explained graphically.

'It must have been,' agreed Quill. 'But about to-night . . .'

'*Mon Dieu!*' Stroganoff pointed a quivering finger at a corner of the stage.

Quill looked at a pretty girl who appeared to be dancing very nicely. But apparently he was wrong, for at that moment Arenskaya leapt on to the stage, sprang at the pretty girl, and dragged her off. The pretty girl burst into tears. In the stalls a large woman rose to her feet and marched with a determined gait towards the foyer.

'*Quelle catastrophe!*' said Stroganoff. 'It is the mother. She come immediate.' He dodged behind a curtain. 'You tell her I am not here,' he begged the dazed Canterbury Brindle.

'About the British Envoy,' said Quill. 'Stroggy—are you listening?'

'*Mais oui, mais oui,*' Stroganoff looked frantically for cover. 'I hear everything. But for the moment the mother she is on the way.'

'The British Envoy,' began Quill again.

'Why you worry me with that now,' said Stroganoff crossly. 'Cannot you see that I prepare to occupy myself with an earthquake?'

The door burst open. The earthquake had arrived.

On the stage the two bluebirds were cooing choreographically at one another. In the box Stroganoff was manfully standing up to the earthquake. On the stage the Bluebirds clove tautly through the air. In the box the earthquake was bringing down the ceiling. On the stage the Bluebirds, furious, were advancing on the conductor. In the box the earthquake was telling the silent Canterbury Brindle to stop interfering. The exhausted Bluebirds chased each other off the stage. An exasperated Quill chased the earthquake out of the box.

All was silent except the orchestra.

'They play well—no?' said Stroganoff, trying to ignore the episode.

'No,' said Canterbury Brindle.

But as usual Stroganoff was not listening. He was engaged in a long-range argument with Arenskaya, who was standing by the footlights. Quill dragged him away. Arenskaya consoled herself by transferring the argument to the conductor.

'Now then,' said Quill. 'Where is the British Envoy going to sit?'

'The Royal Box,' said Stroganoff promptly. 'It is not as large as mine,' he boasted.

'The theatre will be policed, of course?' asked Quill.

'My friend,' said Stroganoff soothingly. 'What for are you so frighten? Have in me the confidence unmentionable. You will be well guarded, have no fear. For this I have engaged a special supervisor who presented himself to me. One,' he announced, 'with much experience of the bump-off. He is an American,' he added, explaining all.

The impartial Brindle roared with laughter.

Stroganoff looked at him enquiringly.

'I make the joke unconscious?' he asked, well pleased.

'I'll say you have,' said Quill. 'Have you engaged anyone else specially for the occasion?'

'Assuredly,' said Stroganoff, beaming. 'It will be for you the surprise gratifying. It is none other,' he paused, 'than our old friend Kurt.'

'Good God,' said Quill.

'*Tiens*—you are surprise,' said Stroganoff. 'But poor Kurt he has fall on the evil days. But,' he drew himself up, 'Vladimir Stroganoff does not forget. Always I remember that once when the Ballet Stroganoff it is up to the neck in the soup the good Kurt try to repair my fortune.'

'With a gold mine,' said Quill.

'It is not his fault,' said Stroganoff hotly, 'that the mine it does not exist.'

Quill let it go. 'What job have you given him?'

'Alas,' said Stroganoff, 'there is not much I could offer my old friend. But I do the best I can. He bears the coffee to the Royal Box.'

'Oi,' said Canterbury Brindle.

The door opened. A shock of black hair came striding into the room, looked round and made for the only stranger present.

'You schange me small scheque?' it asked Canterbury Brindle winningly.

Canterbury Brindle blinked.

'This,' said Stroganoff with pride, 'is Nicolas Nevajno, choreographer of the future.'

There was an uproar from the stage. The orchestra had gone on strike.

*　*　*　*　*

'And I thought that politics were crazy,' said Canterbury Brindle to Quill as they left the theatre.

CHAPTER

14

WHILE the Ballet Stroganoff was convulsing itself into its gala performance the chief Chancelleries in Europe were going through a somewhat similar process.

On the Wilhelmstrasse Hitler had sent for Ribbentrop, who had wisely sent Himmler instead.

The Fuehrer was eating cream buns, but in spite of this he seemed to be in a bad temper. 'Why,' he demanded querulously, 'has Franzi not yet reached Insomnia?' With great presence of mind Himmler blamed it on the railways which had been sabotaged—of course by Winston Churchill. However, he hastened to point out, there was some good news from another quarter. The gallant ship *Stickelgruber* had just triumphantly scuttled itself off West Point.

'Gut,' said the Fuehrer, biting into another cream bun. 'My navy rules the waves.'

'Under the waves,' cracked Himmler, forgetting himself.

His Fuehrer looked at him.

'Our U-boats,' said Himmler hurriedly.

The Fuehrer reached for another cream bun. It was on land, he explained, that he was not so happy. He had only managed to grab half Poland. His *Blitzkrieg* had backfired on him. And his generals, though always quarrelling among themselves, never seemed to agree with him. These stiff-necked Prussians would never let him forget that he was once an Austrian corporal.

Himmler clucked sympathetically.

'So you see,' said Hitler, 'we've got to get the Gardenium.'

Himmler saw.

The great man pondered.

'Maybe,' he decided, 'I'd better see Franzi myself. Bring him to Berchtesgarten.'

'At once, Sire.' Himmler saluted. Almost he felt sorry for the wretched Franzi.

'So you see,' said the Minister of War to the assembled Cabinet, 'we've got to get the Gardenium.'

'I wonder what the hell Stung is up to,' mused the Prime Minister.

The First Lord of the Admiralty lit a cigar. 'I suppose,' he said wistfully, 'you wouldn't let me send a warship?'

There was a commotion outside. A little man in a bowler hat burst into the room.

'You've simply got to listen to me!' The little man appealed to the Cabinet.

'Surely, surely,' said the Minister of War. 'Write to me about it.'

'But you don't understand. . . .' The little man was nearly weeping.

A pair of outraged arms rushed into the room, tackled the little man, tutted apologetically to the Cabinet and dragged him out.

'The I.R.A.?' suggested the Prime Minister, reaching with imperturbable British calm for the fire extinguisher.

'Don't think so,' said the Minister of War. 'He's been trying to see me all week.'

'What did he want?' asked the First Lord of the Admiralty, an inquisitive man.

They looked at him.

* * * * *

At the Ministry of Elimination Sir Humphrey Spratt picked up his newspaper.

'Anglo-Insomnian Talks Proceed in Friendly Atmosphere'

'Good,' said Sir Humphrey, well pleased. 'Excellent.'

He trotted off to tea.

* * * * *

'I'm worried,' said Bauldstok, struggling with his white tie. 'If Hannibal sends that envoy to England we're defeated.'

'Dished,' agreed the Minister of Fine Arts, an uncouth man.

'Leave it to me,' said Al Schenk.

They turned on him.

'A fine mess you've made of things,' said the Minister of Fine Arts.

'Here is Stung, refreshed by all the sleep he's had, turning up at the Opera to-night as big a nuisance as ever,' complained Bauldstok.

'For crying out loud,' said Al, 'is it my fault you wouldn't let me murder him?'

'Our big obstacle,' brooded the Minister of Fine Arts, 'is King Hannibal.'

'Let me look after him,' suggested Al.

'Impossible,' said Bauldstok regretfully. 'The people would never stand for it. If only,' he sighed, 'I had twenty thousand pounds.'

'Why?' asked Al.

'It would keep Hannibal in Paris for a couple of months at least,' said Bauldstok wistfully.

'Well, we haven't got it,' said the Minister of Fine Arts, a brutal man.

'Too bad,' said Al. He sat down and pondered.

'What we've got to do,' said Bauldstok, pulling off his tie and starting again, 'is to keep Stung hanging about here a bit longer. Until Franzi arrives anyway.'

'I'm getting sort of discouraged about Franzi,' said Al.

They sighed.

'But we've got to stop Hannibal sending that envoy,' said the Minister of Fine Arts.

'Quite,' agreed Bauldstok, 'but how?'

They pondered.

'Let me look after the envoy,' suggested Al.

'No more murders,' said Bauldstok severely.

'I feel,' said the Minister of Fine Arts regretfully, 'that the time has come to fall back on Diplomacy.'

'This from you,' said Bauldstok astounded.

The Minister of Fine Arts smirked. 'I've got it all worked out. We'll kid King Hannibal that we've come round to his point of view and coax him away from this envoy whim by buddying up to Stung. Make it look as though we're ready to sign the treaty with him.'

Bauldstok nodded. 'And then, when Franzi does arrive, we sting Stung again,' he chuckled.

'If the detective lets you,' said Al.

They turned on him.

'You look after the detective,' said Bauldstok.

'He's altogether too pally with Hannibal for my liking, anyway,' said the Minister of Fine Arts.

'If you ask me,' said Bauldstok, 'I think he's much more dangerous to us than Stung.'

'He knows too much,' said the Minister of Fine Arts.

'Altogether too much,' agreed Bauldstok.

They looked at Al.

Al sighed. He had known all along it would have to come to this. 'You make me tired,' he said and went.

'I'm glad he's gone,' said Bauldstok. 'That man makes me nervous.'

'Forget it,' said the Minister of Fine Arts. 'Concentrate on being nice to Stung. Think you can manage it?' he asked anxiously.

Bauldstok adjusted his tie and smirked.

'Watch me,' he said. 'I've not been in the political racket for twenty years for nothing. If necessary,' he said, 'I'll even let him tell me a funny story.'

* * * * *

'Is my tie straight?' asked Mr Stung, surveying himself in the mirror in his room at the Hôtel des Ambassadeurs.

'Perfect,' said Quill.

'You know,' confided Mr Stung, 'I'm worried. Dash it all, I ought to have met this Cabinet two days ago.'

'As long as you stay awake to meet them to-night, I'll be satisfied,' said Quill.

Mr Stung looked hurt.

'I know,' said Quill. 'It's my fault. But do me one favour to-night. Forget Protocol. Forget about your warships. Forget that Bauldstok eats out of your hand.'

'But he spent a week-end with me,' objected Mr Stung.

'Don't remind him of it,' said Quill hastily. 'What you've got to do to-night is to get yourself liked. Rely on the boyish charm.'

'Charm!' said Mr Stung, horrified.

'King Hannibal likes me,' said Quill. 'Can't you get Bauldstok to like you?'

This was a revolutionary idea. It took Mr Stung some time to assimilate it.

'You know, Quill,' he said, 'I believe you've got something there. Tell you what,' he came to a decision, 'I'll try it.'

'Don't overdo it,' said Quill.

'Rely on me,' said Stung, fascinated by the unusual quality he was calling on himself to produce. 'I'll have Bauldstok eating out of my hand before you know where you are.'

Quill looked alarmed.

'I'll tell him a funny story,' said Mr Stung, putting on his opera cloak.

*　　　*　　　*　　　*　　　*

'Peof!' said Stroganoff to the exploded conductor, 'your resignation it matters nothing. To-night I wave the baton myself.'

CHAPTER

15

A FEELING of keen expectation galvanized the blacked-out foyer of the Opera House at Rumba-Rumba. There were good friends expecting the ballerinas to get by somehow. There were rivals expecting them to flop. There was the old guard of ballet-goers expecting to find ample grounds for mourning the good old days. ('You ought to have seen Karsavina!') There was the young guard missing Massine. There were the faded faces of one-time favourites, hardly expecting to be remembered and pathetically grateful for a flung smile of recognition. There were mothers swanking before the performance, and mothers who could afford to wait till after the performance to have their fling. There were the critics. There were the photographers. There were the boy friends. There were even some members of the paying public.

So far there is no Arnold Haskell, but let us hope that this is only because his exit permit from England has been slightly delayed and that he will arrive in good time for the unique quadratic groupings of the New Nevajno Ballet *Mélange Maginot*.

And here is Vladimir Stroganoff, gesticulating, embracing, dodging, and promising all over the foyer. It is his firm conviction that the success of his season depends on his personally greeting every one of his audience.

'Good-bye,' he panted, and dashed off to kiss the hand of a stately old lady, whom he imagined, quite wrongly, to be the Countess of Kashkavar, the power behind the throne.

There was Arenskaya, embellished in property pearls and posing for a photographer.

'Amazing,' murmured Mr Stung as Quill hurried him past.

A cannon went off. The belligerents in the foyer jumped. But the nationals remembered that they were Insomnians. Besides, they knew that this was the traditional manner of announcing that the reigning monarch had arrived.

Immaculate in his pale white uniform with the pale blue and gold order of the Fascinated Cow (First Class) slashed across his breast, King Hannibal the Hothead walked aloofly in. He looked exactly like Prince Charming in a Lyceum pantomime—only he had less bosom. On his arm was the Countess de Kashkavar, a dizzy blonde, divinely tall and temporarily fair. Behind them filed the Cabinet, smiling phonily at the public. Bauldstok stuck a hookah in his mouth and posed to a photographer.

* * * * *

Depositing Stung in the ante-room with strict instructions not to speak to anyone till he came back ('in a crisis-nod!'), Quill made a hurried tour of the house. There were no spies in the stalls, no bombs in the boxes, and no ambushes in the upper circle. But on the stone steps leading up to the gallery, there was a recumbent figure. Sasha

Podushkin, impervious to the stampede that was going on all around him, was taking a rest.

'You,' said Quill astonished. 'A balletomane?'

'But certainly,' said Sasha. 'Am I not a White Russian? Never,' he boasted, 'do I miss the Ballet—even when I know that it is going to be bad.'

Quill grinned. 'Come along with me,' he suggested, 'and I'll ask Stroggy for a stall.'

Sasha stared. So must King Cophetua have looked at his wife's relations.

'A stall?' he said coldly. 'A Podushkin at the Ballet in a stall!'

'Why not?' said Quill. 'You don't have to dress.'

'The true intellectual,' said Sasha, 'watches the Ballet only from the gallery. You should have known this,' he added severely.

Quill bowed his head.

'I will meet you at the bar in the *entr'acte*,' said Sasha, struggling to his feet. 'You may buy me a drink,' he added forgivingly.

Crushed, Quill crept away.

*   *   *   *   *

To an encouraging rattle of applause, starting in the orchestra pit, the conductor mounted his rostrum. He was not Stroganoff. Arenskaya had seen to that.

In her stall Mme Pinsk sighed blissfully.

'Sylphides,' she said ecstatically to her dormant husband.

'Is that the one with the overgrown little Lord Fauntleroy?' asked the husband. Resigned, he closed his eyes.

Mme Pinsk jerked him to his feet.

King Hannibal was entering his box and the orchestra had burst into the Insomnian national anthem. It had been their intention to play all seven verses, but at the end of the third King Hannibal sat down firmly.

'A sensible man,' said Sasha Podushkin, following suit.

The house applauded violently. King Hannibal was popular with his subjects.

The bald dome of Stroganoff was seen for a second bobbing between the curtains. Clearly he considered this the right moment to make 'the speech welcoming.' But Arenskaya dragged him back.

The conductor rapped on the desk with his baton.

'Sylphides,' said Mme Pinsk with ecstasy.

Mr Pinsk closed his eyes.

Mme Pinsk jerked him to his feet. The orchestra was engulfing the house in 'God Save the King.' The British Mission had arrived.

Mr Stung was concentrating on charm. He adjusted his monocle and essayed a smile. In the circle a programme-seller swooned.

'And how,' enquired Bauldstok, also concentrating on charm, 'is your so talkative mother-in-law?'

'Talking,' said Mr Stung resigned.

The two men looked at each other and sighed. For a moment they were almost brothers.

The conductor rapped his baton.

'Sylphides,' said Mme Pinsk with rapture.

For the third time Mr Pinsk closed his eyes.

Mme Pinsk jerked him to his feet. Stocky well-cropped heads were marching stiffly into the stage box. The orchestra burst into *Deutschland Über Alles*.

'Heil,' said the German Mission, and sat down.

Mr Stung dropped his eyeglass.

'Can't understand it,' mused King Hannibal. 'Didn't I send them to the cinema?'

'They were showing *Professor Mamlock*,' said the Minister of Fine Arts, a brutal man.

The conductor rapped his baton. Mr Pinsk stood up. Mme Pinsk pushed him down.

'Sylphides,' she said reprovingly.

This time she was right. It happens to everyone once.

* * * * *

On the stage the tableau of exhausted sylphs came creakily to life. King Hannibal adjusted his binoculars.

Manfully the cavalier slung the heavy sylph across his shoulder.

'*Ach*,' said the German Mission entranced. 'Almost it might be the *Merry Widow*.'

In an orderly if ill-timed manner the moonlit sequences succeeded each other until at last the little Lord Fauntleroy leapt clean through the last tableau, missing the reclining ballerina by a hairsbreadth. The curtain fell.

'Pretty,' said Mr Stung with charm, 'but I prefer Vic Oliver.'

There was a certain amount of applause. Little Lord Fauntleroy appeared with a laurel-wreath slung round him. It had a luggage label on it.

'Talking of Vic Oliver,' said Mr Stung, 'reminds me of a fearfully funny story he tells.'

He told it. It was not funny, but then neither had it been told by Vic Oliver.

King Hannibal left the box abruptly. But Bauldstok managed a smile.

'And that,' he said, 'reminds me of another story.'

The Countess de Kashkavar hurried out.

'Two commercial travellers,' said Mr Stung, getting into his stride . . .

Quill fled.

* * * * *

In the Royal ante-room a little man with a large beard was juggling energetically behind the bar. Brandy, angostura, cordials, bitters, and crushed ice cascaded in all directions under his enthusiastic hand. Some of it, however, went into the cocktail shaker. Joyfully the bartender pounced on it, shook, tossed it in the air, only just caught it, opened, poured, plucked a couple of cherries, and with a beaming smile offered the result.

'Skol,' said King Hannibal.

'Skol,' said Quill.

They choked.

'Good gad,' said King Hannibal, 'what's this?'

The barman bowed. 'It is kind of Your Majesty to congratulate me,' he said, 'and I am glad that you are pleased. It is my own invention.'

'I see,' said King Hannibal.

'If you like,' offered the barman, 'I will write down for you the ingredients.' He whipped out a pencil. 'Have I,' he enquired, 'Your Majesty's permission to call it the *Hannibal?*'

'No,' said King Hannibal firmly.

For a moment the little barman looked depressed. But only for a moment.

'I understand perfectly.' He bowed. 'Royalty must not advertise.'

'Mix me a Martini,' said King Hannibal coldly.

'*De suite*,' said the barman. 'It shall be delicious,' he promised.

Picking up a bottle of Benedictine he got to work.

'For the dry Martini,' he told the transfixed monarch, 'there is no one to touch me. I have,' he said modestly, 'the talent natural for mixing the drink.'

'Ah,' said Quill.

'Had I chosen this profession,' said the barman unexpectedly, 'I would have made a very fine barman.'

King Hannibal dropped his eyeglass.

'The finest barman in the world,' went on the very fine barman. With an expressive gesture he knocked over the Martini he had just prepared.

To Quill there seemed something vaguely familiar about the patter.

He peered more closely at the barman. He stretched out a hand and pulled his beard.

'Come, come,' said King Hannibal, shocked. 'You can't do this, you know. Fellow didn't mean to offend you.'

But most of the beard had come away and the mortified face of Kurt Carruthers was almost showing through it.

'You!' said Quill. He wasn't very surprised.

'I do it for my Government,' said Kurt quickly.

'I cannot believe,' said King Hannibal, puzzled but persevering, 'that any Government should have employed you to serve me—um —unique cocktails.'

Kurt beamed. 'That,' he said, 'was just for me the extra pleasure. The reason that I am here,' he stopped, 'but perhaps it is not wise to discuss this. Only tell me,' he turned to Quill, 'when will your Mr Stung be thirsty?'

Quill grinned. 'Not this performance,' he said and led the dazed monarch out of earshot.

Outside the Royal Box they paused.

'Wonder how they're getting on?' said King Hannibal anxiously.

'They were all right when I left,' said Quill, 'if only Bauldstok and Stung would get to like each other. . . .' The King sighed, 'Bauldstok could carry the Cabinet with him.'

Quill opened the door and peeped in. Hookah in mouth Bauldstok was in full swing. Mr Stung caught sight of Quill, lifted a triumphant thumb, and pointed to his cigar. Quill shut the door and tiptoed away.

'They're doing fine,' he said. 'Bauldstok is telling Stung about his first election.'

'Poor devil,' said King Hannibal. 'That goes on for twenty minutes.'

They went back to the ante-room.

Vladimir Stroganoff bounced up from a table and went to meet him. Behind him came a shock of black hair.

'Majesty,' said Stroganoff anxiously. 'Permit that I present Nicolas Nevajno, choreographer of the future.'

Majesty adjusted his eyeglass. He looked. He went on looking.

'See,' said Stroganoff to Nevajno encouragingly. 'You make the good impression.' He leant closer to the monarch. 'The evening dress,' he whispered, 'he has put it on special for the occasion. I had much trouble to persuade him.'

'Ah,' said King Hannibal.

'But at last I succeed,' said Stroganoff. 'Look.' He pointed with pride at the patent shoes, the corrugated socks, the near-white waistcoat.

'The red tie,' he said regretfully, 'I could not induce him to abandon. It is,' he explained, 'his politics.'

Regal calm was almost shaken. Not daring to look at Quill, King Hannibal extended a hand.

Nevajno ignored it.

'Nicolas,' said Stroganoff reproachfully.

But Nevajno was oblivious. He was searching frantically through his pockets.

'*Un petit moment*,' he said and dashed off.

'*Mon Dieu!*' yelped Stroganoff, realization dawning. 'He has gone to fetch his cheque book. *Quelle catastrophe!*' Frantically he turned to King Hannibal. 'When he come back,' he said urgently, 'do not schange the small scheque he will ask.'

'He won't,' promised Quill.

'Only,' pleaded Stroganoff, 'say that this is because you have left at home your pocket-book. So you will not hurt his feelings. Good-bye.'

He darted off.

'You know,' said King Hannibal reflectively, 'in many ways I'm enjoying this evening.'

'Let's get back to the box,' said Quill.

'Ah, yes,' said King Hannibal, 'the love birds! What about all getting tight together?' he suggested.

'An idea,' said Quill.

Arm-in-arm they wandered back to the box.

'Shall we knock?' asked the King playfully.

They knocked.

There was no answer.

Quill turned the handle.

The two love birds were standing up face to face, breathing heavily.

'And as for your Gardenium,' said Mr Stung whitely, 'you know what you can do with it.'

Very deliberately Bauldstok reached out a hand, plucked Mr Stung's cigar from his trembling mouth, stubbed it out and put it back in his own cigar case.

'You're a pompous idiot,' he said, 'and a damned conceited ass.' He strode out and slammed the door.

Mr Stung sagged.

The door opened.

'And what's more,' said Bauldstok, putting his head round the corner, 'I don't care if you do send a warship.'

From the coat-stand emerged Canterbury Brindle.

'Excuse me,' he said, 'I've got to telephone.'
'What happened?' asked Quill.
'We were discussing peace aims,' said Mr Stung apologetically.

* * * * *

On the stage *Mélange Maginot* was being churned out. The atmosphere in the Royal Box was nearly as involved. Depressed by the unaccountable failure of his 'charm' Mr Stung relapsed into moody silence. King Hannibal was trying to persuade the Countess Kashkavar that the ballet must be over soon and Quill was just fed up.

The door opened. Sasha Podushkin came in.

'You promised me a drink,' he told Quill reproachfully.

Quill grinned. 'Sasha,' he said, 'I'm surprised at you. Leaving in the middle of a new ballet to get a drink.'

'But why not?' said Sasha. 'The true balletomane never waits for the end of a new work. He has seen it already at dress-rehearsal. Also,' he admitted, 'they have thrown me out of the gallery. Me—a Podushkin.'

'Podushkin,' said King Hannibal keenly. 'Are you Sasha Podushkin?'

Sasha bowed. 'At Your Majesty's service. Provided, of course,' he added hurriedly, 'that what you demand is not too exhausting.'

'Come outside,' said King Hannibal, ignoring this. 'I've got a job for you.'

CHAPTER

16

'WELL, good night,' said Mr Stung.

'Good night,' said Quill.

'See you in the morning,' said Mr Stung. He fidgeted. 'Don't worry about Bauldstok,' he said. 'I'll deal with him to-morrow. He'll eat out of my hand,' he promised without much confidence.

'Sure he will,' said Quill. He patted Stung on the back and turned despondently towards his own room.

He opened the door. As he was groping for the light switch something hit him on the head. It hit him very hard, but he did not realize this until a few minutes later.

By that time he was lying bound and gagged on the bed and Al Schenk was leaning over him.

'How feeling?' asked Al.

'Gug,' said Quill.

'Too bad your skull's so tough,' said Al. 'I was hoping you wouldn't wake up this side of heaven.'

'Gug,' said Quill.

Al produced an alarm-clock, a black box, and a coil of wire.

'Pardon me,' he said and got to work. 'Time bomb,' he explained. 'Twelve o'clock suit you?'

'Gug,' said Quill.

'You know, sonny,' said Al, 'I'm real sorry to leave you to face death alone, but you know how it is with a bomb. Unhealthy,' he explained.

'Gug,' said Quill.

'Sorry it had to be a bomb,' said Al. 'But a revolver isn't strong enough. You can shoot a guy with a revolver and nothing much happens. Remember Sardinko!'

'Gug,' said Quill.

'But it will take a hell of a lot of diplomacy to patch up an exploded mission,' said Al. He twisted a wire. 'There now,' he said, 'that ought to put the lid on the Anglo-Insomnian Gardenium pact.'

'Gug-gug,' said Quill violently.

'You've got just twenty minutes,' said Al. 'So make your peace.' He paused in the doorway. 'Nothing personal in this at all, sonny, you understand. I'm real sorry to have to blow you up. But,' he shrugged, 'you would come to Insomnia.'

He put out the light and closed the door.

Alone in the dark Quill listened to the grisly ticking of the alarm-clock. He felt horrible. It seemed to him that he must be looking exactly like the hero on the jacket of a ten-cent pulp. Only these heroes always get themselves rescued.

The reflection galvanized Quill with a bump. He began to struggle with his bonds. He writhed, he twisted, and he stretched. He wriggled his wrists, kicked his legs and toppled off the bed. The gag came out but the bonds remained immovable.

He opened his mouth to shout and closed it again. He must not waste his energy. No one would hear him through these thick stone walls. Nothing for it but to die. He hoped he would die like an Englishman. With calm.

Well, it had been a good life. Scotland Yard. The Stroganoff Ballet. And the girl behind the tobacco kiosk. It was a pity perhaps that he had never solved a case, but it was too late to bother about that now.

And anyway England was going to win the war even though he wouldn't be there to see it.

Sixteen minutes to go. That fool Stung.

But England would still win the war—even though it didn't get the Gardenium!

What was this Gardenium, anyway?

Fifteen minutes. He wondered how high he would be blown. And that reminded him. Stung would be blown up too. His first act no doubt would be to ask the Lord Almighty to send a warship.

In spite of himself Quill laughed. The sound rolled round the empty room. As it died the ticking of the clock broke through it.

Not much longer now. Steady. Calm. Remember you are British.

The pounding of blood in Quill's ears sounded exactly like distant footsteps. God, it was footsteps! They were coming closer.

'Help!' yelled Quill, forgetting to die like an Englishman. 'Help!'

The door opened. A lean hand switched on the light.

'Why have you tied yourself up like this?' asked Sasha Podushkin.

* * * * *

'A bomb,' said Sasha incredulously. 'But how interesting. I have never seen a bomb.' He stepped carefully over the prostrate Quill and peered fascinated at the mass of wires. 'How does it work?'

'It goes off at twelve,' said Quill with some heat.

Sasha looked at the clock.

'Fifteen minutes,' he said. 'We have plenty of time.' He picked up a wire and fingered it. 'What happens,' he enquired, 'if I pull this?'

'You blow us up,' said Quill shortly.

'Ah,' said Sasha, dropping the wire. He stepped back over Quill and lay down on the bed. 'I am tired,' he announced. 'Always the Ballet it exhausts my emotions. Never have I used up so much disgust.'

'Yes, yes,' said Quill, waving away the æsthetics. 'But come and untie me now, there's a good chap.'

Sasha opened one eye. 'We have yet thirteen minutes,' he said reassuringly.

Quill groaned.

A thought struck Sasha. 'You are uncomfortable,' he enquired. 'Here is a cushion.' He threw it.

'Don't you realize,' said Quill, 'that if we don't disconnect this damn bomb we'll both be blown the other side of eternity?'

'Eternity,' said Sasha solemnly. 'Death. Oblivion.' Suddenly he became very Russian. 'Had you told me this morning that I was destined to die with you . . .'

'There's no need to go to those lengths,' snapped Quill, 'if we disconnect this damned thing.'

'To die,' mused Sasha, waving this irrelevant comment aside. 'To accept the fate that has cut us off, so young, and to laugh in its teeth —ha! ha!'

'Ha, ha!' said Quill nastily.

'But to a Podushkin,' said Sasha, starting a new train of thought, 'to die young is perhaps no hardship. What is death,' he demanded, 'but a negation—a cessation of activity—and a sleep? Sleep,' he repeated gratefully, and closed his eyes.

'Hey,' said Quill. 'Wake up.'

'I wonder,' said Sasha, eyes still closed, 'how high we will be blown?'

'Will be?' groaned Quill.

'But, yes,' said Sasha. 'I have decided to resign myself to this. If I die I shall not have to go to England as an envoy.'

'Envoy!' said Quill, astonishment swamping his other emotions, which were nevertheless still there.

'But, yes,' said Sasha. 'King Hannibal has commissioned me to go to England with you. I protested, but it was useless. And now,' he finished consolingly, 'we do not have to pack.'

Quill looked at him. As a diplomat Sasha was something new.

'I thought you were a parachute jumper?'

'In peace-time only,' said Sasha. 'Then there was a car to find us when we landed. But now there is no petrol, and they expect us to walk back to headquarters. It is too much. I resigned.' He leant up on one arm. 'Would you not have done the same?'

There were five minutes to go.'

'Untie me,' said Quill, 'and I'll tell you.'

Sasha looked at him dubiously. 'If I untie you,' he asked, 'will you promise not to take me to England?'

Four minutes.

'Sure,' said Quill. 'Sure. Anything you say.'

'We will go to Vienna instead,' promised Sasha. 'You will like Vienna. Also you will like my Uncle Bounya. His bortsh!' He kissed his fingers.

Three minutes.

'If you don't get me out of this,' said Quill, 'you'll never taste it again.'

Galvanized, Sasha leapt from the bed and inspected the bonds.

'Give me a knife,' he demanded.

'How can I?' roared Quill. 'I'm tied up, you blasted fool.'

Sasha drew himself up. 'You insult me,' he said. 'Me—a Podushkin. *Ça-y-est!* I do not speak to you any more. I go.' He turned.

'Come back,' shouted Quill. 'I'm sorry, I apologize, I grovel. Only get me out of this.'

Sasha came back. He looked a little shamefaced.

'I am sorry,' he said. 'I forget that you are about to be blown up. Never shall it be said that a Podushkin had failed his friend. It is unpardonable, what I was about do.' He came closer. 'Can you ever forgive me.'

'Easily,' said Quill. 'Only please get a move on.'

'You are magnanimous,' said Sasha, 'and to be magnanimous it is the greatest virtue of all. I remember once in Vladivostok . . .'

Thirty seconds to get untied, to snatch a knife and to cut the wire. Already there was a horrible whirring in the machine.

'Sasha,' Quill gasped. 'Hurry.'

The whirr thickened to a rumble. The rumble to a screech. The bomb gathered itself together.

It failed to go off.

'*Ersatz*,' said Sasha, with deep disgust.

CHAPTER

17

'VOILA,' said Sasha. 'It is finished.' Exhausted, he fell on the bed.

Quill flung away the last remnants of smouldering rope and surveyed his charred hands ruefully. Like a sorcerer's apprentice, he stood in a circle of burnt matches suffering from anti-climax.

'How my wrists ache,' complained Sasha. 'Never in my life have I struck so many matches. The next time,' he counselled, 'implore them to use string.'

'I'll make a point of it,' said Quill savagely.

'And also,' said Sasha, 'in rescuing you I have become badly injured myself. Look!' He held out a finger on which a minute smudge could just be discerned. 'Have you,' he demanded, 'any butter?'

Quill turned his back on him.

'Vienna,' sighed Sasha, gazing at the ceiling. 'How I have worked to reach you. One hundred and forty-seven matches.'

Quill turned round again. 'You're not going to Vienna.'

'But you will adore it,' said Sasha. 'It is sunny, it is gay, it is sociable. Even the Fuehrer speaks of moving there.'

'I happen to be at war with the Fuehrer,' said Quill.

'That is not important,' said Sasha. 'We will tell no one you are English. You speak Russian, of course,' he enquired.

Quill had had enough of this.

'Look here,' he said, 'if they're really crazy enough to have made you an envoy you're coming to England with me.'

'But you promised,' said Sasha.

'But you didn't rescue me,' said Quill.

In a hurt silence Sasha pointed to the ring of matches on the floor.

'That doesn't count,' said Quill brutally.

The door opened. Canterbury Brindle came bustling in, surveyed the scene, and lit himself a cigar.

'So you're still alive,' he commented between impartial puffs.

Quill looked at him.

'Glad to see you're not rattled,' said Brindle. 'I got quite worried thinking about you alone with that bomb.'

'He was not alone,' put in Sasha. 'I rescued him and now he is taking me to Vienna.'

Quill ignored him. 'You knew about that bomb!'

'Sure,' said Brindle, puffing. 'I knew about it.'

Quill could hardly believe his ears. 'And yet you left me here,' he pursued.

Brindle nodded. 'Had to get the story through,' he reminded him.

'Blast you,' said Quill. 'I know you're impartial, but there are limits.'

Brindle went on puffing.

'I suppose,' said Quill sarcastically, 'you're going to tell me you knew the bomb wouldn't go off.'

'Knew it?' said Brindle. 'I arranged the substitution. Cost me nearly a thousand peccoes in bribes.'

'The Government will reimburse you,' said Quill stiffly.

Brindle waved an airy hand. 'Don't worry,' he said. 'I've put it down in my expenses under Entertainments.'

'Tell me something,' said Sasha, interested. 'When you have a woman, does your paper also pay?'

'Certainly,' said Brindle.

'And how do you describe that?' asked Quill.

'Beauty Culture,' said Brindle.

The telephone rang. Instinctively Brindle made towards the receiver. But Quill beat him to it.

'Yes,' he snapped.

'Is that Quill?' asked a voice.

'Yes,' said Quill. 'Who the hell are you?'

'King Hannibal,' said the voice coldly.

'Oh,' said Quill.

'Listen,' said King Hannibal, 'has Sasha Podushkin arrived yet?'

'He's arrived,' said Quill. 'Sat here and watched a bomb blow me up.'

'Really,' said King Hannibal. He did not sound particularly interested. One gathered that bombs were more or less routine in the life of Royalty.

'Only it didn't go off,' said Quill.

'Splendid,' said King Hannibal, and dismissed the subject. 'Now listen,' he said, 'I've decided to send an envoy to England. He'll have full powers to sign the Gardenium pact. Are you listening?'

'Yes,' said Quill.

'After what's happened between Stung and Bauldstok to-night it's quite hopeless to try and get it signed here. The Cabinet has been dead against it all the time.'

'I noticed that,' said Quill.

'And now Bauldstok will be totally obstructive. So the only hope for me to get to Paris,' said King Hannibal with a chuckle, 'is to get the treaty signed out of range.'

'Quite,' said Quill.

'So,' said Hannibal, 'I'm sending an envoy. You agree?'

'I agree,' said Quill. 'But has it got to be Podushkin?'

'Podushkin!' said King Hannibal. 'What's the matter with Podushkin?'

'He's indolent,' said Quill. 'He's tactless. He wants to go to Vienna. And his heart isn't in the job.'

'That is exactly what I told him myself,' said Sasha with a deep sense of grievance, 'but he would not listen.'

'Sorry,' said King Hannibal, 'but Podushkin is the man for the job. The gods have spoken. So see to it that Sasha Podushkin gets to England in safety. Don't let him be murdered.'

'Ah,' said Quill wistfully.

'I don't expect you'll have a smooth journey,' said King Hannibal. 'In fact, attempts will be made to stop you. But you'll survive them,' he said encouragingly.

'Quite so,' said Quill. 'And what about the German mission?'

'That's all right,' King Hannibal chuckled. 'Franzi Papen has taken a tumble in the Alps. Toboganning,' he added richly.

'Ski-ing,' corrected Brindle, whose ear was almost as close to the receiver as Quill's.

'I want you to be off at once,' said King Hannibal. 'If you hurry you can just catch the eleven a.m. express.'

Quill glanced at his watch. It was a little after midnight.

'How far is this station of yours?' he asked.

'Idiot,' said King Hannibal. 'The train was due this morning.'

'It ought to be along pretty soon now,' said Quill.

'That's what I meant,' said Hannibal. 'So get going.'

'Right,' said Quill.

'Good-bye and good luck,' said King Hannibal.

'Good-bye and thank you,' said Quill.

'By the way,' wheedled King Hannibal, 'do you think you can persuade Sir John Simon to make out the cheque to me personally?'

'I'll do my best,' Quill promised.

He hung up.

'We start at once.'

Sasha made a gesture of despair. 'Impossible to pack in time,' he said starkly.

'That's all right,' said Brindle. 'I've had a man over at your flat to do it for you. He ought to be here any moment now.'

Sasha glared. 'Busybody,' he said, and turned his back on him.

'Well,' said Quill, 'I'd better go and wake Stung.'

'Not necessary,' said Brindle, 'I looked in on him on my way here. He ought to be dressed by now.'

'You think of everything,' said Quill.

There was a knock at the door. Mr Stung entered. In cinnamon plus-fours and a gay pull-over, he looked almost cheerful.

'Well, well,' he rubbed his hands. 'All ready for the journey. You know,' he announced triumphantly, 'I'm not a bit sleepy.'

CHAPTER

18

'BUT,' said Kurt hotly, 'was I to blame that the bomb was *ersatz?*'

'You were,' said Al Schenk.

'The substitution was made under your very nose,' said Señor Centime reprovingly.

The trio were seated at a wooden table in an alcove at 'The Scheming Octopus,' a low dive catering specially for conspirators.

'And besides,' said Kurt defiantly, 'I am pleased that your bomb did not explode.'

'So,' said Señor Centime.

'Never,' said Kurt eloquently, 'would I have fetched the bomb from the address Señor Centime had given me—for which no doubt,' sneered the man of the world, 'he had arranged the rake-off—had I supposed for a minute it was not for stiff-necked Mr Stung. Had I known it was to trap my good friend Quill . . .'

'Friend?' jeered Señor Centime.

'My good friend,' said Kurt firmly. 'And I do not betray my friends. I may,' he conceded, 'sell them the shares unlucky, induce the wager on the horse belated, or pass them on the mine defunct. I will remove their pocket-books. I will effect the blackmail innocuous. I will, if it is absolutely necessary, drug them.' He shrugged. '*Les affaires sont les affaires.*'

'Sure,' said Al. So far he followed perfectly.

'But the assassination—never! Above everything,' said Kurt proudly, 'I am a man of honour.'

'A man of honour,' agreed Al, 'but a lousy spy.'

'I deny it,' said Kurt, furious. 'Always I am the tip-top. Everything I do it is the professional. Even to mix the drinks. Did not King Hannibal himself compliment me on my cocktails?'

'He has no palate, that one,' said Señor Centime. 'It is well known. Also,' he put in, 'an efficient spy should rise above personal considerations.'

'This I do all the time,' said Kurt self-sacrificingly. 'Was I not willing to blow up Mr Stung, even though the cheque he gave me was not yet cleared.'

'Blackmail?' asked Al, interested.

'*Du tout*,' said Kurt. 'Much more difficult. A gold mine.'

'Ah,' said Señor Centime enviously.

'A triumph of technique,' said Kurt, beginning to swank. 'I introduce myself to the British Envoy. I talk to him for ten minutes only, and already I sell him a gold mine.'

'Must be a record,' said Al.

'In its class, perhaps,' said Kurt. 'Only it must be admitted that in 1902 Hayseed Herb sold the Brooklyn Bridge to a rich ranger in seven minutes flat.'

'Gosh,' said Al, impressed.

'It is spoilt only,' said Kurt, 'that he was paid in horses.'

'Bungler,' said Al, and lost all interest in Hayseed.

'We're wasting time,' he said briskly. 'Let's get together and think up some way of stopping the mission getting to England.'

They pondered.

'I have an idea,' said Kurt eagerly.

They waved him away.

CHAPTER

19

THEY were proud of their station at Rumba-Rumba. At first sight it looked rather like the offices of the *Daily Express* in Fleet Street—all glass, glitter, and, of course, stream-lines.

With the glistening electric trains, purring in and out, punctual to the second, the spectacle was impressive. At least it would be in another seven years, when the Insomnian Four-Year Plan, allowing for time-lag, could be expected to reach fruition.

In the meantime passengers had to make do with usual high, wooden, overcrowded suburban steam-trains, and an occasional haughty trans-continental express. Since the war these had been running a little late.

'But do not despair,' the sleepy stationmaster told Quill. 'It will come, you may be certain of that. Wait only a few hours.'

'*Bon*,' said Sasha Podushkin. He made for a luggage trolley, curled himself up, and slept like a child.

The stationmaster looked at him enviously. 'He has ability that one. Alas! that my duties do not permit to do the same.'

'Why not?' asked Quill, looking at the empty platform.

'*Tiens*,' said the stationmaster. 'It is an idea that. You will excuse me.' He stumbled off towards his office.

In the doorway he paused.

'You promise to wake me when the train comes?' he pleaded touchingly.

*   *   *   *   *

There was a thundering, a clanging, and the sound of grinding brakes. The station shook in every limb. Puffing shamefacedly, the Trans-Mittel-Europa Rapide crept into the station at Rumba-Rumba exactly twenty hours late.

'*Pas mal*,' said the engine-driver, elated. '*Bon jour, mon ami*,' he called to the revived stationmaster.

'*Bon jour*,' said the stationmaster. 'And your so charming *petite amie?*' he enquired. 'She is with you on the train as always.'

The engine-driver frowned. 'She was unfaithful *en route*,' he said shortly. 'I put her down at Bucharest. And how,' he enquired, 'is Madame your wife?'

The stationmaster sighed. 'Evacuated.'

'Ah,' said the engine-driver, brightening. '*C'est à peu près la même chose!*'

That concluded the exchange of courtesies.

There is a school of thought which insists that there is something romantic about a trans-continental rapide—any rapide in any continent. Your true believer has only to glimpse a window under the heading of the names of two towns sufficiently far apart, to imagine immediately captains of industry drinking champagne with glamorous spies, while an octi-lingual *wagon-lit* attendant simultaneously prepares their beds and ransacks their luggage. 'To think,' it says, pointing rapturously to a sooty third-class carriage, 'that only three days ago these wheels rolled in Istanbul and here they are pulling up for me in La Bazouche!'

The authors of this book do not for one moment subscribe to this school. One look at the Man from Cook's and they are reminded instantly of Mommas in corridors, a permanent thirst, and frontiers —invariably reached just as they drop off to sleep. There is, you will tell us, the Wagon-Restaurant. Agreed. The French, a sensible race, have shown just what they think of this by perpetually bringing with them their own cold chicken, and in this, as in so much else, we find ourselves in complete agreement with our gallant Ally.

'*En voiture*,' shouted the conductor.

Unflagged, unsung, un-red-carpeted, and dragging with them an unwilling Envoy, the British Mission boarded the train.

'To think,' said Sasha, clinging fiercely to the footboard, 'that all we have to do is to sit quite still in this train and we would reach Vienna! Instead, you make us change three times and we finish up in London.' He spat.

'You have a brother in London,' said Quill, trying to cheer him up.

'Ah,' said Sasha, 'but he does not make bortsh like my Uncle Bounya.'

Quill pushed him in.

The conductor, a careerist, waved a black-out lantern. The stationmaster whistled. The engine-driver pulled a handle and clucked at the engine. Reluctantly the engine pulled itself together. A final combined effort and they were off.

'Safe at last,' said Mr Stung, and sank into a corner of the carriage.

* * * * *

Down the corridor came a very old attendant wearing a very new apron. He was as bearded as a boyard.

'Breakfast,' he said in a genial quaver. 'Very good.'

He did not say it very loudly, but Sasha Podushkin still woke up.

'*Bon*,' he said. 'Bring it.'

'It is in the Wagon-Restaurant,' said the attendant.

'I reserve you three places—yes?' With pride he produced a large book of counterfoils and scribbled. '*Voila*,' he said, 'the places are now reserved.'

'Is it necessary?' asked Quill doubtfully.

'*Du tout*,' admitted the attendant. 'But it is the methodics.'

'Nothing like method,' said Mr Stung with deep approval. 'Stick to it,' he said encouragingly, forgetting the long white beard, 'and you will go far in your profession.'

'It is not a career that interests me,' observed the attendant unexpectedly. 'I have other ambitions. But come,' he said, 'the coffee waits.'

'Coffee,' said Sasha dubiously.

'Have no fear,' said the attendant. 'I make it myself. There is no one in the world,' he boasted, 'makes better coffee than I.'

He turned and ambled away, rheumatism in every rattle.

Quill looked after him puzzled.

'Come,' said Mr Stung jovially. 'Breakfast. You know,' he confided, 'I'm peckish—'pon my soul I am.'

They went out into the corridor.

One of these days somebody will get on a train and find, to his astonishment, that his carriage is right next door to the wagon-restaurant. So far we have not yet met anyone who has claimed this distinction. To the ordinary passenger the trek to nourishment is made up of a fine collection of bruises, a recurring vista of disappointment and an ecstasy of '*Pardons!*' As he struggles to the end of each corridor and stands swaying in the concertina-like connecting aperture, there rises the resurging hope that Mecca, appetizingly sprayed with the smell of vegetable soup, awaits him on the other side. No amount of experience can quell this hope. And the sight of yet another long corridor, all cluttered up ahead, disappoints him just as shatteringly as though he had not already traversed seven others exactly like it. But half-way past the flattened-out Mommas, not one of whom seems to want to stay in the seat she has taken so much trouble to reserve three weeks in advance, hope rises afresh. This time, of course . . .

Eventually he arrives. He is led firmly past the pretty girl sitting alone at a table and plonked down opposite a voluble, child-accompanied, and not-yet-eating Momma.

Three cluttered corridors, and the British Mission lost Sasha. Five corridors later they found this out. Quill sighed and made his way back through a trail of '*Pardons!*' noticeably less ecstatic. To make it worse he had to peer into every compartment in case Sasha had elected to rest in it.

He found him eventually lolling in the conductor's seat in the *wagon-lit*.

'I get tired,' he explained simply.

'Come,' said Quill and jerked him to his feet.

They went.

A very weary conductor sank gratefully into the empty seat.

Back through the cluttered corridors, into the swaying concertinas, past the flattened-out Mommas, went our heroes, leaving behind them a trial of muttered: '*Ah! ça c'est trops!*'

'Young man,' said a truculent Momma, refusing to flatten. 'Do me the favour of making up your mind in which part of the train you wish to travel.'

Sasha looked at her.

The Momma flattened.

* * * * *

In the dining-car the aged attendant came forward with a flourish.

'You have been very long,' he said reprovingly. 'This way.'

He waved the British Mission forward.

Save for an elderly coffee-sipper with a fierce expression the dining-car was empty. Like the Reich to a Minority, the attendant made for him. Once there his resolution faltered.

'*Pardon, M'sieur,*' he said.

The coffee-sipper looked at him. The attendant wilted.

'Pardon,' he repeated. 'This place is reserved.'

The coffee-sipper glared.

'It is true,' babbled the attendant. 'See! He held up the book of counterfoils so recently annotated. 'Numbers twenty-seven, eight, and nine—that is this table,' he pointed out incontrovertibly.

'I am sitting in number thirty,' said the coffee-sipper, a diehard.

The attendant shrugged and went back to the British Mission.

'Impossible to argue with him,' he confided to Quill. 'He has been here since dinner and still he drinks black coffee. However, I will try again.' He braced himself.

'Don't bother,' said Quill. We can sit somewhere else.'

'But no,' said the attendant outraged. 'You have reserved the seats and you are entitled to sit in them.'

He strode over again.

'M'sieur,' he said. 'Once again I implore you to leave the carriage.'

The coffee-sipper lifted the coffee-pot. 'Empty,' he observed. 'Bring some more.'

The aged attendant brooded. Inspiration came.

'Impossible,' he said in triumph. 'The Dinner Service is finished. It is now time for the Breakfast to begin.'

'*Bon*,' said the coffee-sipper instantly. 'Then I will have breakfast. Bring me,' he reflected, 'some coffee.'

The attendant's beard wriggled with emotion. 'If you will go to your carriage,' he pleaded, 'I will bring you some coffee myself to your seat—*Bien chaud*,' he promised.

'My compartment,' said the coffee-sipper, 'is seven carriages away. How, then, keep it hot?'

The aged attendant was baffled.

'Gentlemen,' the coffee-sipper addressed himself to the British Mission, 'I will be honoured if you will take breakfast with me—at your table.'

'*Enchantay*,' said Mr Stung with charm.

'Waiter,' ordered the coffee-sipper. 'Bring,' he pondered, 'four coffees.'

'And some toast,' said Sasha.

'And some marmalade,' said Mr Stung.

The aged attendant crept away, a beaten man.

'Permit me to present myself,' said the coffee-sipper. 'General Jodpur of the Fifth Insomnian Foot—at your service.' He clicked his heels under the table. 'Retired,' he added regretfully.

'You were wise to resign,' said Sasha approvingly. 'All the marching—it is no life for an old man. Far better to travel by train.'

General Jodpur glared.

'And even here,' said Sasha, gazing at him with admiration, 'you have a technique for saving energy. Each time one wishes to eat on a train there lies ahead an arduous journey through flattening *Mamushkas*. How much more sensible to stay in the dining-car throughout.' He bowed.

'Not at all, sir,' barked General Jodpur. 'In my compartment there is an old lady who knows how to win the war. She does not get out until Timsk,' he added, explaining all.

The aged attendant came back with coffee.

'Delicious,' he said, putting it on the table. 'I have made it myself.'

Mr Stung jerked up. He was remembering all the coffee he had drunk in Insomnia.

'Have no fear,' said the attendant unexpectedly. 'It is not drugged.'

He wandered away. Quill looked after him. Had the story travelled so far?

Clearly it had. General Jodpur had exploded into a series of cackles.

'Heard the story about the British Envoy?' he asked. 'Dashed funny.'

Mr Stung signified faintly that he had.

'They drugged him,' said General Jodpur with relish.

'Drugged him all over the place,' he gloated.

There was an awful silence.

'And quite right too,' went on General Jodpur, oblivious. 'The impertinence of these English. Trying to corner our Gardenium—whatever it is. Nothing personal, sir,' he assured Mr Stung.

Mr Stung bowed.

'Amazing race the British,' the General brooded. 'At war three months and haven't decided yet whether they're fighting Germany or Russia.'

Quill grinned.

'How do you expect us to be on your side,' demanded the General, 'if you won't tell us which it is?'

'A neutral,' said Mr Stung severely, 'has no right to take sides. He should confine himself to selling to the belligerents.'

'That means us,' explained Quill.

The General leant forward. 'Confidentially, sir,' he announced, 'I can tell you that the British Mission is wasting its time.'

'Agreed,' said Quill.

'I have it on the highest authority,' said the General, 'that Bauldstok would never permit such a treaty to be signed. So the Mission might as well go home.'

'They've gone,' said Quill.

'Excellent,' said the General. 'Good riddance. Nothing personal, you understand,' he said and passed his cigar case to Mr Stung.

'Only,' said Quill, enjoying his triumph, 'they've taken with them an envoy with full plenipotentiary powers.'

Mr Stung looked at him reproachfully. 'Careless talk may give away vital secrets,' his eyebrows said.

Quill blushed.

'They'll never get through,' said General Jodpur undismayed. 'Our Gestapo,' he boasted.

'You think so,' said Sasha Podushkin brightening.

'Certain of it,' said General Jodpur. 'Even at this moment,' he gloated, 'as they sit snug and well-fed in some train, imagining themselves on the way to accomplish their mission, the trap is being prepared.'

'We seem to have stopped,' said Quill absently.

'Take no notice,' said General Jodpur. 'Ever since I got on this train yesterday morning it's been stopping. Disgraceful!'

'Why don't you go by aeroplane?' asked Sasha.

'Don't believe in aeroplanes,' snorted the General. 'Except, of course,' he added broadmindedly, 'for bombing military objectives.'

There was a convulsive jerk. The General's coffee spurted in every direction.

'We've started again,' said Quill.

The General mopped himself up. 'What was I talking about?' he asked.

'The British Mission,' said Quill.

'Ah, yes,' said the General. 'You know,' he confided, 'if it were not for the fact that I can't stand the English, I'd feel quite sorry for that Mission. So they imagine they can get our envoy out of the country, the poor fools.'

'I believe they do,' said Quill.

'They'll be stopped,' said the General. 'Stopped good and proper. Only wish,' he said wistfully, 'that I could be there to see their faces when it happens.'

Mr Stung bowed.

Quill had had enough of this. He stubbed out his cigarette, walked to the other end of the carriage, and looked out of the window. The train was nosing its way among the bare hills.

The General was still talking about what was going to happen to the British Mission. Mr Stung was still bowing.

To hell with them both, thought Quill. He would go back to his compartment and try to get some sleep.

He opened the blacked-out door of the dining-car.

He nearly stepped out into nothing.

*   *   *   *   *

Quill's first thought was that someone had been careless and left the rest of the train behind.

His next reflection was not nearly so comforting. Even in wartime a trans-continental train did not attempt to economize coal by lightheartedly shedding its carriages as it went along.

The General was right. Something was happening to the British Mission.

He went back to the table. General Jodpur was still talking.

'And, finally,' he was saying, 'let me point out that it is not beyond the ability of our Gestapo to uncouple the coach in which the British Mission is travelling.'

'They've done it,' said Quill.

The General sprang to his feet. A horrible doubt was beginning to dawn.

'Who are you?' he demanded.
'The British Mission,' said Quill.

*   *   *   *   *

The British Mission had been stopped. Stopped good and proper. And what is more their faces were well worth looking at. But General Jodpur was far too worried to make the most of his opportunity.

'I wonder,' he said in some trepidation, 'where they're taking us.'

'You should know,' said Quill savagely. 'It's your Gestapo.'

Not unreasonably he was annoyed. He had drunk too much bad coffee, he was being made to look a fool in front of a foreigner, and, worst of all, he loathed the smirk on Sasha Podushkin's face. The British Mission was about to get it in the neck and so would he, thought Quill, if they ever got out of it.

And what would they have to say about this in Downing Street? . . .

*   *   *   *   *

'At sea,' said the Prime Minister, addressing a crowded house, 'we continue to pursue the U-boats with gusto.'

From the Front Bench the First Lord of the Admiralty scowled. It was the one description he himself had not yet used. As a matter of fact he had been saving it up for next week's broadcast.

'On land,' continued the Prime Minister, oblivious to this near-breach in the Cabinet, 'leeway and even progress has been maintained. Our armaments are massing up—a formidable arsenal that no neutral need fear. Even now a further consignment of aeroplanes lies in readiness in the harbours of that friendly Power, America, awaiting only the necessary formalities for its dispatch.'

'Cash,' muttered the Chancellor of the Exchequer sadly.

'And now,' said the Prime Minister, 'I have some further encouraging news. The British Mission in Insomnia has to-day left for England.' He beamed. 'But this is not all,' he continued lusciously. 'They bring with them an envoy with full powers to sign the treaty delivering to our control eighty per cent of the world supply of that invaluable mineral, Gardenium.'

'What is Gardenium?' asked the member for the Isle of Wight.

But the Prime Minister could cope with this sort of thing in his sleep.

'It would not be in the public interest,' he said smoothly, 'to divulge at this juncture the exact properties of Gardenium. But the honourable member may rest assured on one point. When the Envoy reaches these shores there will be no dilly-dallying.'

'What arrangements,' asked the Member for the Isle of Wight, 'have been taken to safeguard the Envoy?'

The Prime Minister stuck a benevolent thumb in the lapel of his coat.

'The house can take it from me,' he said, 'that throughout his journey, the Envoy from Insomnia is being well looked after.'

* * * * *

The well-looked-after Envoy from Insomnia poured himself out the last of the coffee, and sipped it complacently.

'My good General,' he was saying, 'why are you so upset? Wherever they take us it cannot be worse than London.'

'I wasn't going to London,' snapped General Jodpur. He pressed the bell violently.

Moving with extraordinary speed the aged attendant came running up.

'More coffee?' he asked. '*Bon*. I bring.'

'Stop,' bawled the General. 'Come back. Do you know that they've uncoupled this car?'

'Already?' said the attendant. He seemed pleased.

'My luggage is in the other part of the train,' said Mr Stung sadly.

'Where are you taking me?' barked the General. 'Stop immediately. Take me back.'

The attendant made a gesture of despair.

'I demand,' said the General, 'that you take me back and couple me to the rest of the train.'

'But did I not beg you to leave the dining-car?' said the attendant. 'Did I not plead with you all the time. You would not listen. And now,' he shrugged, 'it is too late. Even I can do nothing.'

Quill looked at him.

'Be patient,' said the attendant. 'Resign yourselves. And to pass the time we will play some cards.' He pulled out a pack. 'Poker?' he suggested hopefully.

Quill looked at the old man again. He peered. He stretched out a hand and grasped him by the beard.

'I say,' said Mr Stung horrified.

The beard came away. Once again Quill looked at half the face of Kurt Carruthers.

'I ought to have guessed it,' he said exasperated.

'Do not blame yourself too much,' said Kurt soothingly. 'As an actor I have the talent natural. Had I gone on the stage . . .'

'Oh, shut up,' said Quill, 'and tell us where we're going.'

'This I cannot tell,' said Kurt. 'But I have some good news for you. I am going with you to organize your comfort. As an organizer . . .'

'I know,' said Quill. 'You have the talent natural.'
Hooting excitedly the train dived into a tunnel.
'What is going to happen to us?' mused General Jodpur.
'What is happening to my luggage?' mourned Mr Stung.

CHAPTER

20

'HEIL,' said the Gauleiter.

'Heil, sonny,' said Al Schenk good-naturedly. He climbed out of his car. 'Take me to the Gauleiter.'

The young man looked reproachful. 'I am the Gauleiter,' he said.

'Well, well,' said Al. He examined the five-foot-ten of spit, polish, and ramrodry clicking its heels in front of him. It must have been eighteen years old if a day.

This was the ideal spot for his purpose, thought Al, glancing approvingly at a tangle of storm-troopers, struggling with the mechanism of an ancient drawbridge that led to a formidable castle. The castle was isolated, the walls were high, the drawbridge looked as though it needed a regiment to handle it, and even Quill would never persuade Sasha Podushkin to swim the moat.

Here the British Mission could be held in security, and if possible comfort, until such time as they had repaired the bridge leading from Germany to Insomnia, which Franzi Papen had carelessly ordered to be blown up at almost the exact time his train reached it. Of course he had missed the train.

'*Heil*, Hitler,' said the Gauleiter, seeking around for a conversational opening.

'Just as you say,' agreed Al. 'Now, sonny, I've only got five minutes and . . .'

'Time,' said the Gauleiter, 'is on our side. Dr Goebbels—Nuremberg—1939.'

'Quite,' said Al. 'But the British Mission isn't.'

'Perfidious Albion,' said the Gauleiter. 'Hitler—Munich—— After the explosion,' he explained.

Al nodded. 'Rooms prepared?'

The Gauleiter saluted. 'The cells await. Each cell,' he boasted, 'has a plank, straw, and there is room for one man if he does not stand up.'

'This won't do,' said Al sharply.

The Gauleiter looked pained. 'They have them at Dachau!'

'Now get this clear,' said Al. 'I want you to hold this Mission at your headquarters until I tell you to let them go. But apart from that I want them housed in comfort and treated as guests.'

'But they're British,' said the Gauleiter puzzled.

'Sure,' said Al. 'But they're friends of mine—one of them.' Now that the Mission was no longer a menace he was glad Quill had escaped that bomb, and he wasn't going to have him worried.

'See that they have plenty to read,' he ordered. '*Esquire*,' he suggested.

'*Mein Kampf*,' said the Gauleiter. 'Only,' he paled at the thought, 'if I lend them my signed copy what will they do with it?'

'Guess?' said Al.

'The British,' said the Gauleiter, 'are aggressive, grasping, and cowardly. Ribbentrop—very often. But have no fear,' he promised. 'The Mission need expect no mercy from me. It is a pity only,' he mused, 'that my rubber truncheon is broken.'

'Broken?' said Al.

'I was practising on a sack,' said the Gauleiter. '*Ersatz*,' he explained.

'Now look here,' said Al. 'You Insomnian Nazis are very enthusiastic, very Reich-minded, and,' he looked at the fledgling Foerster, 'very young. And it isn't every day a British Mission falls into your hands for,' he sought the happy expression, 'practice.'

The Gauleiter nodded rapturously.

'I understand perfectly,' said Al. 'I sympathize. But do me a favour, sonny. Don't beat up the British Mission.'

The Gauleiter looked dashed. But he was young and hope dawned.

'And should they attempt to escape?'

'Stop them,' said Al. 'Stop them firmly.'

The Gauleiter clicked his heels.

'But gently,' said Al. 'Remember Insomnia is fighting for its neutrality.'

'A neutral,' said the Gauleiter with conviction, 'who is not on the side of the Reich is against it. *The Nazi News*,' he sighed. 'Only this morning.'

From his pocket he pulled out the Insomnian edition.

Al waved it aside.

'What arrangements have you made for collecting the British Mission at the station?'

'Ah,' said the Gauleiter, 'I am glad you have asked me that. I am taking two detachments of our crack Shwartze Korps. You would like to inspect them?' he asked eagerly.

Al saw no way out.

The Gauleiter shouted an order in a shrill pipe.

The crack Shwartze Korps abandoned the drawbridge to its predicament and fell-in smartly in parade order. Erect, motionless, every button a mirror, they stood awaiting further commands.

Poor little beggars, thought Al. Hardly one of them over fifteen, trained to snap into orders from their cradle. Trained not to reason. And not a grimy face among them. Gosh!—what lousy business men they would make.

'Pretty,' he said, feeling something was expected of him.

But the Gauleiter was scowling. He shouted something in a childish guttural. Nothing happened. He shouted it again.

An uncouth little boy emerged from under the drawbridge. His cap had come adrift, his bootlaces had never been done up, and his tarnished buttons hung perilously by the few remaining threads. He looked guiltily at the Gauleiter.

'Can't find my bugle,' he mumbled.

The Gauleiter blushed for him. 'It is Hansel,' he explained. 'He is a disgrace to our Korps. But what can we do?' He sighed. 'His mother does our laundry for nothing.'

'Ah,' said Al. 'Mind if I have a word with him?' He led the dubious Hansel to one side.

'Listen, sonny,' he said, 'like to make some money?'

'I got plenty,' said Hansel unexpectedly, 'but I can always use more.'

'Just how I feel,' said Al.

Two kindred spirits arrived at an understanding.

'What are you doing with this outfit, anyway?' asked Al.

'It's my ma,' said Hansel. He sighed. 'She doesn't want me around.'

Al looked at the uncouth little boy. 'Maybe she knows something. But it's tough on you.' He pondered. 'Say, how would you like to be batman to the British Mission?'

Hansel looked wary. 'What would I have to do?'

'Hang around,' said Al. 'Look after them. Run their errands. And if they give you any letters to post re-address them to me.'

'What's it worth?'

'One hundred peccoes,' said Al, 'and what you pick up in tips.'

Hansel pondered. 'Will it get me off parade?'

'I'll arrange that too,' promised Al.

'Oke,' said Hansel.

'And listen, sonny,' said Al. 'Whenever they make an attempt to escape 'phone me up.'

'Charges reversed?' asked Hansel.

'Sure,' said Al.

'Oke,' said Hansel and shuffled away.

The Gauleiter intercepted him.

'Here,' he said, 'is your bugle. Try not to play it too loud.'

'Oke,' said Hansel and shuffled on.

Al Schenk climbed into the driving-seat of his car.

'Well, sonny,' he said. 'So long.'

As the car started off the Gauleiter piped a command. The Korps leapt to attention and extended their right hands in the Nazi salute. They held them there while Al turned the car, straightened up, stepped on the accelerator, and drove straight into the moat.

They had forgotten to let down the drawbridge.

* * * * *

'Halt!' shouted the Gauleiter.

The two crack detachments of the Shwartze Korps came to a stop in the station yard. All except Hansel that is. He made straight for the chocolate machine.

The Gauleiter wiped his brow. It had been a heavy morning.

At 5.30 a.m. he had been awakened by the unearthly noise made by Hansel blowing the 'Reveille.' There had followed the usual strenuous routine recommended by the Reich to all healthy neutral Nazis. P.T. to the Hamburg radio. A swim in the moat. (They were using the swimming-pool to breed fish in.) No breakfast ('Learn to starve for the Reich.' Goering—Karlsbad—1937). Button polishing. Instruction in Spontaneous Cheering and Mass Enthusiasm. One cup of cocoa—unsweetened. And now there was the added predicament of fishing a voluble Al Schenk out of the moat. The Gauleiter had come well out of this. Save for a tiny splash his uniform was speckless and he had shown authority and resource in a crisis by picking a telephone number at random and terrifying the householder into sending his car for Al forthwith.

A puff of smoke appeared on the horizon. The Gauleiter piped an order. The two picked divisions of the Shwartze Korps lined themselves along the platform. They stood tense and alert. Almost they might have been expecting Unity Mitford.

The huge engine with the solitary dining-car attached to it came to a halt.

'*Alors*,' said the engine-driver. 'Uncouple me. I have to get back to the rest of the train,' he explained.

The door of the dining-car opened. Quill peered out. The Gauleiter sprang forward and pushed him back.

'*Verboten*,' he said severely, 'prisoners must not step out as though they were passengers. You have to come out struggling.'

Quill was in no mood for *chi-chi*. 'Have it your own way,' he said. He picked up the Gauleiter, swung him, and threw him into the arms of his crack Korps. Three of the crack Korps sat down very hard on the platform.

There was a hoarse laugh from the chocolate machine.

Pale with emotion the Gauleiter struggled to his feet to find himself facing the unbelieving monocle of Mr Stung.

'How d'you do,' said Mr Stung, preserving face.

The Gauleiter gawked, blinked, and pulled himself together.

'Surround them,' he ordered.

The crack Korps leapt to it.

There was a bellow of rage. Two of the troopers had boarded the dining-car and were emerging with a purple-faced, irate, and reluctant General Jodpur.

The Gauleiter climbed on to the platform of the car and held up his hand. The crack Shwartze Korps waited expectantly for one of his famous fighting speeches.

The Gauleiter cleared his throat.

'*Achtung*,' said Hansel, and blew his bugle.

This seemed to put the Gauleiter off. He faltered and changed his mind.

'The prisoners,' he said curtly, 'will accompany me to the car.'

'Ridiculous, sir,' said General Jodpur. 'Call your men off. I demand . . .'

'Silence, dog of an Englishman,' thundered the Gauleiter in childish treble, and spat at him. But his aim was bad.

With perfect calm, Mr Stung mopped himself up.

'Confound you, sir,' roared the General. 'I didn't come here to be insulted. I'm not an Englishman!'

'Why are you holding us?' said Quill. 'This is a neutral country.'

'I demand an apology,' said the General.

'I demand an explanation,' said Quill.

'I demand,' said the engine-driver, 'that you uncouple me.'

The Gauleiter looked stern. Somehow he must stop the rot or his authority would be permanently undermined.

'To the car,' he thundered.

'Which way?' asked Mr Stung courteously. They escorted him.

Mr Stung looked at the youthful crack trooper by his side. Might as well make friends, he reflected.

'Cigarette picture?' he offered with charm.

On the platform General Jodpur was preparing to sell his life dearly. It took a detachment to liquidate him.

Quill decided to go quietly. But the crack Korps was taking no chances. They frog-marched him.

The car was pretty full. Quill and the Gauleiter shared the dickey seat.

The Gauleiter shouted an order. The troops fell in. Hansel blew a dismal call on the protesting bugle.

'March,' ordered the Gauleiter.

Like a perfect machine, the column moved forward. Only Hansel was out of step.

The Gauleiter gave them a start. He enjoyed whizzing past his toiling troops.

'Now,' he told the driver.

The car moved slowly out of the yard.

'Hey,' said Quill, 'haven't you forgotten something?'

'What?' The Gauleiter was up in arms.

'The Envoy,' said Quill.

* * * * *

It took ten minutes to hoist Sasha into the dickey. ('Me—a Podushkin.') Slowly the car moved off.

The Gauleiter embarked on his speech.

'Gentlemen,' he said, 'you are now in the hands of the Insomnian Nazi Party. Our aims . . .'

'Useless to tell me,' said Sasha, waving him away. 'You cannot induce me to join. You march too much.'

'An army,' said the Gauleiter, 'marches on its stomach—Napoleon. The stomach will probably be empty—Goering.'

The car was running through a range of bare hills. Quill looked about him.

'Where are you taking us?' he asked.

'Castle Gelt,' said the Gauleiter. 'Our headquarters,' he explained with pride.

'I do not care for castles,' said Sasha, depressed. 'They have long corridors, and there is never a lift. Could we not,' he pleaded, 'go to a hotel?'

The Gauleiter looked at him contemptuously. 'Pampered democrat,' he said, and braced himself against the rebound of the insult.

Sasha bowed. 'Granted,' he said. 'I have never laid claim to being a Spartan.'

The Gauleiter gaped.

'To tolerate discomfort,' said Sasha, 'is one thing. A man may do this and not be a fool. But to set out to achieve it takes . . .' he pondered, '. . . a Nazi.'

The Gauleiter beamed. 'We are tough,' he said smugly.

'How far is headquarters?' asked Quill.

'This I am not allowed to say,' said the Gauleiter, 'but I may tell you that it has high walls and a moat.'

'Fine,' said Quill.

The Gauleiter looked at him doubtfully. ('The English have no sense of humour'—Ribbentrop.)

'Impossible to escape,' he said severely.

'Excellent,' said Sasha. 'What are the beds like?'

'You are to be treated as guests,' said the Gauleiter regretfully. 'The best of everything. You will even,' he pointed out, 'be allowed to walk in the grounds.'

'I doubt,' mused Sasha, 'if I will avail myself of this privilege.'

'You will enjoy the privilege for one hour every day,' said the Gauleiter firmly. 'I have my orders. "The good Nazi," ' he adumbrated, ' "obeys and asks no questions. Too often there is no answer. —Dr Schact—Berne, 1939." '

'How long are you going to hold us?' asked Quill.

The Gauleiter pondered. 'There is no reason why I should not tell you this,' he decided. 'You are to be held until His Excellency Herr von Papen signs the Treaty.'

'To travel hopefully is better than to arrive,' quoted Quill.

'Who said that?' asked the Gauleiter suspiciously.

'Stalin,' said Quill.

'Ah,' said the Gauleiter. He produced a note-book and scribbled. His smile as he turned to Quill was quite appealing.

'Do you know any more patriotic quotations?' he asked hungrily.

Quill grinned. 'Come to my cell to-night and I'll think up a few.'

The car had caught up with the crack Shwartze Korps. Hearing it, they abandoned their slouch and leapt nimbly into the goose-step.

The car slowed down for the Gauleiter to take the salute.

Hansel was still out of step.

'The finest body of men in Insomnia,' boasted the Gauleiter as they left the column behind. 'And this is only the beginning.'

'The beginning of what?' asked Sasha, interested.

'The return to the Reich,' said the Gauleiter richly. 'Our numbers increase daily and soon also we will have money.'

'Doesn't the Reich subsidize you?' asked Quill.

'This they have promised to do,' said the Gauleiter. 'But somehow it has not yet come.' He looked wistful.

'Tough,' said Quill.

'But we manage,' said the Gauleiter, warming to sympathy. 'Already we are operating a system to obtain credit by threat.'

'And does it work?' asked Quill.

'Not always,' admitted the Gauleiter. 'But it will go better when we get our machine-gun from the Fuehrer.'

'Can he spare it?' asked Quill.

'To further the return of Insomnia to the Reich,' said the Gauleiter, 'there is no sacrifice the Fuehrer will not make. He might even,' he said ambitiously, 'spare us a tank.'

'Why don't you pal up with Great Britain?' suggested Quill. 'They might spare you a warship.'

The Gauleiter looked puzzled.

'Take it easy, old man,' said Quill. 'It's a joke.'

'You should not make a joke in a serious discussion,' said the Gauleiter reprovingly. ' "Wit," ' he quoted, ' "is the beginning of decadence"—Goebbels.'

'It is only the decadent that know how to live well,' said Sasha. 'Always I have regretted that I was not alive in the Roman Empire —when it was already declining.'

The car left the road and began a laborious ascent up a donkey track.

The Gauleiter abandoned polite conversation and embarked on the steep history of the Nazi Movement in Insomnia.

The car lurched over a rut. The Gauleiter nearly got bogged down by that part of the story which dealt with the ruthless oppression of the German minority by the good-natured Insomnians.

The car turned and twisted among the brambles. The Gauleiter plucked the thorns of neutrality, prosperity, and the popularity of King Hannibal from the swaggering Nazi path.

The car described a parabola over a boulder.

The Gauleiter described the glorious header of the first Nazi plunge into an Insomnian rally. The principal speaker should have been Herr von Papen.

'But he didn't arrive,' said Quill.

A tyre burst.

The Gauleiter went flat.

'No,' he admitted.

Throughout the repairs the Nazi Movement surmounted one predicament after another, and it was not long before the car was on its way again and the party had received the first consignment of *ersatz* shirts. (They were brown as long as you did not wash them.) And with the arrival of one thousand signed copies of *Mein Kampf* (Cheap Edition) the party had turned the corner and was climbing full speed ahead. So was the car. The radiator began to bubble. The Gauleiter began to babble. Great names squirted from his conversation like ink from an octopus. The engine sizzled. The Gauleiter remembered his glorious visit (together with three hundred and forty-seven other promising Gauleiters) to Berchtesgarten. They had had tea—with sugar—in the summer-house, and the Fuehrer himself had peeped down at them from his study window for fully a minute. How the Gauleiters had cheered! Those were the days, Quill was given to understand.

Outside the frowning castle the car jerked to a stop. So, regretfully, did the Gauleiter.

'I will tell you the rest some other time,' he promised the sleeping Sasha. He climbed down. 'The party,' he ordered, 'will please to emerge.'

The party obliged. Quill looked round him. It was isolated all right.

'A castle, by gad,' said Mr Stung, cheering up. 'Nice little place to spend a week-end. Wonder who owns it?'

Still purple and badly bruised into the bargain, General Jodpur gazed with disapproval at the rather streaky group of brown-shirted boys pathetically struggling to get Al Shenk's abandoned car out of the moat, while a further group, almost too tired to watch them, sat on the bank.

'No morale,' he snorted.

'I deny it,' said the Gauleiter hotly. 'Our discipline is perfect.' He strode to the drawbridge and tugged a bell.

Nothing happened.

Furious, he tugged again.

An old man in a skull cap emerged from the castle, hobbled over to the portcullis, and got busy with a winch. The drawbridge, which had defied the efforts of the brown shirts, creaked into place.

'It is Herr Kaleb Krust, your host,' explained the Gauleiter as the party crossed. 'A very great patriot,' he said reverently.

'Why,' demanded the great patriot in tones of fury, 'do you ring the bell twice? It wears out the ropes unnecessarily,' he explained to Mr Stung.

Mr Stung adjusted his monocle.

'Sensible,' said Herr Krust, eyeing it approvingly. 'If you are short-sighted in one eye only, spectacles are a waste.'

A small boy who had been gazing at Mr Stung with some awe, made up his mind, leapt to his feet, clambered up the bank, and pelted over.

'Excellency,' he panted. 'Your autograph.' Appealingly he held out his album.

'Go away,' said the Gauleiter crossly. 'This is not Herr von Papen.'

But the flattered Mr Stung was already writing.

CHAPTER

21

'HAVE some wine,' suggested Herr Krust expansively. 'Mind you, it's against my principles to offer it, but,' he beamed, 'shall we call it a special occasion?'

'The blockade?' enquired Quill sympathetically.

'Not at all,' said Herr Krust. 'I'm a miser.'

Mr Stung's eyeglass fell with a clatter on the table.

'And anyway,' said the miser defensively, 'it's *vin du pays*.'

The British mission, plus the cooling-off General Jodpur, were seated at a long stone table in a long stone hall. It was not entirely medieval and not at all modern, but somehow managed to combine the bareness of both. The room was lit by candlelight, great branched candlesticks sprouted from the table like fountains from Versailles, and, though not all of them were lit, the shapes of the relaxed British mission threw strange shadows on the stone walls.

The floor was carpeted with rushes, the table laden with thick peasant ware, and the great fireplace, with its immense wooden logs, had not yet been lit. A pair of bellows, deflated of expectation, lay defeated beside it.

'If you move closer,' said Herr Krust to Sasha Podushkin, 'we should not need so many candles.' He stooped over and blew one out.

'Why do you not install electricity?' asked General Jodpur. 'More convenient,' he explained.

'I'd do it like a shot,' said Herr Krust. 'Only,' he shrugged, 'my Press agent won't let me.'

'Your Press agent!' said Mr Stung.

'An excellent man,' said Herr Krust. 'Worth every penny I pay him.'

Quill grinned. If it hadn't been for the thought of what they must be saying about him in Downing Street, he would have been enjoying himself. Their wing was quite comfortable. The food might easily have been worse. And the local characters provided all the richness he could well digest. In the glow induced by the *vin du pays* even the Gauleiter seemed a decent lad who, given the advantages of an L.C.C. upbringing, might easily have been a Boy Scout. Not since his first breathless encounter with the Stroganoff Ballet had he been plunged into such a silly symphony of a world. It seemed almost a pity that from now on all his efforts must be concentrated on escaping from it.

It had been a pleasant day, punctured only by Mr Stung lamenting for his luggage. The lamentations had reached a climax with Herr Krust's invitation to dinner. 'How,' demanded Mr Stung of the inattentive Sasha, 'can I come down to dinner in a strange castle wearing only plus fours when it isn't even Sunday evening? What will the servants think?'

But there was only one servant, cunningly disguised as an old retainer, and if he was shocked he did not show it.

Even General Jodpur seemed to have simmered down under the soft fingers of the candlelight. Though still indignant at being held, he had stopped clamouring to be let out. And Sasha Podushkin seemed quite happy in any place as long as it was not on the way to London.

What was wrong with London, anyway, thought Quill, that this languid cosmopolitan should show such an aversion to sleeping in it?

The aged retainer bent over Herr Krust and said something in a low voice.

'Show him in,' said Herr Krust.

A storm-trooper strode smartly over the floor, clicked his heels, saluted, and held out an envelope.

'Stop clicking your heels,' said Krust crossly. He ripped open the envelope.

'Ah,' he said. 'Good news. Professor Guggenheim, my new financial adviser, will be here to-night. I am told,' he added expectantly, 'that the professor claims to be the shrewdest judge of stock markets in the world.'

Quill blinked.

'You may go,' Herr Krust told the storm-trooper, who was still standing to attention.

The storm-trooper clicked his heels and saluted.

'Stop clicking your heels,' said Herr Krust irritably. 'You're wearing out the carpet.'

'But,' said Sasha logically, 'how does one wear out a carpet which does not exist?'

'Ah,' said Herr Krust with satisfaction. 'One of my best ideas. A carpet of straw. Just as warm and much cheaper. And when it gets dirty the horse eats it.'

'Horse,' said Mr Stung, brightening.

Herr Krust nodded. 'I bought one specially.'

'There is something here that I do not understand,' said Sasha Podushkin, pondering deeply. 'To buy a horse specially—this is not the operation of a born miser.'

'I'm not a born miser,' said Herr Krust. 'I'm self-made.' He looked round with all the defiance of the parvenu. 'I adopted it as a profession.'

'*Tiens*,' said Sasha, impressed. 'But it is an idea that.'

'Oh, it just came to me,' said Herr Krust modestly. 'You see,' he explained, 'on my mother's side my family is French.'

'Ah,' said Sasha, well satisfied. But Mr Stung was still trying to work it out.

Herr Krust leant back in his oak chair. His voice took on all the contentment of a narrator launching into his favourite story.

'When I was eighteen,' said Herr Krust, 'my parents became much concerned about my future. Every month they called a *conseille de famille*. There was Tante Matilde who wished that I should enter a monastery, and there was her husband who dwelt on the certain profit of running a brothel. There was my Cousin Henri who wanted me in his business, and Uncle Guillaume who wouldn't have me at any price. There were my parents who wanted me to be an engineer, a lawyer or even a psycho-analyst. And presiding over them all was Grandmère—strong, implacable, and though she had not as yet any ideas of her own, disagreeing with everybody else's.'

'My grandmother was like that in Ekatarinaslav,' said Sasha. 'Always she disagreed about having children. But the poor one—it availed her nothing. For here I am,' he said.

Mr Stung blushed.

'So,' resumed Herr Krust, 'every month the *conseille* met and every month they could come to no decision. And every month I sat there while my Uncle Ko-ko made his jokes. They were terrible.' He shuddered at his recollection. 'Never shall I forget his favourite story. It went like this . . .'

'No,' said Sasha Podushkin firmly. 'We too have had our uncles.'

'Then you will understand,' said Herr Krust, 'how it came about that I could endure it no longer. So, one day when they were shaking their heads, I arrived and told them that they need agitate themselves no more. I had decided on my profession. I would be a miser.'

He looked up to make certain that he was holding his audience. He was.

'Never,' he said lusciously, 'has there been such a brou-ha-ha in the family since Tante Louisa came back with her coachman. "Ungodly," said Tante Matilde. "Impossible," said Cousin Henri. "Fantastic," said Uncle Guillaume. "It is a bad joke this," said my Uncle Ko-ko crossly. For once the family were united. Maman wept and Papa looked so cross that to this day I am certain that the only reason he did not threaten to stop my allowance was that he had omitted to make me one.

'But all this time Grandmère sat very still at the head of the table. And then suddenly she lifted her hand and everyone else stopped.

' "The boy is right," she said. "It is a prudent profession this. Misers," she pointed out, "always have money—even the poorest of them."

'And so,' said Herr Krust, 'it was arranged, and I began to study for my new profession. To-day,' he paused, 'I am the most famous miser in the whole of Insomnia. You should see my Press cuttings,' he boasted.

He leant back, selected a cigar, looked at it longingly and lit a cigarette.

From outside came the muffled sound of shouted orders. A bugle wailed dismally. The creaking of the drawbridge could be heard even through the mullioned windows.

'Ah,' said Herr Krust, 'that will be my new financial adviser. I hope,' he looked worried, 'he's had dinner.'

The doors of the dining-hall swung open to reveal a corridor lined on both sides with the crack Shwartze Korps standing at the salute.

Through the avenue of honour, heiling with considerable vigour, came the financial adviser.

He was Kurt Carruthers. This time he did not even bother to wear a beard.

*   *   *   *   *

'You!' said Quill.

'You, sir!' said General Jodpur.

'My luggage?' said Mr Stung.

Kurt beamed. 'Have no fear,' he said. 'I have fulfilled my promise. Even now it awaits you in the hall.'

'Excuse me,' said Mr Stung. He dashed out.

'Ah,' said Herr Krust. 'I see that you have met Professor Guggenheim.'

'Often,' said Quill.

General Jodpur was gradually getting back to his normal shade—a cherry-diffused purple. But before he reached boiling-point Professor Guggenheim turned, put a finger to his lips, and unleashed an avalanche of winks.

Confused, the General decided to postpone his explosion.

There was a sound of muffled orders. Once again the doors of the dining-hall were flung open, to reveal the corridor lined with the crack Shwartze Korps at the salute. Through the avenue of honour came a magnificent figure.

It was Mr Stung, in evening dress.

*　*　*　*　*

The wing, allotted after some deep pondering to the British mission, was isolated from the rest of the castle and overlooking a courtyard. There were three rooms, two small and one large, each furnished as comfortably as was consistent with a miser's prestige. By common consent Sasha and General Jodpur had been allotted the single rooms, while Quill and Mr Stung shared the large room.

They were in it now.

Mr Stung, reunited to his blue-striped pyjamas, was sitting up in bed, reading with growing astonishment the copy of *Mein Kampf*, thoughtfully provided by the Gauleiter.

'The man's a lunatic,' he summed up, and threw the book over to Quill's bed.

'You ought to read this, Quill,' he said. ''Pon my soul, you ought. Make you think, 'pon my soul, it will.'

Quill, who felt that in the present predicament he needed no outside stimulus, nodded absently.

Here he was in an impregnable castle, faced not only with the problem of getting out himself but taking with him an unwilling envoy and a bright light from the Foreign Office. He was damned if he was going to take General Jodpur with him too.

'You'll like it,' said Mr Stung, pointing to the volume. 'Haven't enjoyed anything so much since *Lorna Doone*.'

Quill nodded. He had to plan an escape and he had to plan it soon. Any day Von Papen might arrive in Insomnia. It wasn't very probable, but he might.

'Read that bit where he promises to blow up France,' urged Mr Stung. 'Very exciting.'

'I've read it,' said Quill, and kicked the book off the bed.

'Can't understand why they don't make a film of it,' mused Mr Stung.

There was a knock at the door. The Gauleiter came in. He had with him a large note-book, a pencil, and a pair of spectacles. He sat down on the edge of Quill's bed and arranged all three.

'I have come,' he said, 'to hold you to your promise.'

'What was that?' asked Quill crossly. Last night a bomb. To-night a Gauleiter. Was he never going to get any sleep?

'The patriotic quotations,' said the Gauleiter reproachfully. 'You promised you would tell me some.'

Quill groaned. But Mr Stung had suddenly remembered his Shakespeare.

'Hath not a Jew ears, nose, and throat?' he asked a little muddled.

'I have not heard of this,' said the Gauleiter coldly.

Out of the corner of his disapproving eye he caught sight of *Mein Kampf* lying on the flagstones. He sprang passionately to his feet.

'Who,' he demanded, 'has floored my Fuehrer?'

Quill buried his head under the bedclothes. Oh! Hell! They would be gloating on Wilhelmstrasse. They would be wondering vaguely what had come unstuck at Downing Street, and the Gauleiter was obviously set to stay the night.

The Gauleiter had retrieved *Mein Kampf* and was now wiping its face and crooning over it.

'Dashed amusing book,' said Mr Stung encouragingly. 'You ought to read it some time.'

* * * * *

The silver ball (counts double) whizzed along the companion-way, ricochetted off a bumper, hesitated over a hole marked 'Prince blows kiss—2,000,' took one look at the pins defending the highest score of all, got discouraged, and dropped smoothly into the groove marked 'out.'

'The Merry Widow' was the ultimate masterpiece of the Insomnian Pin Table Company. Not only did it contain more gadgets to light and more bells to ring than any other machine extant, but the ball in its progress illuminated the voluptuous if jerky widow in the primary stages of her famous staircase waltz. As a further attraction (20,000 and over), she came up and took a bow in the extreme right-hand corner of the screen.

A machine that any amateur would be proud to play.

But at the moment it was being played by Adolph Hitler with Goering kibitzing. In a corner, chewing the end of his tie, sat the Economic Adviser to the Greater Reich, Herr Funk.

Another ball zoomed into the pretty, wanged against a bumper, and shot straight into the groove marked 'out.'

'*Ach*,' said Hitler with disgust. 'It has not even lit the third position.'

Goering chuckled. 'These machines, Adolph,' he said richly, 'call for a steady hand. Here, I'll show you.'

He pushed the Fuehrer aside, took careful aim, and with all the delicacy of a French pastry-cook, released the trigger.

All the lights went on. There was a chime of bells. The Merry Widow dashed wildly up and down the staircase, came back, and bowed three times.

'See how it's done,' said Goering smugly.

Herr Funk trembled for him. Really, Herman was getting above himself. Just because they had made him stand-in to the Almighty he not only said what he liked to the Fuehrer, but even went out of his way to be rude to Ribbentrop.

'Your luck is in,' sneered Hitler.

'My eye is in,' said Goering. 'Isn't that so, Funk?'

Herr Funk pondered. 'Well, yes and no,' he produced, looking apprehensively at both of them.

'I'll play you a match,' said Hitler, trembling with rage.

They got down to it.

In his corner Herr Funk was biting his tie again. Soon he would be called upon to produce a score to prove irrefutably that both opponents had won. Oh, to be back, juggling with the so much simpler economics of the Reich!

The door burst open. Hitler ducked quickly behind Goering.

But it was only an excited Himmler brandishing a telegram signed 'Schenk.'

'The British mission,' he gloated. 'Held in a castle.'

'*Gut*,' said Goering. 'The Gardenium is in the bag.' He frowned. 'Now where the hell's Franzi?'

Himmler shifted uneasily. 'In Budapest,' he confessed. 'Got himself arrested for one of his own spies.'

'Again,' said Goering annoyed.

'I'll have him out,' promised Himmler, 'as soon as I can lay my hands on a Hungarian to swop him for.'

*   *   *   *   *

At No. 10 Downing Street the Prime Minister scratched his head.

'Curious,' he mused. 'Very curious. Not a word from the mission.'

'Rummy,' agreed the First Lord of the Admiralty.

'Wonder if anything could have happened?' said the Chancellor of the Exchequer, an apprehensive man.

'Impossible,' said the Prime Minister shortly.

There was a scuffle outside. A little man in a bowler hat wriggled his way through the door. Almost immediately a pair of massive arms engulfed him.

'You must listen to me,' he gasped as the commissionaire pulled him out.

'Really, we'll have to do something about this,' said the P.M. 'Can't have him interrupting every time the Cabinet meets.'

'Wonder what he wants?' mused the First Lord of the Admiralty, a curious man.

A messenger came into the room and handed the Prime Minister a chit.

'Ah,' said the Prime Minister opening it. 'From the Intelligence. Latest about the British mission.'

'What does it say?' asked the First Lord of the Admiralty.

'They've lost it,' said the Prime Minister, sighing heavily.

The First Lord of the Admiralty leant over and thumped with his fist on the table.

'Does nobody know where this blasted mission has got to?' he roared.

* * * * *

But one man knew. In the middle of the night a heavy-eyed Quill was dragged out of bed to receive a telegram.

It read:

      HARD LINES—CANTERBURY BRINDLE.

CHAPTER

22

IT was a beautiful morning. There was a lot of light, a nip in the air, and the birds had stopped singing.

Outside the castle walls the newly appointed sentry strode enthusiastically up and down. He was bursting with pride. Three weeks a Nazi and already he had been chosen to guard the prison wing. A grave responsibility. But he would not let his Gauleiter down.

He reached the end of his beat, turned round, clicked his heels, and set off over the beat again with impeccable tread.

From the window Sasha Podushkin watched him with growing incredulity.

* * * * *

In Quill's room there was a jovial gathering. General Jodpur and Mr Stung had decided to have breakfast together. The two old gentlemen, deep in reminiscence, were eating most of the toast. On the starving outskirts, six foot two of Adam Quill waited in vain for a break in the conversation that would give him a chance to ask them to pass the marmalade.

There was no knock on the door. A heavily-breathing Hansel came staggering in with a large pitcher.

'Your shaving water,' he announced. 'I forgot to heat it,' he remembered.

'Your shoes!' said General Jodpur, looking at him with deep disgust. 'Your hair! Your buttons! Tcha!—you'll never make a soldier.'

'That's what I think,' agreed Hansel cheerfully. 'Only Ma won't listen.'

'No keenness,' said Mr Stung, ranging himself on the side of authority. 'No team spirit. Even my fag at Eton,' he recalled, 'never dared show up like this.'

'Pass the marmalade,' said Quill.

Deep into his pockets Hansel delved, rummaged, and emerged triumphant with a piece of dirty rag. He then picked up one of Quill's shoes and breathed on it thoughtfully.

'Boy,' said Mr Stung, 'drop that shoe and fetch the valet.'

Hansel scowled. 'I am the valet.'

'Good gad,' said Mr Stung.

'They appointed me specially,' said Hansel. 'They said you'd tip me.'

'Ah,' said Mr Stung coldly.

'Also,' said Hansel, perking up a little, 'it gets me off parade.'

This went big with General Jodpur.

'Pass the marmalade,' said Quill.

Hansel had crossed to Mr Stung's plus fours and was inspecting them with every approval. 'Don't need brushing.'

'I think,' said Mr Stung thoughtfully, 'I'll press my own trousers. By Gad, I will.'

'Thank you,' said Hansel gratefully.

The two old gentlemen looked at one another.

'Will you *please* pass the marmalade?' said Quill.

'What's that?' said Mr Stung. He turned, focused, and blushed. 'Sorry, old man,' he admitted. 'We seem to have eaten it all.'

* * * * *

From his window Sasha Podushkin was still watching the sentry. But he had drawn up a chair to do it.

The sentry turned, clicked his heels, and marched purposefully over the ground all over again.

'Incredible!' said Sasha Podushkin to himself. Should he enquire further into this phenomenon? He decided it was worth the effort. He flung open the window and leant out.

'*Bon jour, mon ami*,' he said affably.

The sentry halted, swung round, and levelled his rifle.

'Stay where you are,' he said warningly.

'My good fool,' said Sasha, 'if I were about to escape would I draw your attention to me first?'

'That's as it may be,' said the sentry sullenly.

'Also,' said Sasha, 'I am not an acrobat.'

The sentry turned this over in his mind, found the argument sound, shouldered his rifle, and resumed his beat.

Sasha waited patiently until he was level again.

'*Un petit moment*,' he said.

The sentry finished his beat, turned, clicked his heels, and marched strongly back.

'It is *verboten*,' he said as he drew level, 'with the prisoners to converse.'

Sasha pondered, hit on an idea and delved in his pockets. The next time the sentry reached the window there was a slab of chocolate lying enticingly on the ledge.

The sentry looked at it hungrily, fought temptation, remembered the Gauleiter, won, and strode on. But presently he stopped. Sasha had broken off a section of the chocolate and was eating it with a great show of enjoyment.

'Milk?' asked the sentry.

Sasha nodded. 'With nuts,' he added fiendishly.

He broke off a bar and threw it down.

The sentry was lost.

'What is it you wish to know?' he asked, ready to pay his debt.

'But it is tiring to shout,' said Sasha. 'Why do you not come up here where we can converse like reasonable beings.'

The trooper looked shocked. 'I am a sentry,' he said reproachfully. 'It is my duty to see that you do not escape. I have been promoted to do this,' he explained, brushing some chocolate crumbs from his tunic.

Sasha eyed him warily. One false move and this rare and curious specimen might escape him.

'With this,' he said soothingly, 'I have no quarrel. I see at a glance that you are efficient. But,' he wheedled, 'could you not guard me

143

just as well in my room? Sitting down . . . at your ease . . . with a cushion?'

The sentry winced.

> 'Sybaritic Luxury——
> The downfall of Democracy.
> Our Gallant Fuehrer views with scorn
> Any toe without a corn.'

he chanted sternly.

Sasha realized he had made a bloomer. He readjusted the pitch.

'Also,' he said, 'I have a cigar.'

'A good Nazi,' said the sentry, 'does not smoke. Did you say cigar?' he asked wistfully.

'Corona-Corona,' said Sasha.

'*Ach!*' said the sentry. He disappeared into the castle.

* * * * *

'Then,' said Hansel lusciously, 'there was blood. Gallons of blood. Single-handed Aleric the Awful fought the baron's men. The battle raged for hours . . .'

'Why didn't they try a pincers movement?' asked General Jodpur with keen interest.

'They did,' said Hansel unexpectedly. 'That's how they captured him.'

'And what happened next?' asked Mr Stung agog.

Quill, returning from the bathroom, rubbed his eyes. Somehow, during his short absence, Hansel had managed to launch into what sounded like The Legend of Castle Gelt, and what was more he had carried the two old gentlemen in his wake.

'Next,' said Hansel, 'they tortured him. Tortured him like hell. Thumbscrews, racks, and,' he reflected, 'rubber truncheons. And still Aleric the Awful would not speak. So they flung him into the haunted wing. This wing.'

Mr Stung shuddered deliciously.

'Only of course,' said Hansel, 'it wasn't haunted then.'

'Go on,' said General Jodpur eagerly.

'For years he lay in his cell,' said Hansel. 'This cell. And every day the baron came and gloated at him through the bars. And then one day he came and Aleric wasn't there.'

'Dead?' asked Mr Stung apprehensively.

'Vanished,' said Hansel. 'Vanished without a trace. That is,' he said, 'if you do not count his body which they found in the moat three days later.'

For the first time Quill began to take an interest in the story.

'How did he get out?' he asked.

'He dug himself out,' said Hansel. 'And he'd have got clean away only he forgot that he could not swim the moat with his chains.'

'Short-sighted,' said Quill.

'No,' said Hansel seriously. 'That was the baron. He did not notice the missing flagstone and fell into the tunnel. It was in this very room,' he said.

'Ah,' said Quill.

'And now, every year,' said Hansel, 'on the night of his death the villagers have permission to come to the castle to gather in this room, and to wait for the ghost to walk.'

'And does it?' asked Quill.

'No,' said Hansel, a truthful boy.

Mr Stung looked relieved.

Hansel rose regretfully from Quill's bed, picked up a dustpan and ambled over to the door.

'Got to be going now,' he said.

'Sure, sonny,' said Quill. 'Run along.' He rather wanted to be left with this secret passage in the room from which it had started.

'Got to tidy up the Council room,' confided Hansel. 'The Gauleiter has called a meeting there for to-night.'

'Puppy,' said General Jodpur.

Hansel frowned. 'The worst thing about this Return to the Reich,' he said, 'is all the meetings we keep on having about it.'

He ambled off.

'Half a mind to go to that meeting,' brooded General Jodpur. 'Half a mind to tell them what I think of them.'

'Gad,' said Mr Stung. 'Half a mind to go with you.'

This understanding arrived at, they both looked with some astonishment at Quill, who was lying on the floor and trying to carve it up with a breakfast knife.

'What are you doing,' they asked puzzled.

* * * * *

'But,' said Sasha Podushkin persuasively. 'Do you not realize the flaws in the arguments you have been advancing?'

The sentry leant back in his chair.

'No need to argue,' he said comfortably. 'We are good friends.'

He puffed his cigar.

Sasha went back to the beginning.

'Reflect, my friend. How far did you walk this morning in your duties outside my wall? Five miles? Six miles?'

'Seven,' said the sentry, working it out.

'And where were you when you had finished?' demanded Sasha. 'Just where you had started. To walk to a destination—that is bad enough. But to walk when you are already there—that is unbelievable.'

'But I've been promoted,' said the sentry. 'It's an honour,' he argued.

'This I understand,' said Sasha. 'But why do you walk all the time in the same place?'

'It's my beat,' said the sentry. 'I must not leave it.' He puffed luxuriously.

'But,' said Sasha, 'suppose for argument I placed this chair under my window. Would this be on your beat?'

The sentry was sound on this point. 'Yes,' he said.

'And if you sat in it would you be on your beat?'

The sentry pondered. 'I suppose so.'

'Then why do you not do it?' demanded Sasha.

The sentry examined the idea. It had its attractions. After all there was no passage in *Mein Kampf* that said a sentry should not sit down.

* * * * *

Ten a.m. Regretfully the Gauleiter laid aside the *Nazi News* (Insomnian Edition). It carried the Fuehrer's latest broadcast in full. He had devoured every word and still his quotation book lay unopened. If it had not been heresy he might almost have started to think that the old man was repeating himself.

He brightened as he remembered how well everything was going. He had escorted the British mission safely to the Castle. He had it on highest authority that the machine-gun would arrive soon. And the morale of his men was excellent. He wondered how his new sentry was getting on. He buckled on his belt and went out to see. . . .

The commotion brought Sasha to the window. Beside an overturned arm-chair, a sheepish sentry was volubly trying, but obviously failing, to remember the many arguments so recently learnt in favour of seated sentry-going.

Sasha opened the window and helped him out.

CHAPTER

23

'Got it,' said Quill triumphantly, sticking the marmalade knife into a chink in the flagstone.

The knife broke. He hadn't.

The two old gentlemen were still trying to puzzle out Quill's sudden assault on the floor. They consulted together. They agreed on a strategy. They decided to risk a question.

'What are you doing?' they asked.

'Chasing the Baron,' said Quill. He dug another knife into another crack. The knife broke.

He'd find that blasted tunnel if he had to break every knife in Castle Gelt. Viciously he dug into another flagstone.

'Take this,' said a voice at Quill's elbow.

Quill sprang up. It was the ancient retainer thoughtfully offering a formidable clasp knife.

'Thanks,' said Quill.

'Don't mention it,' said the ancient. 'It cost only twenty peccoes.' Inescapably he focused Mr Stung's eye.

Mr Stung blushed and passed him fifty. The ancient retainer pocketed it with the relieved air of a Lady Bountiful not having to give away gruel.

'Mind,' said Mr Stung warningly, 'not a word of this.'

'Not a word,' agreed the ancient retainer happily and ambled off.

Quill flattened out again.

The ancient retainer came back.

'I almost forgot,' he said. 'The young master invites you to a glass of sherry.'

'The young master?' asked Quill.

'Master Kaleb,' said the ancient. 'I served his grandmother in Paris, I served his mother at Nantes, and now I serve the young master at Castle Gelt.'

'Ah,' said Mr Stung reminiscently, 'I myself have an old nurse in Scotland . . .'

'*Je suis pederaste*,' said the ancient retainer coldly and ambled off.

* * * * *

'Sign here,' said Kurt Carruthers blissfully.
Kaleb Krust signed.

'Your full name,' said Kurt, looking at the very small initials with some doubt.

'Never,' said Herr Krust forcibly. 'It wastes too much ink.'

Kurt looked worried. 'But initials alone are not a legal signature.'

'Mine are,' said Herr Krust proudly. 'By special arrangement with the Government of Insomnia,' he boasted. 'Cost me a fortune.'

Relieved, Kurt pocketed the document.

'And now,' he said, extending his hand, 'allow me to congratulate you on a magnificent investment.'

'What's going on here?' asked Quill, who had elected this moment to lead in the British mission.

Kurt backed apprehensively.

'Ah,' said Herr Krust. 'You have arrived just in time to drink to the success of my new venture—a gold mine.'

'A gold mine,' said Quill accusingly.

'By gad,' said Mr Stung. He dropped his eyeglass.

Kurt who had been trying to bob into the conversation changed his tactics. He leapt forward, clutched the miser, and dragged him to a corner.

'It is unwise,' he hissed frantically, 'to discuss the business confidential with the strangers.'

'Nonsense,' said Herr Krust walking back again. 'These gentlemen are my friends. Besides,' he added irrefutably, 'they are prisoners and cannot tell anybody.'

'They might escape,' argued Kurt.

'By that time,' said the miser, 'these shares, as you have pointed out, will already have gone clean through the ceiling, so what does it matter.'

'That's got you,' said Quill with some satisfaction.

The miser delved into the sideboard, and produced a cobweb-covered bottle.

'Tokay,' he said. 'We use it for special occasions.' He looked at it lovingly and put it back.

'What year?' asked General Jodpur, unwilling to give in so easily.

The miser told him. The General licked his lips.

'If only,' said the miser wistfully, 'it was my birthday.'

'It's mine,' said Quill firmly.

The miser beamed. 'But this is good news,' he said warmly. 'Now we have every reason to broach the bottle.'

They broached it.

'Gentlemen,' said Herr Krust, 'I give you a toast. To my good friend the Detective coupled with the greater prosperity of the Upper Trinidad Gold Mining Company.'

Kurt Carruthers wriggled.

'Civil,' said Mr Stung. 'Deuced civil.' He rose to his feet. 'But tell me, sir, how did you know that . . .'

'Gentlemen!' Kurt had taken a flying leap on to a chair and was trying to create a diversion. 'I give you the toast of . . .' he thought furiously.

'Extraordinary kind,' said Mr Stung, continuing his train of thought. 'Can't think how you knew that I . . .'

'Gentlemen,' said Kurt desperately. 'I give you the toast that we all wish to drink, the toast that is nearest to our hearts, the toast of . . .' He paused.

'Kind,' said Mr Stung who had a one-track mind. 'But tell me,' he asked the miser, 'how did you know I owned fifty-one per cent in the Greater Trinidad Mining Company?'

'No, no,' said the miser kindly. 'You are mistaken. I own fifty-one per cent in the mine.'

'Maybe you both own it,' suggested Quill helpfully.

'But that makes one hundred and two per cent,' said the General who had been busy working it out.

The two investors looked at one another.

'Allow me to inform you sir,' said Herr Krust in a cool, clear voice, 'that I have just bought the controlling interest in the Trinidad mines from Professor Guggenheim.'

'And I,' retorted Mr Stung aggressively, 'bought the controlling interest in the Trinidad mines from him four days ago.'

They glared at one another. Doubt began to dawn.

'By gad,' said Mr Stung, worried, 'you don't suppose we've been swindled?'

'No doubt about it,' said General Jodpur delighted.

Murderously the two controllers turned to look for the financial expert.

Something brushed against Quill's knee. Quill looked down. It was the financial expert crawling for the door. He put his finger to his lips and crawled quickly on.

'Over there,' shouted Mr Stung, catching sight of a disappearing boot and launched himself in a flying tackle.

He brought down Sasha Podushkin who had arrived a little late.

'Got him,' said Mr Stung triumphantly.

* * * * *

'But,' said Sasha, ten unmollified minutes later, 'I still understand nothing. First the good Kurt crawls past me in the passage and bids me say nothing, and then, before I can even obey, you knock me down.'

'Sir,' said Mr Stung stiffly, 'I've already tendered my apologies.'

'Yes, yes,' said Sasha. 'This I remember. But should the urge to play Le Rugby seize you again,' he said earnestly, 'promise me that you will play with the Gauleiter. He is energetic that one.'

'You're a fool,' said Herr Krust, whose nerves had got the better of him. 'Your good Kurt has swindled us.'

Sasha was not surprised. He said as much, adding a rider that he was astounded only that it had taken Kurt so long. He also pointed out soothingly that should his brother Misha ever have the good fortune to meet a sucker half as crass as either, he would live in luxury for the rest of his days.

From outside came the sound of a splashing of oars. Kurt was rowing himself across the moat.

'Bad style,' said Mr Stung, his disapproval swamping his other troubles.

'Couldn't have been at a rowing college!' said Quill.

General Jodpur had an idea. 'Why don't you chase him?' he enquired.

'Too late,' said Quill. 'He's getting into his car.'

Dejected, Herr Krust walked away from the window and sank into a chair.

'It isn't the money that I mind,' he told Quill, 'but what will my public say?'

'What indeed,' said Quill.

'I cannot understand,' said Mr Stung reproachfully, 'how you, a man of the world, came to be taken in by a common confidence trickster. Why, he wouldn't have deceived a schoolboy.' Then he remembered and blushed.

Herr Krust turned on him. 'I am a miser,' he said, 'not a business man.'

'I congratulate you,' said Sasha, who had mellowed since finding the Tokay on the table. 'You are like us. No Podushkin has been a business man since my Uncle Vasilli in Ekatarinaslav. And that one,' he gloated, 'went bankrupt so often that he rented the flat outside the receiver's court to save himself the droshky fares.'

'As a man of business,' said Herr Krust, 'I am no good. This has been proved over and over again.'

'One more mistake,' said Quill, 'and you won't be able to afford to be a miser.'

Herr Krust looked alarmed. 'But,' he pointed out, 'as a miser I am most ingenious. No one else could find such economies as I do. For instance,' he boasted, 'how many people have seriously considered the wear and tear on a lock each time a key is turned in it?'

'I cannot say that I have pondered this,' admitted Sasha. 'But I have thought often that a waistcoat has too many buttons.' He sighed at the sadness of life.

'When first I heard you were coming,' said Herr Krust, 'I was alarmed. Four keys turning in four locks six times a day. It was too awful to contemplate.'

'I can see that,' said Quill.

'But I found the solution,' said Herr Krust proudly. 'I have put you all in one wing and your doors are unlocked.' He chuckled. 'But should you try to escape by way of the corridor you will get a surprise.'

He glanced at his watch.

There was a thud at the door.

'Ah,' said Herr Krust, 'that should be the surprise.'

The door opened. The surprise bounded joyously in, knocked over the Tokay, sighted Herr Krust, made for him, and bit him in the pants.

It was a Labrador.

'Come back, you,' said a sturdy peasant in the doorway. 'Don't move,' he warned Herr Krust, 'or he'll bite you again.'

'He's only playing,' said Mr Stung, who liked dogs.

Herr Krust, rubbing his thigh, was not convinced.

'He's a great biter,' said the peasant with relish. 'He'll guard your prisoners well.'

The Labrador growled rapturously. In a burst of energy Sasha climbed on to the table.

Mr Stung was perturbed. He hated to see a dog worried.

'Come here, old boy,' he invited, clicking his fingers.

'Useless,' said the peasant. 'He obeys no stranger. He does not even obey me,' he added sadly.

'That,' said Herr Krust testily, trying to free himself, 'is evident.'

Mr Stung ignored them. 'Come here, then,' he urged. 'Come here, old boy.'

The Labrador considered the matter, came cautiously across, and sniffed Mr Stung's trousers.

'Stand still,' said the peasant warningly. 'Maybe he will only bite you in the leg.'

The Labrador sprang.

'*Mein Gott*,' said the peasant. 'He will eat him.' He rushed forward to pull the dog off.

'Bravest thing I ever saw,' said General Jodpur from the mantelpiece. 'Why don't you help him, sir?' he demanded of Quill.

Quill stepped forward gingerly.

'Go away, both of you,' said Mr Stung annoyed. 'Can't you see we're playing.'

* * * * *

A peaceful afternoon.

In his study the miser opened his safe, pulled out a bag of gold, and practised trickling it through his fingers. He was getting better at it.

In the courtyard Mr Stung and General Jodpur were taking the Labrador for a walk. Behind them, carefully keeping his distance, paced a once-bitten storm-trooper.

In his office the Gauleiter was waiting for the postman. If the speech from Goebbels did not arrive damn quick he would have to write his own for to-night's mass-meeting. A grave responsibility.

In his cell Sasha was entertaining the sentry (demoted), and two of his friends, to tea.

By the moat rival sections of the crack Shwartze Korps took it in turns to lower and pull up the drawbridge.

Everywhere everyone was amusing himself after his own fashion.

But in his cell the conscientious Quill lay on his stomach and stabbed at the floor with a chisel.

* * * * *

Dusk gathered over Castle Gelt. The storm-troopers scuttled about the place like busy black-beetles. They pulled up the drawbridge for the night. They swept the courtyard. And they polished up the handle on the big front door. And then as though compelled by some strong magic they staged a spontaneous demonstration outside the British wing. (Could this be orders?)

'Puppies,' said General Jodpur.

'Not puppies,' contradicted Mr Stung, stroking the Labrador, 'brats.'

'Puppies,' said General Jodpur obstinately. They had served vodscht with dinner and he was in no mood to mince matters.

In the courtyard they were polishing off the Horst Wessel. The Labrador joined in.

'Nice tune,' said Mr Stung, beating time.

In a one-two movement the spontaneous demonstration turned smartly and goose-stepped off to the meeting-place.

'Cocky,' said General Jodpur. 'What's more I'm off to tell them so.' He got up.

'Where are you going?' asked Mr Stung interested.

'I'm going to the meeting,' said the General grimly. 'I'm going to get on the platform and I'm going to tell those young puppies what I think of them.'

'Good,' said Mr Stung. 'I'll come with you.'

'Take care of yourselves,' said Quill looking up from his floor.

Down the corridor went the two old gentlemen. Mr Stung had developed a shadow. It had four legs and it thumped its tail.

Inspiration came to the General.

'Tell you what,' he said to the arrested Mr Stung. 'When I'm through telling them what I think of them I'm going to take the Gauleiter by his ear and throw him out. How's that?'

Mr Stung pondered. 'I should sling him out first, old man,' he suggested.

'Excellent,' agreed General Jodpur. 'Action, not words.'

The old gentlemen strode strongly forward.

Outside the meeting-place they stopped. A shower of words came pouring through the doorway. Goebbels had sent a pippin and the Gauleiter was going strong.

The old gentlemen frowned.

'Seditious nonsense,' said Mr Stung. ''Pon my soul, it is.'

But General Jodpur had got another inspiration.

'Tell you what,' he said, 'I'll go in there and I'll throw the lot of them out.'

'Will you, by gad,' said Mr Stung impressed.

'The lot of them,' said the General, taking off his coat. 'One by one,' he promised lusciously. 'And you,' he directed, 'shall stay outside and count.'

He rolled up his sleeves and went in.

There was a sudden silence—a lull. Then the storm broke. There was the sound of startled voices. The crashing of wooden benches to the ground. A flurry of scuffling bodies. The door opened. A form came hurtling through the air and landed in the corridor. The Labrador pounced on it.

'One!' counted Mr Stung.

'Stop counting,' said General Jodpur testily. 'It's me.'

*   *   *   *   *

Outside the door of Quill's cell two chastened old gentlemen looked at one another.

'Not a word of this,' said General Jodpur.

'Rely on me,' said Mr Stung.

Even the Labrador nodded.

They threw back their shoulders, puffed out their chests, and, chins up, went into the cell.

It was empty.

But on the floor, where Quill had lain, was a large dark hole.

The old gentlemen looked at it.

The old gentlemen looked at one another.

'Kidnapped, by gad,' said Mr Stung.

*   *   *   *   *

In the bowels of the castle Quill was groping around. He was wet, he was muddy, he was frozen.

And he was as merry as a grig.

*   *   *   *   *

Snug in his bed Sasha Podushkin was asleep. There was a blissful smile on his face. We cannot think what he was dreaming about, but it certainly did not include two worried old gentlemen dropping candle grease on him.

With a yell Sasha Podushkin woke up.

'I am innocent,' he declared. 'I did not know she was your wife.'

They shook him.

'Wake up,' said General Jodpur. 'Listen. They've taken Quill.'

'Kidnapped him,' explained Mr Stung.

'But this is interesting,' said Sasha politely. 'Very interesting.' He yawned. 'It was kind of you to come here to tell me.' He turned over and went to sleep again.

They shook him.

'What had we better do?' asked Mr Stung.

'Go to bed,' said Sasha. It seemed simple to him.

They shook him.

'Now look here,' said Sasha, sitting up crossly. 'A joke is a joke. But this has gone already too far.'

'They may be murdering him,' said Mr Stung passionately.

Sasha considered. 'It is possible,' he admitted. 'But in that case he is dead already, and we can do nothing.'

They shook him.

Nothing happened.

General Jodpur had been brooding. With a deep sigh he produced the result.

'Tell you something,' he observed. 'Don't think this fellow is going to be much help.'

'Maybe you're right,' agreed Mr Stung gloomily.

They sat down on either side of him.

'If only we had a battery,' said the General wistfully.

'Or a battleship,' said Mr Stung.

They looked at one another. They sighed.

'Poor Quill,' said Mr Stung, shaking a doleful head. 'He was a fool, but I liked him.'

'An idiot,' agreed General Jodpur. 'But a nice one.'

The door opened. A mass of mud stalked into the room and sat down on Sasha's bed. Inside it was Quill.

'Got it,' he said triumphantly.

'Quill!' said Mr Stung overjoyed. ' 'Pon my soul, it's Quill.'

'*Mais voyons!*' said Sasha Podushkin sitting up indignantly. '*V'la du propre!* First you get yourself murdered—which is inconsiderate. Next you send your friends to tell me the news. And now you have risen from the grave in the middle of the night. Not even original.' He spat.

Quill ignored him.

'To-morrow,' he gloated, 'we start digging.'

'Digging!' said Sasha jerked wide awake at last. 'My good Quill, you must be mad!'

CHAPTER

24

As though determined to spite the astrologers Monday was a quiet day.

The Western front was so peaceful that General Gamelin did not even bother to send a communiqué. ('*À quoi sert?*')

Hitler had been sent to Berchtesgarten.

Winston Churchill was opening an aquarium.

And the Pope was keeping Mussolini waiting.

But in Castle Gelt activity was feverish. The Nazis had taken themselves for a route march. (He who faints last gets a prize.) Herr Krust was going over his accounts. And Hansel, who had made a point of fainting first, was sitting on the drawbridge practising his bugle.

The British mission were digging themselves out. Beside them, watching with interest, was the ancient retainer who had brought up a further supply of heavily-bribed tools.

Since the days of Aleric the Awful the passage had got itself choked, and many relays of strenuous digging lay ahead of our heroes.

It was General Jodpur's turn with the spade. He thrust, he heaved, and he turned beetroot colour.

The ancient retainer clucked disapprovingly. 'You'll never make a gardener,' he said.

By the mantelpiece Mr Stung was limbering up. It would be his turn to take over in twenty minutes.

On his bed the exhausted Quill slept like a child.

By common consent Sasha Podushkin had been sent to Coventry. He was lying on his bed toying with the idea of translating *Mein Kampf* into Russian.

* * * * *

Tuesday was altogether livelier.

In London the worried little man in the bowler hat once again eluded the commissionaire and got into the Cabinet meeting just as the First Lord of the Admiralty was enquiring with some heat into the well-being of 'that damn fool Stung.'

'You've got to listen to me,' said the little man despairingly.

Inevitably they slung him out. As an afterthought they sacked the commissionaire.

The Wilhelmstrasse had its troubles too. A fight had broken out between Goering and Ribbentrop, and Himmler was winning it. They telephoned the Fuehrer. The Fuehrer left Berchtesgarten, saw a civilian, and scooted back again.

At Castle Gelt Sasha had been brought forcibly back from Coventry. He was livid about this.

Quill was looking at his corny hands. Mr Stung had a backache. But General Jodpur claimed to be feeling twenty years younger.

In relays they had been digging for twenty-four hours. But the gallant little tunnel still held out manfully against the aggressors.

In his study the miser had sent for the Gauleiter.

'I notice,' he said, 'that you have omitted to pay any rent since you moved in.'

' "A loan," ' said the Gauleiter, ' "is better than annexation"—Himmler.'

'Much,' agreed the miser. 'But you haven't paid a pecco for eighteen months.'

' "The Reich," ' said the Gauleiter, ' "will pay you back in full"—Hitler to Poland.'

'Quite,' said the miser. 'But when?'

'To-morrow maybe,' said the Gauleiter, as one who waits for the dawn. 'Every day now we expect the party funds to arrive from Herr Funk.'

'Well, I don't press you,' said the miser, 'but . . .'

Outside the castle the new sentry blew up his Li-Lo, spread it out, looked guiltily round, and lay down.

The rot was setting in.

* * * * *

Wednesday was hectic.

The tunnel was getting discouraged. So was the Labrador. His master (Mr Stung) had oddly forbidden him to knock down General Jodpur.

They had put Hansel on sentry-go. The Gauleiter himself stood over him to see that he did not sit down. Ten storm-troopers had taken advantage of this to have tea with Sasha Podushkin. One of them had brought a banjo. Very soon they were sitting round the fire and singing 'Otchi Tchernia.' Outside the Gauleiter frowned. He had no ear for music, but he could have sworn this was not the Horst Wessel.

In his study the miser was frowning over his accounts. He sent for the Gauleiter.

'Don't you see,' he said persuasively, 'that, as a miser, I cannot allow you to live here for nothing?'

'To-morrow,' promised the Gauleiter vaguely. 'Or perhaps next year.'

In his Palace King Hannibal sat gazing with ecstatic unbelief at a thick bundle of dollar bills that had fluttered out of an envelope. He counted them. He held them against the light, he counted them again.

'Paris,' he breathed.

Lovingly he stuffed the notes into his pocket-book.

'This,' he said, 'is the sort of anonymous communication I like.'

The Wilhelmstrasse was having an awful time. Hitler had arrived from Berchtesgarten to find Ribbentrop sitting on Goering's stomach.

'Now will you listen to me?' he was saying.

* * * * *

On Thursday Quill wrote to Canterbury Brindle claiming his co-operation in their escape. A well-bribed Hansel promised to post the letter. He did—after readdressing the envelope to Al Schenk.

The tunnel had almost capitulated. By to-morrow night they would be through.

And wouldn't Downing Street be delighted?

At the moment the Prime Minister was addressing the House. Like a conjurer who looses a pigeon to distract the audience while the vanishing lady climbs out at the back, he had brought up the stern subject of restless evacuees to take the members' minds off Insomnia. But, as sometimes happens to conjurers, the trick came unstuck.

'Where,' demanded the ubiquitous Member for West Hampstead, 'is the British mission?'

'Where,' demanded Hitler, back at the Wilhelmstrasse, 'is Franzi now?'

'On his way,' said Himmler glibly. 'A direct train to Insomnia,' he added. 'I put him on it myself. This time there can be no mistake.'

On the lonely platform of a country halt, very angry, very cold, Herr von Papen was marching up and down. Seventeen hours to wait. What on earth could have induced him to get out at a place like this?

* * * * *

At the castle the Gauleiter locked himself in his room and dialled Al Schenk. He was almost in tears.

'Cannot you take the British mission away?' he pleaded.

'Why?' asked Al.

'They are undermining the morale of my Korps,' said the Gauleiter passionately.

'Too bad,' said Al.

'This morning,' said the Gauleiter, 'twenty-seven of them refused to go on a route march. Useless, they argued, to walk so many miles only to have to walk back again.'

Something suspiciously like a chuckle came over the wire.

'Terrible,' said Al. 'I'm ashamed of them.' He hung up hurriedly.

Depressed, the Gauleiter stalked into the corridor. From Sasha's room came the sound of voices raised in song. Down the passage came the Labrador chasing Hansel.

The Gauleiter sighed. Everyone was happy except himself.

The choir burst strongly into the Imperial Russian National Anthem.

The Gauleiter paused outside the door. He opened it. He hesitated.

'Come in,' said Sasha Podushkin cordially. 'We have been expecting you.'

CHAPTER

25

ON Friday morning the tunnel surrendered unconditionally. By Friday night the British mission was all set to escape.

'What on earth are you up to?' asked Quill, entering the room to find Mr Stung bent double over two valises.

'My luggage,' said Mr Stung.

'Don't be an ass,' said Quill. 'We've got to crawl through a tunnel.'

Mr Stung sighed. 'Well, I'll just take one,' he conceded.

'You English,' said General Jodpur contemptuously. He puffed out his chest. 'An old campaigner like myself can travel comfortably with a rucksack.'

He produced one.

'The ancient retainer,' he explained. 'Fifty peccoes.'

'Ah,' said Mr Stung absently. He was suspended in an agony of indecision between his valises. One was genuine pigskin, but the other had labels from every capital in Europe.

'Travel light,' said General Jodpur, strapping himself into the rucksack. 'One toothbrush, one night-shirt, and no fal-lals. Aren't I right, sir?'

'You would be,' said Quill, 'if you were coming with us.'

' 'Course I'm coming,' said the General. 'Did my share of the digging, didn't I?'

'Quite so,' said Mr Stung absently. He was saying good-bye to three silk shirts.

'But there's no need for you to come with us,' Quill pointed out. 'The moment we've gone no one is going to stop you from just walking out. Isn't that so, Stung?'

Mr Stung shook his head. It was quite impossible to take both his dress shirts and his dressing-gown.

'Nonsense,' said General Jodpur warmly. 'Did my share of the digging.'

'But,' said Quill, 'you're an Insomnian. No one will want to hold you for anything.'

The General was unmoved. 'Did my share of the digging,' he repeated obstinately. 'If you've got to leave someone behind why not Podushkin? He shirked,' he said accusingly.

'And why not?' said Sasha Podushkin from the doorway. 'It is a good idea that. I am comfortable here, the food is tolerable, the storm-troopers like me, and, best of all, it is not on the way to London.'

Quill rounded on him. 'See here, Podushkin,' he said. 'You've been given the job of Envoy. You've been paid to do it. So the fewer squeaks out of you the better. You understand?'

'*Mais oui*,' said Sasha, dazed. There was nothing in his technique to cope with this. Meekly he sat down on Mr Stung's white waistcoats.

This helped a little. Hitherto Mr Stung had been unable to decide whether white waistcoats without dress shirts would be useful or not. Now he would take his patent-leather shoes.

'After we sign the Gardenium Treaty,' said Quill, pressing home his advantage, 'you can go and bust yourself on your Uncle Bounia's bortsh, but until then,' he thumped the table, 'you obey orders.'

'Ashamed of you, Podushkin,' said General Jodpur. 'Letting the regiment down. Look at Mr Stung and me. Twice your age and make light of hardship. Eh, Stung?'

'Come over here,' said Mr Stung, 'and jump on the lid.'

The General did. It relieved his feelings.

'How's that?' asked Mr Stung, fixing the last strap.

'Fine,' said General Jodpur. 'Keep your tobacco dry and travel light.'

'Precisely,' said Mr Stung. He picked up the valise. He staggered.

'All set?' asked Quill.

'Ready,' said General Jodpur promptly.

Sasha rose obediently to his feet. The telling-off appeared to have done him good.

'You first,' said Quill, who was taking no chances.

'*Entendu*,' said Sasha, resigned. He gazed apprehensively at the wooden steps leading into a mass of mud. 'In there?'

'In there,' snapped Quill.

'Ah, *bon*,' said Sasha, and went clambering down.

Staggering under his valise, Mr Stung followed.

Quill turned to say good-bye to General Jodpur. He was horrified to find him nearly in tears.

'Now look here,' said Quill. 'You don't really want to come with us. It'll be most uncomfortable.'

'Nonsense,' said the General gruffly. 'Used to roughing it. Old campaigner,' he pleaded. 'Travelling light. Besides,' he pointed out as an afterthought, 'did my share of the digging.'

'Oh, all right,' said Quill. 'Have it your own way.'

'Thanks,' said General Jodpur gratefully and clambered down like a schoolboy.

*   *   *   *   *

A blob of mud that had been marking time for two hundred and fifty years seized its opportunity and fell with a plop on Mr Stung.

The British mission on all fours was on its way. Progress was slow. It was dark. The lantern had gone out. There was a lot of mud. They had to crawl through it. And there were noises. Frequently Quill, in the lead, had to stop to listen to them. He could never be sure whether the noise had been made by an incautious crawler in his own party or hot pursuit shuffling after him.

Sasha was being unusually good. Not once had he reminded Quill that he was a Podushkin. But as against this there was Mr Stung's valise. At one stage its owner had almost decided to abandon it. But General Jodpur would not hear of this. They took it in turns to slither it along.

At last a thread of moonlight pierced the tunnel. Heartened, the British mission crawled faster.

'Courage,' said Sasha to himself. 'It is nearly over.'

Quill, too, was feeling better. A little luck now and they'd get clean away.

He halted the party.

'Remember now,' he said, 'not a sound until we're through.'

'Our safety depends on your silence,' said Mr Stung. 'Gad,' he added, impressed by his own phrase, 'but that's good.' Forgetting, he looked round for the Gauleiter.

Quill crawled cautiously out. It would be heartbreaking if anything went wrong now.

He peered into the darkness.

A shadow sprang out and knocked him flat.

Grimly he grappled. The shadow barked enthusiastically and rolled over on its stomach. It was enjoying this game.

'Awfully sorry,' said Mr Stung, helping Quill to his feet. 'You're a bad boy, sir,' he told the wagging Labrador.

The Labrador went dim.

'What the hell is this?' asked Quill, annoyed. 'First a valise and now your Teddy bear. Is this the British mission or a blasted nursery?'

'Couldn't leave him behind,' said Mr Stung unhappily. 'Lonely,' he explained.

'Perhaps,' said Quill, 'you'd like us all to come back and keep him company?'

'No, no,' said Mr Stung. 'He's coming with us—aren't you, boy?'

The Labrador nodded.

'Oh, is he?' said Quill.

'Brought him down specially,' said Mr Stung. 'Knew you'd object,' he admitted with bravado, 'so I put him in the tunnel when you weren't looking.'

'Clever,' said General Jodpur.

'I'm looking now,' said Quill through his teeth, 'and you can damn well put him back.'

'Oh, no,' said Mr Stung, shocked. 'Can't break a dog's heart.'

He peered at Quill anxiously. Surely even a policeman could see that?

'He won't be any trouble,' he pleaded optimistically.

Up the slope a lamp came wavering towards them.

'The enemy,' said General Jodpur warningly.

'By gad,' said Mr Stung. 'At him, sir,' he snapped.

The Labrador sprang.

'Call him off,' said Quill. 'It's the ancient retainer.'

But Mr Stung was loath to call off any fight that his dog was so obviously winning.

'Ah,' he said cleverly, 'but are you certain he is on our side.'

'He's rowing us across the moat,' said the exasperated Quill. 'I've paid him heavily.'

'You will have to pay him more now,' said Sasha, brightening for the first time that evening.

The Labrador came strutting back. He was carrying the lantern.

'Well done, boy,' said Mr Stung, and patted him.

The ancient retainer was distinctly cross. If he had known this was going to happen, he told them, he would have given them the keys to the castle and washed his hands of the whole affair.

Quill swallowed. 'Have you got the keys to the castle?'

'But who else?' said the ancient retainer. 'You didn't suppose that I would trust them to the little boys who play all day at soldiers?'

'Let us get this clear,' said Sasha Podushkin. 'You stand there. You allow me to dig for six days. And all the time with a flick of the wrist you could have let us out?'

The ancient retainer nodded.

'*Pfui*,' said Sasha. 'What could I not say of your grandmother?' He spat.

'Gentlemen,' said the ancient retainer, 'you are not reasonable. In what way am I to blame that you did not ask me for the key?'

'But dammit, man,' said Mr Stung. 'You watched us dig?'

'The English like exercise,' said the ancient retainer irrefutably. He picked up the lantern, in which the Labrador had by now lost interest, and led the way.

On the moat, moored to the bank, was an old punt.

'No cushions,' said Sasha disapprovingly. He climbed in and selected the only dry spot. He was returning rapidly to normal.

Mr Stung and General Jodpur shared the suitcase.

'Knew it would come in handy,' said Mr Stung.

'Snug as a bug,' agreed the General.

'Oh no you don't,' said Quill to the Labrador, who was trying to follow the party in.

'Don't worry,' said Mr Stung coldly. 'He'll swim.'

The Labrador looked worried.

'Come on, boy,' said Mr Stung, clicking his fingers as the ancient retainer pushed off.

The Labrador looked at the moat, shook his head, and whined.

'Come, come, sir,' said Mr Stung sharply. 'Don't be a coward.'

On the receding bank the Labrador wailed dismally. The situation was getting desperate.

'Sorry,' said Mr Stung. He snatched Quill's hat and flung it into the water.

There was a colossal splash. All enthusiasm now, the Labrador had taken a dive.

'There,' said Mr Stung triumphantly.

Swimming strongly, the Labrador reached Quill's hat, ignored it, and swam on.

Sasha stirred uneasily. An awful thought had occurred to him.

'What happens,' he asked, 'when we get to the other side?'

'Do not worry,' said the ancient retainer soothingly. 'I have arranged for transport.'

The moonlight, the lapping water, the moist river smell took Mr Stung back to an earlier age. They did something to him.

In a throaty tenor he burst into the Eton Boat Song.

'Shut up,' said Quill. 'Do you want to wake the castle?'

Even General Jodpur looked reproachful.

Silence descended upon them.

'*Voilà*,' said the ancient retainer, bringing the punt gently in. 'We have arrived.'

He held up the lantern and lit the party to the shore. The little candle did not throw its beam very far, but it shone distinctly on his outstretched palm.

Mr Stung fumbled.

'Well,' said the General with deep satisfaction. 'River forded. Party landed in good order. No casualties.'

'Fine,' said Quill indulgently.

'Morale excellent,' gloated the General. 'Men in good health and dry as a biscuit.'

The Labrador landed on the bank in good order and shook himself joyfully all over the General.

His morale was excellent.

*　　*　　*　　*　　*

'Transport?' said Sasha hungrily.

'The other side of the hedge,' said the ancient retainer, and led the way.

It was a night of shadows. Somewhere in it a bull-frog obligingly croaked. The moon had gone behind a cloud. The hedge was a blur.

'Visibility poor,' said General Jodpur.

The ancient retainer came to a halt. '*Voilà*,' he pointed.

Propped against the hedge, spokes agleam, pedals outstretched to welcome the succulent legs of local hornets, a bicycle thinly stood.

'Tandem, by gad!' said Mr Stung. He pounced.

'Mechanized transport,' said General Jodpur, equally delighted.

'Transport,' said Sasha, who had been looking at it in a daze. 'Impossible.'

'I would have lent you my car,' said the ancient retainer apologetically, 'but my coupons are finished.'

Mr Stung fingered the handle-bars lovingly. 'Haven't been on one of these,' he observed, 'since I courted Augusta. Used to cycle down to the Star and Garter at Richmond every Wednesday. Fell in love with her back,' he said proudly.

'You English!' said Sasha Podushkin. 'To exhaust your energy on a bicycle before you go to bed.'

'Sir,' said Mr Stung. 'The lady is my wife.'

'Better,' said General Jodpur unexpectedly, who had succeeded in wresting Mr Stung's valise from the Labrador.

Mr Stung looked at the gleaming bell. He wondered if it worked. He tried it.

'*Assez de chi-chi*,' said Sasha. 'I am getting cold. Where,' he demanded, 'is your transport?'

'Ah,' said the ancient retainer. He hobbled over to a haystack and came back with another tandem.

'Reinforcements,' said General Jodpur approvingly.

Sasha Podushkin turned pale. Now, for the first time, it occurred to him that he was expected to ride this spinning spider. He turned awfully on Quill.

'You are mad,' he said and sat down.

He had gone right back to normal.

'It's only for ten kilometres,' coaxed Quill. 'Then Brindle will be meeting us with a car.'

'You go there,' said Sasha unbelievingly, 'and bring it back.'

'But I wrote to him. The whole thing's fixed.'

'I do not stir,' said Sasha flatly.

Quill sighed. 'Why can't you co-operate, Podushkin? A tandem isn't so terrible. Look at the two old gentlemen.'

He pointed to where Mr Stung and General Jodpur, considerably hampered by the Labrador, were practising starts.

'Great fun,' said Mr Stung, picking himself up. 'Soon get the hang of it,' he promised.

'We stand firm,' said the General incorrectly.

They climbed on again.

'Bless their hearts,' said Quill.

'You may bless them all you like,' said Sasha, 'but I will not ride on that machine.'

'Yippee,' shouted Mr Stung. 'We're off.'

They wobbled unsteadily past, hit a boulder, and collapsed.

'We're improving,' said Mr Stung.

From the ditch the General nodded happily.

'*Voyons donc*,' said the ancient retainer, losing his patience with Sasha. '*Essayez un peu.* Am I to stay up all night for three hundred peccoes?'

'Come on,' urged Mr Stung. 'You'll like it,' he tempted.

'Good for the liver,' said General Jodpur.

Sasha shuddered. 'You do not realize what you ask,' he said pathetically.

'Look here, old man,' said Quill. 'Don't think I'm taking this thing lightly. I know what it must mean to you to get on a bicycle. You—a Podushkin. Believe me,' he said truthfully, 'if I could see any other way out I wouldn't ask you to do it. But what is there left to us?'

'Nothing,' said Sasha, resigned. 'It is fate.' He brightened at the very sound of the word.

'Let us sit down and discuss the situation like reasonable beings,' he suggested. 'Supposing—for the sake of argument only,' he postulated, 'that I mount this machine. . . .'

'Got it,' came the triumphant voice of Mr Stung.

The two old gentlemen had mastered the start and, taking no further chances, were wobbling off down the road. Around them, barking excitedly, pranced the Labrador.

'I do not like this,' said Sasha. 'The two old ones alone in the night. They will fall down and hurt themselves.'

Unexpectedly he climbed to his feet.

'For what do we wait,' he said to Quill. 'Come on.'

Quill reeled. But clearly this was not the moment to enquire into miracles.

'Hurry,' urged Sasha. 'We cannot allow the old ones to get lost.'

'Hey!' called the ancient retainer, hurrying after them. 'Wait a minute.' From the recesses of his green baize apron he produced an enormous key. 'Take this,' he urged.

'Why?' asked Sasha distastefully.

'It is the key to Castle Gelt,' said the ancient retainer. 'I thought maybe you would like it as a memento. Only fifty peccoes.'

At the memory of six days' digging, Sasha spat.

'Come on,' he said, leapt into the saddle, and set a pace that was much too hot for Quill.

'For a Podushkin,' said Quill admiringly, 'you turn a rapid pedal.'

'But yes,' said Sasha. 'When I was much younger my brother and I won the six-day bicycle race. At Vladivostok,' he added, hoping to mitigate the blot.

He churned steadily on.

Even in the darkness you could feel him blushing.

* * * * *

'Tell you what,' said Mr Stung. 'We'll race you to the top of the hill.'

Wavering wildly, the two old gentlemen put on a spurt. They appeared to have found their form.

'Come on,' said Quill to the flagging Sasha. 'Can't let the old boys put it across us. Remember Vladivostok,' he urged.

For three miles now Sasha had been in constant danger of forgetting it. Miles that lingered up hills, rushed down ravines, and twisted giddily round corners. Twice Mr Stung's valise had come off his bicycle. Twice General Jodpur had expressed considerable surprise at this. ('Tied it on myself!') Twice the Labrador had lagged so far behind that Mr Stung had insisted on going back for him. And Quill was sick of ordering Sasha to take his feet off the handlebars.

The old gentlemen wobbled their way to the top of the hill, turned to wave, and fell off. Goaded, Sasha put on a spurt.

'Can't be far now,' said Quill encouragingly.

The party collected itself for a final effort. One more gruelling climb up a hill, one more dive down a ravine, one more whirl round a corner. And there—solid, welcoming, and ample—stood a car.

'Almost I believe in God again,' said Sasha.

With a sigh of relief General Jodpur dismounted. He was feeling very tired and now he would not have to admit it.

'Good old Brindle,' said Quill. 'Knew I could count on him.'

Gratefully the party clambered into the car.
'No,' said Sasha explosively. 'Not the Labrador.'
But Mr Stung was firm.
The car moved off. Quill relaxed.
'Safe at last,' said Mr Stung with keen satisfaction.
'Sure you are!' said Al Schenk from the driver's seat.

CHAPTER

26

A LOVELY journey.

Quill was smouldering with anger. To dig for six days, strenuously and persistently. To coax his assortment of charges through the tunnel. To lever Sasha on to that blasted bicycle. And all to end up a prisoner in a car, rushing wildly through a mountain pass, with everything in the world piled up on one side and nothing in the world left on the other, while Al Schenk explained smoothly how things had gone according to schedule. (His schedule.) How the letter addressed to Brindle had arrived with the right breakfast tray (Al's). And how the ancient retainer had telephoned through the hour of their escape. (A hundred peccoes.)

Had it not been for the two old gentlemen (not to mention the Labrador) Quill would have risked a grab at the wheel. But the hairpin bends, with sickening regularity, kept coming up.

'Now take it easy, sonny,' said Al fiendishly, guessing what was in his mind. 'If you do anything rash now you won't be here to regret it later.'

'On my stomach!' said Sasha, who had been brooding since the ride started, and was now livid. 'I dig. I crawl. And I ride a bicycle. And all the time you wait to capture us.' He spat. 'Why,' he demanded, 'did you allow us to escape?'

'Well,' said Al, 'if you must know it was your own fault.' He chuckled. 'You were retarding the return to the Reich.'

'Me,' said Sasha, dazed.

'Sure,' said Al. 'You got that bunch of dead-end kids eating out of your hand. You know,' he confided, 'that got me worried for a bit. I was durn glad to hear you were escaping. All I had to do now was to fix up a snug hide-out to hold you until Franzi Papen shows up.'

'Hasn't he come yet?' said Quill sharply. Time was still on their side.

'He is indolent, that one,' said Sasha with deep disapproval. 'Goes to sleep on the job.'

'What's that?' said Mr Stung, sitting up at the familiar word. He was very tired and must have closed his eyes for a minute.

The Labrador looked at his master beseechingly. One more lurch and he would be as sick as a dog.

A lovely journey.

But General Jodpur was quite happy. He had no treaty to sign. He did not have to go to London. He had no need to escape from anywhere.

He only wanted to be with Mr Stung.

* * * * *

'Blast!' said Al Schenk.

A large tree had fallen across the road.

The car slewed to a halt.

'Come on, you guys,' said Al. 'Help me shift this thing.'

General Jodpur rose to his sleepy feet. He was muttering something about being an old campaigner.

'Not you, sonny,' said Al kindly. 'Quill and Podushkin can manage.'

'Sure,' said Quill. 'I'd love to help you clear the way to your fancy concentration camp. But as for Sasha,' with more than Russian resignation he shrugged.

A flight of dark shapes flocked from the bushes and surrounded the car. A Mexican hat bared its teeth at the window.

'Ambushed, by gad!' said General Jodpur.

What was even more surprising, he was right!

The Brigand rested his gun on the driver's window.

'Climb out,' he ordered.

The Labrador obeyed rapturously. He sniffed the Brigand, he liked him, he wagged his tail.

'Heel, sir,' said Mr Stung, disappointed.

The swarthies surrounded the party, and urged them out. Sasha sat down on the log.

'Five,' said the Brigand, counting the captives. 'Five thousand peccoes a head. How much is that?'

A swarthy in spectacles pulled out a pencil and began to calculate.

'Twenty thousand,' he announced.

'That's a bargain,' said Al, a man of business even in a crisis.

The Brigand spoke. 'Impossible to keep you all here,' he announced.

'You will eat away my profits. I will keep only one as hostage. You may,' he granted a favour, 'decide among yourselves which.'

There was no doubt in Quill's mind. 'That one,' he said, pointing to Al.

'*Bon*,' said the Brigand. 'Then I will hold him till you send the ransom.'

'Sure,' said Quill, 'and don't let him go until you hear from us.'

'Hey,' said Al Schenk. 'Wait a minute. . . .'

'I see,' said the Brigand coldly, 'that you are not acquainted with our customs. . . .'

'Never release without ransom,' said the swarthy in spectacles. 'That's our slogan.'

'We may,' conceded the Brigand, 'occasionally release an ear, but . . .' He shrugged.

'Listen, you pack of thugs,' said Al. 'You can't intimidate me. Wait till my Government hears of this.'

'*Tiens!*' said the Brigand. 'You have a Government, too! Already at the base we have one prisoner who has a Government. For six days now we wait for his ransom to arrive. You will like him,' he promised Al. 'So Courteous. So modest. And so helpful with the finance. You would scarcely believe,' he announced, 'that he is the greatest spy in the world.'

For the first time that night Quill and Al were in complete agreement.

'Kurt,' they said as one man.

The Brigand gave an order. The swarthies surrounded Al and led him away.

'Remember,' said the Brigand. 'Twenty thousand peccoes or you never see him again.'

'We have your word for this?' asked Quill.

'You have my word,' said the Brigand gravely. He motioned them into the car.

Quill took over the driver's seat. The British mission settled themselves in.

'Come, sir,' said Mr Stung to the Labrador, still sniffing happily around the Brigand.

The Labrador looked shattered. An idea dawned. He would persuade his two good guys to travel together. He seized the Brigand by the sleeve and tried to drag him forward.

'I like your dog,' said the Brigand. 'I will buy him.'

'No!' said Mr Stung convulsively. 'Here's his ransom.'

He held out some banknotes.

The Brigand patted the Labrador regretfully and pushed him in. Business was Business.

'What about moving this tree?' asked Quill.

The Brigand signed to his men. They seized the tree and gave the car scraping room.

Like a beetle at a funeral, the car moved through the leaves.

'Careful,' said General Jodpur. 'You'll scratch the paint.'

'You'll be all right,' the Brigand encouraged Quill, 'and like this it is less trouble to put the barricade back again.'

They were through.

'Well, so long,' said Quill.

Remembering his manners, the Brigand took off his Mexican hat and bowed.

'Straight ahead,' he said. 'The frontier is only forty kilometres.'

The car moved off.

'Wait a minute!' shouted the Brigand.

The car stopped. 'What is it now?' asked Quill.

'Almost I had forgotten,' said the Brigand. 'My address.'

He handed Quill a visiting card. It read:

> PUEBLO DEL SIERRA
> *Experienced Brigand*
> Dial DESert 347

'Engraved,' said the Brigand with pride.

'Thanks,' said Quill.

The car gathered speed.

From the hollow came a thin halloo.

'Don't forget to write,' shouted Al Schenk.

* * * * *

Through a mountain pass, down into a valley, round a frozen lake.

In the back of the car the old gentlemen slept. But, like a true son of Russia, Sasha, who had slept throughout the hold-up, finding it was the middle of the night, woke up and started to talk.

'If,' he argued, 'you turn to the left after we cross the frontier we will soon reach the *autobahn* to Vienna.'

Quill ignored him.

'If you like,' offered Sasha generously, 'I will get out at the first post office and send my Uncle Bounya a cable that we are coming.'

Quill took a hump-back bridge with unnecessary violence.

'Now,' complained Sasha, 'my stomach has got left behind. But perhaps,' he added philosophically, 'this does not matter as we go to England.'

What with escapes, bicycles and brigands, Quill was a bit on edge.

'Now look here,' he said violently. 'What have you got against England?'

Sasha leant back. 'First,' he said, 'there is London.'

'And what's wrong with London?'

'Useless to explain,' said Sasha, 'if you cannot see it for yourself. Besides,' he added, 'I do not wish to get married.'

'Don't change the subject,' said Quill, for once allowing himself the luxury of being as thoroughly disagreeable as he felt.

'I am not changing,' said Sasha. 'I am explaining. It all happened a long time ago. It began,' he pointed out, 'in Ekatarinaslav.'

'It would,' said Quill.

'I was very young,' said Sasha. 'And very poor. And very good-looking. So I decided not to get married.'

Quill skidded a corner.

'To achieve this,' said Sasha, 'I had to find a girl. A rich girl, you understand.'

'Well, I do and I don't,' said Quill.

'But it is simple,' said Sasha. 'My reputation in Ekatarinaslav is terrible. I play cards, I eat with all the married women and—worse— it is well known that I long for the revolution. I was very young,' he explained apologetically.

A rabbit ran across the road. For the next few moments Quill fought one-handedly with the Labrador. Sasha waited politely.

'So,' he resumed as the Labrador subsided, 'you will understand why I am not considered the eligible bachelor.'

'Perfectly,' said Quill. 'But what has all this to do with your dislike of London?'

'Patience,' said Sasha. 'I am coming to that. As I have told you I am poor. To cure this there are three possibilities. I can inherit—but all the Podushkins live long. I can win a lottery—but even in Russia you cannot always be certain of this. Or I can be bought off.'

Through a village. Along an embankment. Under a tunnel.

'And that is how,' Sasha was saying, 'I came to woo the rich Elisavetta Bolvanova. She was plump, she was stupid, and she was very rich. It is certain, I tell myself, that her father will be horrified.'

'Go on,' said Quill. He was beginning to get interested in the story for it's own sake.

'I woo her energetically,' said Sasha. 'Every afternoon we go to the lake and I watch her skate, and every night we sit together while she plays to me on the guitar. And sometimes I sing.' He sighed.

'Ducky,' said Quill.

'If you mock me,' said Sasha crossly, 'I will tell you no more.'

Quill pulled up. They had reached the frontier of Insomnia. The custodian was asleep. Quill went on again.

So did Sasha.

'Presently,' he said, 'she could resist me no longer. "I love you," she said. So I put on my worst suit and went to see her father.'

Quill pulled up again. They had reached the frontier of the Republic of Astoria. The custodian was asleep. Quill went on.

'I was very confident,' said Sasha. 'Already, I was being off-hand to my creditors and spending the money the pappa would give me to give her up. And I was going to be firm, I decided. Hard-hearted. No parental tears would induce me to consider a cut price in renunciation.'

'Sound,' said Quill.

'He received me,' said Sasha, 'in the pink drawing-room.'

'Revolting,' said Quill.

'On the table was a bottle of champagne. Fool that I was I did not realize it's significance. "M'sieur Bolvan," I said. "I love your daughter. I wish to marry her." I bowed my head and I waited for the storm.'

'Ah,' said Quill.

'But instead,' said Sasha, 'he kissed me.'

Quill raised an eyebrow.

'Russian fashion,' said Sasha, 'on both cheeks. "My boy," he said, "you have made me very happy." I recoiled. But it was too late. "Take her," he said. "She is a fine girl and only a little pregnant." '

Pavements, telegraph poles, an early morning milk cart. They were running into Splitz, the capital of Astoria.

'The days passed,' said Sasha. 'Everyone is happy. My creditors are expectant. Elisavetta buys her trousseau. And the two mothers no longer talk. But me—*moi qui vous parle!* I am miserable. A Podushkin to marry for money—and so little money at that. Unthinkable! Every day I seek for a new plan to escape but each one needs capital. So every night I play *vint* and my capital gets less. And presently it is the day of the wedding.'

Tramlines. A roundabout. The main street.

'I get up,' said Sasha. 'I put on my best suit. My father gives me twenty roubles. I get into a drosky. "To the church," I say resigned. But on the way we pass the railway station.'

He leant back. The narrative was finished.

'Very nice,' said Quill. 'But what has all this to do with London?'

'My good Quill,' said Sasha astounded. 'Is it possible that you have forgotten the revolution? Elisavetta and her father are now in London. Muswell Hill.' He spat.

The Hôtel Neutralité. To look at it was to want to wash its face. But it was the best hotel in Splitz.

Quill pulled up.

In the entrance stood a bulky figure.

'You're right on time,' said Canterbury Brindle.

CHAPTER

27

IT was three o'clock in the afternoon when Canterbury Brindle entered Quill's room at the Hôtel Neutralité carrying his early morning tea. Quill was still asleep. Almost he might have been Sasha.

The ruthless Brindle shook him. 'Time to go to press,' he said.

Quill came reluctantly to life, yawned, stretched, gulped down his tea and felt a little better.

'So it's you,' he said.

'It is,' said Brindle placidly. 'But it was a darned near thing. I was on my way to Paris when I heard you were coming.'

Quill remembered something he had been much too tired to enquire into last night.

'How did you hear?' he asked.

'The Brigand telephoned me,' said Brindle. 'He's a friend of mine.'

'Sorry,' said Quill. 'I ought to have guessed it.' He chuckled suddenly. 'He's a friend of mine, too, only he doesn't know it. He's holding Al Schenk.'

Brindle shook his head. 'Only till to-night,' he said warningly. 'I've just cabled his ransom.'

Quill spilt his tea. 'What the hell did you do that for?'

'Now be reasonable,' said Brindle. 'Al Schenk makes news. I can't have him locked up in a brigand's camp. You do see that—don't you?'

'Damned if I do,' said Quill. 'But if Al Schenk is loose I've got to shift.' He leapt out of bed.

'Now take it easy,' said Brindle. 'You're got twenty-four hours' start. What more do you want?'

'I want a plane,' said Quill. 'I want a machine-gun. And,' he picked up his mudstained trousers, 'I want a new suit.'

* * * * *

In the dining-room, Mr Stung and General Jodpur were having a farewell breakfast. Mr Stung, who had called on his valise, was immaculate but the General looked as though he had gone through a hedge backwards. Their impending parting hung heavily upon them. Neither had any real appetite, but they were making a brave show.

On the floor, pecking unhappily at a bone, lay the Labrador. He did not know what had gone wrong but he was very sad.

'Thirty minutes,' said General Jodpur. 'Time for me to be off.'

Mr Stung looked at him miserably. 'Tell you what,' he said. 'Come to England and spend the week-end with me.'

The General looked wistful.

'Come on,' urged Mr Stung. 'You'll love it. Bauldstok's been, and we gave him a wonderful time.'

But the General shook his head.

'There's a crisis this week-end in Insomnia,' he said. 'Never get an exit permit.'

'But you're out already,' said Mr Stung. 'This is Astoria.'

'Got to go back,' said General Jodpur. 'Country calls.' He got up.

Mr Stung understood. 'Tell you what,' he said. 'I'll see you off at the station.'

'Will you really?' said General Jodpur, overjoyed.

Arm-in-arm the old gentlemen started off. The Labrador came too. But the taxi-driver, who had a phobia against being bitten, refused to take him.

Sadly the Labrador went back to the hotel and bit the concierge.

At the station the train was waiting. Mr Stung tucked the General into a first-class compartment, wrapped a rug round him, and rushed off to the bookstall. He came back looking disappointed.

'They didn't have *Punch*,' he explained. 'But here's the *Sunday Times*.'

General Jodpur could read no English but he wasn't letting on.

'Just what I wanted,' he declared, and turned to James Agate. His French wasn't too bad.

The engine whistled. The old gentlemen looked hungrily at each other.

'Well,' said General Jodpur, 'you'll write, won't you?'

'And you'll come to England, won't you?' said Mr Stung.

They exchanged a solemn promise.

'Well,' said General Jodpur, 'I'll never forget this week.'

'All good things come to an end,' agreed Mr Stung.

'But it's been fun,' said the General.

'Won't be so much fun without you,' said Mr Stung gloomily.

The engine whistled again.

'Bong voyage,' said Mr Stung and held out his hand.

The General swallowed the prejudices of a lifetime. 'Good-bye,' he said. 'And I hope that England gets the Gardenium.'

'What's that?' said Mr Stung. 'Ah, yes, yes—the Gardenium—of course.'

* * * * *

The little salesman twitched the bow tie, smoothed down the lapels, stepped back to survey the effect and was carried away by it.

'*Epatant*,' he announced.

Quill looked dubiously at the fluted sports suit—too tight under the arms—the brown bow tie and the speckled trousers without turn-ups, that comprised the only suit that would fit him in Splitz.

'If,' said the salesman ecstatically, 'M'sieur will play the mannequin and tell his envious friends where he acquired the suit, we will make him a reduction.'

Quill grinned. 'They'll be applying for permits and coming in flocks,' he promised.

Canterbury Brindle appeared.

'My,' he said, looking at Quill, 'won't this go big in Bond Street.'

'Just what I tell him,' said the salesman happily. '*Un petit moment*.' He scuttled away.

'Well!' said Quill.

'Bad news,' said Brindle jovially. 'You can't get near a plane. They're all being used to defend the local neutrality.'

'How about a car?' asked Quill.

'Impossible,' said Brindle with deep satisfaction. 'No petrol.'

'Then what about a train?'

'Well, there is a train,' ceded Brindle. 'Direct to Holland. But,' he pointed out, 'it'll take you three days. As a matter of fact,' he finished, 'I am travelling on it myself.'

There was a bellow of rage from the adjoining cubicle. The little salesman emerged breathing heavily. He was carrying a cascade of top hats.

'He is not fair that one,' he complained. 'In what way is it my fault that his head is too large?'

A morning coat, a lavender waistcoat, a perfect cravate and the infuriated face of Sasha Podushkin strode into the cubicle. He was pale with rage.

'Very well,' he announced. 'I will go to Buckingham Palace like this.'

Defiantly he jammed on a beret and strode out of the shop.

The salesman sat down.

Quill turned to Brindle.

'So you're going to Holland,' he said. 'Don't tell me Hitler is about to invade it again.'

'Just to check up on a peace plot,' said Brindle. 'From there I go to Paris and write up King Hannibal.'

Quill was alarmed. 'King Hannibal in Paris?'

'Three days ago,' said Brindle. 'Got hold of some money and buzzed right off.' He rubbed his chin. 'One of the things I've got to find out is where he got it.'

Quill hated the sound of this.

'And what's going to happen to my treaty?'

'What can happen?' Brindle shrugged. 'They can't sign a sausage until the King gets back. And that,' said Brindle, 'depends on how much money he's got with him.'

'And while you're finding things out,' said Quill, 'you might enquire into that too.'

* * * * *

'Poor little woman,' said Mr Stung sympathetically. 'How you must have suffered. Have some champagne.'

'You are so kind,' said his companion in a suppressed soprano. She patted her sleek hair, adjusted a jade ear-ring, fitted a long cigarette into an even longer holder, crossed her legs, leant back in her chair and arranged herself in Our Recommended Pattern for A Beautiful Spy. She was not very beautiful, but neither was she a very good spy. That is why after starting ambitiously at Geneva, muffing it at Monte Carlo, and collapsing altogether at Constantinople, she had ended up in Splitz. It had been either that or becoming a governess.

Mr Stung, lonely for the General, had fallen an easy victim to her technique. Returning from the station solitary and dim, he collected the Labrador ('you're all I've got left, old boy') and wandered off to the American Bar for a bracer.

The beautiful spy sitting at the counter had spotted him immediately. She dropped her handkerchief. The Labrador sniffed it and turned away. He did not care for Coty.

The beautiful spy asked for a light. But Mr Stung was remembering the bicycle race. The barman obliged.

Baffled, the beautiful spy turned to the Labrador.

'Nice dog,' she said.

The Labrador spat.

In desperation the beautiful spy knocked over Mr Stung's whisky, apologized to him sweetly, and, before he could say 'General Jodpur' he had found himself installed at a little table and sharing a bottle of champagne.

Soon it was evident that the beautiful spy had a secret sorrow. But she was very brave about it, and refused to confide in Mr Stung until the second bottle.

It was a sad story, if faintly familiar. It included a gambling father, a finger-to-the-bone momma, and a brother, who, true to his heredity, preferred debt to dishonour. And then she fell in love.

The Labrador hunched a shoulder.

Armand was handsome, gallant, and generous. In spite of this they stood him up against a wall and shot him.

But it was not until she was in Budapest, fighting for her honour, that Quill and Brindle came in and meanly sat down at the adjoining table. The beautiful spy frowned at them crossly. But Mr Stung was too busy filling her glass to notice.

'Poor little lady,' he said. 'Alone in the big city.' He sighed. 'I, too, know what it is to be alone!'

The Labrador looked dismal.

'The gay old so-and-so,' said Quill indulgently.

'Sucker!' said Canterbury Brindle in disgust.

By this time the beautiful spy was losing her honour all over the place. She leant forward and whispered.

'He didn't,' said Mr Stung horrified. 'I can hardly believe it.'

Even the Labrador looked doubtful.

Feeling her style was being cramped the beautiful spy turned to Mr Stung.

'The sorrows of the world oppress me,' she said. 'I would cry them away on your shoulder. But we are not alone'

'Aren't we?' said Mr Stung. He turned round, caught sight of Quill for the first time, scowled, and turned away again.

'Tell you what,' he suggested. 'Come upstairs and help me pack.'

* * * * *

'What a beautiful room,' said the beautiful spy, looking around as though she had never been in a hotel bedroom before.

'Not bad,' said Mr. Stung. He pulled out his valise and opened it.

The beautiful spy peered anxiously in. But Mr Stung was not up to the secret documents stage of his packing yet. He was carefully folding a claret dressing-gown with polka dots.

The beautiful spy sighed. Evidently she would have to lose her honour again. Languorously she spread herself on the bed.

Socks in hand, Mr Stung looked up.

'Tired, m'dear,' he said. 'That's right. Put your feet up.' He opened the cupboard and produced an armful of shirts. 'Don't worry about helping me. I can manage.'

The beautiful spy kicked off her shoes.

'That's right,' said Mr Stung. 'Make yourself comfy. How do you like this tie?' He held it up.

'Bloody,' said the beautiful spy viciously. 'I mean,' she corrected, 'lovely.'

'Had it five years,' said Mr Stung, stowing it tenderly away.

'It's warm in here,' said the beautiful spy. She wrestled herself out of her clinging gown.

'Is it?' said Mr Stung. 'Thought it was rather chilly. However . . .' He strode to the window and obligingly threw it open.

The beautiful spy gritted her teeth and climbed, unassisted, out of her suspender belt. Mr Stung went on packing.

'Throw me my pyjama case,' he said absorbed.

'Come and get it,' said the beautiful spy playfully.

Mr Stung turned.

Compellingly, the beautiful spy flickered her eyelashes.

'Good gad,' said Mr Stung. 'You'll catch pneumonia.'

There was a knock at the door.

Mr Stung looked at the beautiful spy. Suddenly the full horror of the situation dawned on him.

'Your husband!' he gasped. 'Hide!'

Again that knock.

Mr Stung braced himself. After all, his conscience was clear. He had never thought of the woman in that way. But another thought struck him. Would a Continental husband understand?

Gingerly he turned the handle.

'Come on, you old buzzard,' said the comfortable voice of Quill. 'Our train goes in forty minutes.'

* * * * *

'Can't come in,' said Mr Stung, waving Quill away.

He was out in the corridor. His back was against the door. And his heart was still thumping.

'I wasn't meaning to come in,' said Quill blushing. 'I only wanted to tell you to hurry up.'

An awful thought struck Mr Stung.

'Good gad,' he said looking everywhere except at Quill. 'You don't think that I . . . ?'

'Of course not,' said Quill, looking everywhere but at Mr Stung.

'Tell you what,' said Mr Stung, deciding to risk a confidence.

'Terrible predicament. Woman taken off all her clothes. Don't know what to do.'

'Er,' said Quill.

'Tell you what,' said Mr Stung. 'You go in and tell her to put them on again.'

Quill backed. 'You go in,' he suggested.

'Tell you what,' said Mr Stung. 'We'll both go in.'

Together they advanced, refrained from looking at one another, and turned the handle.

As they went in the bathroom door opened. The beautiful spy tiptoed stealthily into the corridor. Under one arm was Mr Stung's valise. Under the other her suspender belt.

'Vanished, by gad,' said Mr Stung.

'Thank God,' said Quill. 'Let's get going.'

Mr Stung looked round for his valise. He stopped. He pondered. He let out a yell of agony.

'My silk shirts,' he moaned. 'She's taken them.'

Quill grasped the situation. 'What else did you have in your valise?'

'Ties,' said Mr Stung. 'Pyjamas. A silk dressing-gown,' he added, a broken man.

'What about your dispatches?' asked Quill.

'Oh, them,' said Mr Stung absently. 'I left them behind at the fortress. No room in my case,' he explained.

CHAPTER

28

THE station saddened Mr Stung. He had been there before. Here was the booking office where General Jodpur had bought his ticket. Here the very platform where, only a few hours ago, the train had stood that carried General Jodpur away. And—with a fresh wave of nostalgia—the smell hadn't changed at all.

But it was all new to the Labrador.

'What we want,' said Mr Stung, 'is a compartment with plenty of room for my dog.' He walked anxiously down the crowded train, peering into every carriage.

Canterbury Brindle had an idea. He selected a full compartment and pushed the Labrador into it.

Pretty soon there was room for everybody.

The British mission settled in.

But hardly had the Labrador subsided on the floor than an ancient bonnet came stubbornly back, picked up a left-behind packet of sandwiches, counted them, glared at Mr Stung, and hobbled off again, entirely forgetting the basket of fruit that it had managed to salvage from the funeral, which had been so hard to settle in the hat-rack.

'Tell you something,' said Mr Stung, looking at Quill for the first time since the embarrassing episode of the beautiful spy. 'Candidly, old man, I don't like your suit.'

'It is terrible,' agreed Sasha, ramming on his beret.

A thickly bearded stranger, who had clung to his seat despite the onslaughts of the friend-making Labrador, nodded.

'If you like,' he said, 'I can recommend you to a very fine tailor.'

Quill looked at him.

'Mine,' said the stranger, stroking his revolting broad stripe.

Mr Stung shuddered.

'I can get it for you wholesale,' said the stranger. 'With two pairs of trousers,' he offered

'Tempting,' said Quill.

The guard blew his whistle.

'Are you Mr Kalliputsky?' A fierce little man had materialized outside the window, and was glaring at the bearded stranger.

The bearded stranger nodded.

'Then take this,' said the little man. He wound up his arm and donked him on the nose.

The bearded stranger sat down on the Labrador. The Labrador bit him.

Gathering speed, the train beat a well-timed retreat.

'I certainly fooled him that time,' said the bearded stranger struggling to his feet. 'I'm not Kalliputsky.'

'Aren't you, by gad?' said Mr Stung impressed.

The man who was not Kalliputsky examined his trousers.

'You'll need that second pair now,' said Quill.

With an airy hand the man who was not Kalliputsky waved this detail aside.

'It matters nothing,' he said. 'I have a large wardrobe. The largest in the world,' he boasted.

Quill jerked to attention. He peered. He leant forward and seized the bushy beard firmly with both hands.

But the man, who was not Kalliputsky, was not Kurt Carruthers either.

*   *   *   *   *

'Phew!' said Quill.

It was a relief to get to the dining-car, leaving behind an erupting stranger, whose real name, curiously enough, had never managed to get itself established.

At a corner table another bearded stranger was puffing a luxurious cigar, but Quill was too dispirited even to try a tweak.

'Good gad,' said Mr Stung apprehensively. 'We've stopped.'

Quill looked out of the window. Slinking in on the adjoining track came a sleek, well-groomed, and altogether pampered train.

'The Istambul Express,' said Brindle. 'Insomnian Section.'

'I have never been to Istambul,' said Sasha sadly.

The pampered train slid to a stop. Two dining-cars faced each other.

From his morass of Potage St Germain Mr Stung found himself looking at a well-groomed, grey-haired woman with three waiters hovering around her.

'Chicken à la King,' said Mr Stung enviously.

With a charming gesture the pampered traveller raised her glass and solemnly toasted Canterbury Brindle. Like a startled buffalo Brindle sprang to his feet.

'Hell,' he said, 'it's Tabouis. Bet your boots she's on to something.'

He dashed out. A moment later he had thrust aside the conductor and was clambering aboard the pampered train.

'*Sa femme?*' asked Sasha interested.

'Ass,' said Quill. 'That's Genevieve Tabouis, the political journalist.'

The pampered train pulled out.

'I knew a journalist once,' mused Mr Stung. 'Borrowed a fiver. . . .'

* * * * *

During the night the Hague *rapide* almost lived up to its name. It whistled, it produced—on the straight—quite creditable bursts of speed, and it ignored one large-sized town. The last was a mistake. Its stationmaster had been furious.

But with the dawn it weakened and by ten in the morning it pulled up panting at a country halt miles from anywhere.

The man who was not Kalliputsky threw open the window. He seemed to have regained much of his buoyancy. He had combed out his beard, the attendant had cobbled up his trousers, and his nose was hardly red at all. He smiled affably at Quill.

'A wonderful morning,' he said, making it quite clear that he had forgiven him.

Down the platform lumbered a sulky porter. He was tough. He

had bought a bottle of red wine. And yet all last night Marie had refused.

He scowled at the telegram he was carrying.

'Mr Kalliputsky?' he shouted.

The man who was not Kalliputsky lifted his head like a horse at a battle cry.

'Here,' he said beckoning the porter cockily.

'Careful,' warned Quill.

'Do not worry,' said the man who was not Kalliputsky. 'I never repeat myself.'

The porter glowered at him. 'Mr Kalliputsky?'

The man who was not Kalliputsky chuckled.

'No,' he said and, overcome by his own sense of humour, roared with laughter.

'So!' said the porter. He wound up his arm and donked him on the nose.

The man who was not Kalliputsky sat down very hard on his own bowler.

'Fooled him again,' said Mr Stung admiringly.

* * * * *

A bell rang. A small boy appeared on the platform carrying an enormous blackboard. It announced, in inspiring chalk letters:

> *ARRÊT MOMENTAIRE*
> Votre Courage
> Votre Esprit
> Votre Resolution
> Gagnera le jour

Behind strutted the translator. He was the stationmaster.

Quill beckoned him over.

'What's all this about?' he asked.

The stationmaster looked hurt. 'Is it not clear?' he reproved.

'No,' said Sasha. He leant out, plucked a piece of chalk from the stationmaster's pocket, and adjusted a comma.

Furious, the stationmaster rubbed it out again.

'What's gone wrong?' asked Quill.

'But do you not see,' said the stationmaster crossly. 'He has interfered with my composition.'

'Yes, yes,' said Quill. 'But what's holding up the train?'

The stationmaster shrugged. 'Who knows? Maybe a bridge has fallen down, maybe a tunnel is no longer empty, or maybe it is the English sending help to the Finns at last. But,' the stationmaster spread resigned hands, 'it is more likely that we wait for the important one who is staying in the village. For many days now,' he confided, 'he has hurried to the station, but always he has been just too late to catch the train.'

'Hallo,' said Quill. 'Sounds like Franzi Papen.'

The stationmaster looked round.

'You are right,' he said. 'It is Herr von Papen. But do not tell anyone. It is the big secret.'

'A bad traveller,' said Mr Stung reprovingly.

'Ah,' said the stationmaster. 'But what a charming personality.' He sighed.

A gendarme came striding down the platform. He conferred with the stationmaster. The stationmaster shook his head.

'*Sais pas*,' he said and retreated to his office.

The gendarme walked down the train, caught sight of Quill's suit and swung himself into their compartment.

'Mr Kalliputsky?' he enquired truculently.

The man who was not Kalliputsky shifted uneasily. The Gendarme swung round to glare at him.

'Are you Kalliputsky?' he accused.

The man who was not Kalliputsky thought it over, rubbed his nose, and played for safety.

'Well,' he essayed, 'maybe—yes, maybe—no.'

'Trying to be funny, eh?' grunted the gendarme.

He wound up his arm and donked him on the nose.

The man who was not Kalliputsky staggered, failed to regain his balance, and sprawled on the floor. On the rack the basket of fruit, saved from the funeral, abandoned its poise and cascaded all over him.

'Tell you something,' suggested Mr Stung, picking up a cantaloupe. 'Maybe he'd heard the joke already.'

*   *   *   *   *

For a wayside halt the booking-hall contained an unusual number of assorted temptations on its poster board. There was an excursion to the Kiel Canal. ('See the German Navy.') A joy party whirling giddily on the Great Wheel. ('It's Bitter at Blackpool.') And an invitation to the principality of Monte Carlo, warmly seconded by the entire French treasury.

But on the last poster sabotage had reared its ugly head.

Across the façade of the Casino, in vivid red chalk, was written:

Qui joue Roulette
A toujours son regret,

while the green turf of the Jardins Publique sprouted the reminder that:

> *Qui joue Baccara*
> *Bientôt partira.*

And the autobus that went to Nice bore the unexpected warning:

> *Qui joue au Boule*
> *Perdra sa poule.*

The stationmaster was not a gambler.

Adjoining the booking office was a room marked 'Chef de gare.' Over it a dismissed messenger boy had carved the traditional Gallic jeer.

'What does "cocu" mean?' enquired Mr Stung interested.

'Ask your wife,' said Sasha Podushkin, 'and if she does not turn pale maybe she still loves you.' He roared with laughter and slapped Mr Stung on the back.

They went into the office.

At his desk the stationmaster was deep in composition. He looked at the British mission and failed to see them.

'Listen,' he said and read:

> *Qui voyage sur le mer*
> *Peut pas oublier la guerre.*
>
> *Qui par avion va vite*
> *N'aura pas bon appetit.*
>
> *Prends la Rapide. Souviens toujours*
> *C'est très commode pour faire l'amour.*

'How do you like it?' he asked expectantly.

'Fine,' said Quill, who had not understood a word.

'What does "*faire l'amour*" mean?' asked Mr Stung.

Sasha made an expressive gesture.

'Oh,' said Mr Stung blushing.

Quill turned to the stationmaster. 'Any news about our train?'

The stationmaster looked at him, recognized him, and returned reluctantly to reality.

'Bad news,' he said. 'You will be here for many hours. A German train blocks the line.'

'An accident?' asked Mr Stung.

'*Du tout*,' said the stationmaster hotly. 'It has run out of coal.'

'Careless,' said Quill.

'That is what I think myself,' said the stationmaster. 'They should be more cautious. Especially now that we have signed a trade treaty with the Allies which gives them all our coal—only we have to ship it to Newcastle.'

'Sound scheme,' said Mr Stung.

'Then where will the German train get its fuel?' asked Quill.

'Russia,' said the stationmaster.

'Then we are here for always,' declared Sasha. He sat down and put his feet up.

'Come,' said the stationmaster consolingly. 'It is not so bad as that. They are efficient, the Germans. Already they have organized the passengers to cut down the trees in the forest and wait only now for saws. Have courage,' he urged, 'by to-morrow you will be on your way—or the day after that at the latest.'

'Grand,' said Quill bitterly.

'But,' said the stationmaster, remembering his official duties, 'it is time that I told the other passengers the news.' He crossed to the blackboard and picked up the chalk.

'What,' he demanded, 'rhymes with "immobilisé?" '

* * * * *

The lonely halt was not so lonely that it did not contain an *estaminet*. It had no vodscht, but the Pernod was grand.

Feeling much better the British mission started back for the station. In their present optimistic frame of mind it seemed quite an idea to buzz in on the stationmaster and help compose a few more cantos.

Even the Labrador was staggering.

'Who's that?' asked Mr Stung, pointing down the road at a figure advancing towards them.

'I have an idea,' said Sasha. 'Let us sit down and he will come up to us.'

'Sound,' said Mr Stung.

They sat.

The figure came closer. It wore its hair *en brosse* and was carrying a flying helmet.

'*Tiens*,' said Sasha. 'An aviator.'

The aviator came level with the British mission, clicked his heels, and bowed from the waist.

'Fleigel-Hauptmann Schmidt,' he announced. 'At your service.'

'I doubt it,' muttered Quill, gazing at the swastika embroidered on his arm.

'I would be obliged,' said Herr Hauptmann Schmidt, 'if you would direct me to a butcher.'

'Hungry?' asked Mr Stung, interested.

'*Nein*,' said the Herr Hauptmann coldly. 'It is for Herr von Papen.'

'Is Von Papen hungry?' asked Mr Stung, still interested.

Herr Hauptmann Schmidt frowned. 'Herr von Papen,' he said, 'has unfortunately possessed himself of a black eye, and until it is better I cannot fly him to Insomnia.'

'Oh ho,' said Quill. 'So they've sent a plane for Franzi.'

'It was necessary,' said Herr Hauptmann Schmidt. 'Herr Himmler was becoming impatient. My instructions are to fly him to Insomnia direct. But now, with this black eye, we are delayed again.'

'Embarrassing,' said Mr Stung. 'Definitely embarrassing.'

From their ditch the British mission chuckled richly. Schmidt looked surprised.

'How did he come by it?' asked Quill.

'Quite suddenly,' said Herr Hauptmann Schmidt naïvely.

It appeared that a man, who was not Mr Kalliputsky, had wound up his arm and donked Von Papen first.

The story went well. The British mission grew limp with laughter. Even the Labrador shook a little.

'Fooled him again,' said Mr Stung, tears rolling down his face. 'And I wasn't there to see it.'

Herr Hauptmann Schmidt looked at them. They were mad, he decided, mad as Englishmen. He bowed stiffly and walked off down the road.

'You know,' confessed Mr Stung two laughter-swept minutes later, 'I still don't quite see the point of his joke.'

'You will never understand it,' said Sasha. 'It is Armenian.'

The British mission lay back in the ditch and started laughing all over again.

* * * * *

'An aeroplane,' said Mr Stung. 'By gad, it is!'

By gad it was.

Gloriously alone in a field, streamlines, silver wings, swastika, and all.

'Race you to it,' said Quill.

The Labrador won.

'Wonder,' mused Mr Stung, fascinated, 'if it's got any bombs?'

'Imbecile,' said Sasha, who had come in an easy last. 'No aeroplane lands with bombs. Unless, of course,' he amended, 'the pilot has forgotten he is carrying them. Also,' he added, 'this is a passenger plane and has no bomb rack.'

'How do you know?' asked Quill.

'But I know a lot about planes,' said Sasha modestly. 'Did I not jump out of them once.'

Like a flash the idea came to Quill. He would pinch Von Papen's plane.

'Sasha,' he said, 'can you take this dragon-fly up?'

'But certainly,' said Sasha. 'It is not difficult, this. I will show you.'

He clambered in.

'Come on,' said Quill to Mr Stung.

'Come on,' said Mr Stung to the Labrador.

The Labrador looked at Sasha messing about with the controls, and shook his head doubtfully.

'Come on,' urged Mr Stung. 'Be a sport.'

The Labrador looked at Mr Stung. He thought it over. 'Well,' said his eyes, 'for your sake.' He bounded in.

'Look here,' said Quill, reasoning with Mr Stung. 'They'll only put him in quarantine when we get there.'

'I could visit him,' said Mr Stung, clutching the dog obstinately.

Sasha had found the self-starter. The engines whirred into life. The plane shot somewhat convulsively across the field, missed the haystack, and took to the air.

'To Vienna,' shouted Sasha optimistically.

CHAPTER

29

'I SAY,' said Observer Corps, on the telephone to Fighter Command. 'There's something fishy over the Channel. It sounds like a German. It looks like a German. But it's steering the rummiest course I've ever seen anybody try.'

'New tactics,' snapped Fighter Command. 'Up and intercept it, boys.'

'May I sound the sirens?' asked the new assistant hopefully.

'What!' said Fighter Command. 'And have everybody out in the streets. . . .'

* * * * *

Three eager Spitfires sped defiantly through the air.

Where was this Jerry?

It proved unusually easy to find him.

With perfect precision the three Spitfires co-ordinated their plan of attack, took up position, and zoomed at four hundred miles an hour to the point where Jerry should have been if he were a gentleman. But contrary to all rules of aerial warfare he had ignored them and kept a straight course, so, naturally, they missed him in comfort.

Astonished, the three Spitfires spiralled for another stab.

Zoom!

Twenty-four machine-guns were cocked at the doomed plane. Three fingers tightened over three triggers.

Deciding not to argue further, Quill detached Mr Stung from his white silk shirt and waved it out of the window.

He was only just in time.

*   *   *   *   *

It had been a terrible journey. For the first hour they had progressed entirely in circles while Quill pleaded with Sasha not to take them to Vienna and Mr Stung assured the Labrador that 'it wouldn't be long now, old chap.'

Quill had opened confidently with an appeal to Sasha's family affections. He reminded him of his brother Misha alone, and sleeping heart-brokenly at the Ministry of Elimination. But Sasha countered strongly with an ageing Uncle Bounya, alone in a Vienna bed-sittingroom, with no one to share his bortch.

Next Quill had tried a spot of emotional blackmail. He painted a pathetic picture of himself at a German concentration camp with a raging Snarl in London, only waiting for him to escape to sack him from Scotland Yard. There were tears in the Labrador's eyes and Mr Stung wept a little too, but Sasha said that was okay with him.

As a forlorn hope Quill tried a personal appeal. Hadn't they always been friends? 'No,' said Sasha coldly.

It was the compass that had saved the day. It turned out that Sasha could not read it. So, promising faithfully to pilot him to Vienna, Quill had taken firm charge of it.

But he was not so hot with a compass himself. Twice they found themselves flying over Vesuvius. (*On revient toujours à son premier amour.*) The English Channel was a welcome sight.

'Safe at last,' said Mr Stung.

Zoom!

At this point had begun the struggle for Mr Stung's shirt. It was agonized if not protracted, and included a pathetic effort by Mr Stung to fob Quill off with a tie. Even after it was all over Mr Stung could still not understand 'why our own chaps had attacked us—dammit!'

He sat in his seat, hugging the Labrador, and glaring at the young puppies in the Spitfires that kept flitting past to have another look.

And so they came to the city.

'*Tiens*,' said Sasha as they flew over St Paul's, 'how Vienna has changed!'

CHAPTER

30

'You have deceived me,' said Sasha crossly. He was livid over Hendon. 'This is not Vienna.'

'Guessed it,' said Quill.

'London, old boy,' said Mr Stung to the Labrador. 'Look....' He pointed to Golders Green.

The Labrador sniffed.

'Come, come, sir,' said Mr Stung sternly. 'No anti-Semitism.'

They seemed to be leaving Hendon aerodrome behind.

'What about landing?' asked Quill.

Sasha nodded. 'It is an idea,' he said. He got up and started to rummage.

'What on earth are you doing?' asked Quill.

'The parachutes?' said Sasha, anxious. 'Where are they? Ah!' He pounced.

'But look here,' said Quill. 'We aren't going to jump out. We're going to land.'

'You may do as you like,' said Sasha indifferently, 'but for my part I do not trust you to bring the machine down safely.'

'Me?' said Quill, startled. 'I've never brought a machine down in my life.'

'Neither have I,' said Sasha with profound satisfaction.

'But dammit, sir,' said Mr Stung, who had been listening with growing horror. 'You can't expect my dog to jump.'

Quill lost his temper.

'Of all the blithering asses,' he snapped. 'Pretending to be a pilot!'

With infuriating calm Sasha laid aside his parachute, sat down, and lit a cigarette.

'You are unfair,' he pointed out. 'I made no such claim for my aeronautics. You asked me only if I could take this plane up. You did not enquire if I could bring it down.' Exquisitely he blew a smoke ring. 'Was I to guess that you considered this important?'

'Oh, my God,' said Quill. 'Are you really certain you can't land?' he pleaded.

'Positive,' said Sasha implacably. 'You see,' he explained, 'I am a parachutist. Many times have I gone up in an aeroplane and seen how it is done. But when it is time for the plane to come down—*voyons*—I have already jumped.'

'Exciting, by gad,' said Mr Stung. He looked round for General Jodpur. If only they could be jumping together. 'What do we have to do?' he asked eagerly.

'But it is easy,' said Sasha. 'You pick up a parachute.' He picked one up. 'You strap on the harness.' He strapped it on the excited Mr Stung. 'You jump off, you rest a little, and you pull the rip-cord.'

'But you can't expect my dog to pull a rip-cord,' said Mr Stung, strapping a parachute on the puzzled Labrador.

'You must pull it for him,' said Sasha, and turned to strap in the stunned Adam Quill.

'Do not be nervous,' he said soothingly. 'It is simple, pleasant, and not energetic. I will go first and show you.'

He clambered out on to the wing.

'Watch me closely,' he said. 'Now!' He stood poised.

'Hey!' shouted Quill frantically. 'Come back. You've forgotten your parachute!'

*   *   *   *   *

It was a beautiful afternoon. Puffy clouds, like dolphins, disposed themselves about the sky. The gulls dipped and wheeled over the lake. And the vistas in St James's Park had never looked greener.

Even the Snarl, walking home from Scotland Yard, relaxed and was seen to smile at a child who had nearly knocked him over with a scooter. Terrified, the child fled howling away. It did not realize the Snarl had unbent.

A beautiful afternoon. The Snarl sniffed approvingly at the keen winter air. It put a snap into him. A pity, thought the Snarl, he couldn't put a snap into Quill. Born idiot—disappearing like that and taking the British mission with him. Only wait till he got back.

At the thought of what he was going to say to Quill the Snarl brightened again.

A lot of people seemed to be staring up at the sky. The Snarl craned his neck. Some silly ass was coming down by parachute. Idly the Snarl wondered where he would land.

By Jove, he was going to land quite near him! Only a few yards away! Not even that!

The Snarl ducked.

But he was too late. The parachutist had landed and was being carried over the ground. The Snarl, tangled up in the parachute, bumped with him. They came to rest in a rhododendron bush.

They disentangled themselves. They looked at each other.

'Quill,' said the Snarl accusingly, 'what are you doing in that suit?'

* * * * *

Sasha Podushkin slid nonchalantly through the air and alighted in good order on the roof garden of the Ministry of Elimination.

In a corner, stretched on a chaise-longue, Misha Podushkin was snatching a siesta. He opened one eye and recognized his brother.

'*C'est toi,*' he said, pleased.

'*C'est moi,*' agreed Sasha, climbing unassisted out of his parachute.

He found a deck-chair, pulled it alongside, and sank into it.

The two brothers looked at one another.

'*Alors,*' said Misha. '*Ça va?*'

'*Ça va,*' said Sasha. '*Et toi?*'

'*Ça va,*' said Misha.

Two minutes later the brothers Podushkin were asleep.

* * * * *

Swaying uncomfortably in the wind, the Labrador was thinking bitter thoughts. What a position to put a dog in.

It seemed years since his master had whispered to him, 'Take care of yourself, old boy,' pulled the ring, and pushed him off into an existence where there was nothing to stand on and nothing to smell.

The wind rushed past his ears, his tummy was empty, and at any moment the earth was going to come up and hit him.

It was rushing upwards. Frantically the Labrador struggled to get away. Useless! Soon the earth was bumping him.

The Labrador came to rest on a green patch entirely surrounded by faces. They were surprised and shouting.

The Labrador blinked.

Could this be Wembley Stadium?

A white bundle, wobbling furiously, shot past him. 'By gad,' thought the Labrador. 'A rabbit! 'Pon my soul it is!'

He chased it.

But the parachute hampered him.

The six greyhounds rounding the bend abandoned the rabbit, which they darkly suspected of being phony anyway, and enthusiastically chased the Labrador.

The cads!

*   *   *   *   *

From a barrage balloon Mr Stung peered pathetically down. He hoped his dog was all right.

CHAPTER

31

'HERE they come!'

The Great British Public watches its processions, eyeing with equal indulgence its Lord Mayors, its Ducal Weddings, or the current Eastern Potentate trundling dazedly past.

To-day they had turned out to greet their Insomnian Saviour. The custodian of eighty per cent of the world's Gardenium—whatever that was.

The gallant envoy who had braved such perils to reach their shores and hand over victory.

That most neutral neutral who was so firmly on the right side—theirs.

The man who with pomp and pageantry was to be honoured that day by a civic banquet at the Guildhall.

The man who later that afternoon would take a taxi to the Board of Trade and with a single flourish of his pen sign the treaty they were so sick of hearing about.

In short, Sasha Podushkin.

Outside dear old sooty, reassuring Buckingham Palace the crowds roared and surged. Already the Procession was forty minutes late.

The Snarl breathed heavily. Gosh, if he could only lay his hands on Quill. He'd push him out on to the world-famous balcony and watch him trying to explain to the crowd that the Insomnian Envoy was still asleep.

In the courtyard the postillions dismounted from their steeds.

'Have to bring out the cars,' an official apologized.

'And abolish the speed limit,' said the Head Chauffeur sourly.

By the Admiralty Arch the crowds were in a better temper.

They were being amused by a series of news vans that kept rushing up with intriguing posters that had nothing to do with the war.

'KING HANNIBAL THROWN OUT OF PARIS NIGHT CLUB,' proclaimed the *Evening Standard*.

'HANNIBAL KISSES FOLLIES GIRL.'

'SLUGS HUSBAND,' announced the *Star*.

'HANNIBAL TIGHT AGAIN,' said the *Evening News* shortly.

The Great British Public had taken King Hannibal to their hearts. He reminded them of King Edward the Seventh; they did not quite know why. They could hardly wait for the next editions.

Ah!—here was another van.

But it was only the Procession.

Jerked back to their sense of duty, the Great British Public transferred its weight to the other foot and cheered lustily.

'It is silly, this lunch,' observed Sasha to the bowing Prime Minister. 'Never do I have stomach till the night.'

'Bow,' hissed the Prime Minister.

Scowling horribly, Sasha nodded his head to left and right.

'My neck aches,' he complained. 'Already I have bowed seventeen times.'

'In a British Procession,' said the Prime Minister, 'you do not leave off for a minute. You bow all the time. Like this.' He flashed a smile and motioned the top-hat that had not touched his head since they started.

The Procession whizzed round Trafalgar Square.

In the Haymarket King Hannibal had promised emeralds to a strip-tease dancer. But in Oxford Street he had interviewed Cartier without success about them. Outside Marshall and Snelgrove's he was still arguing with the Jewellers when the Procession flashed past.

The crowd shouted approval. It was almost as good as a dirt track.

Mr Stung, riding with Quill in the third car, looked suddenly worried.

'Hope Podushkin doesn't upset the P.M.,' he said uneasily. 'Funny fellow the P.M.,' he pointed out.

'Very funny,' agreed Quill.

Thirty seconds to get through Hyde Park. The chauffeurs stepped on it.

But they slowed down at Hyde Park Corner where King Hannibal had cut a dinner date with Daladier.

'Smile,' hissed the Prime Minister, working overtime at the cheering populace.

But Sasha Podushkin had produced a map and was poring over it.

'Correct me if I am wrong,' he said politely, 'but are you sure we are taking the shortest way?'

* * * * *

The Guildhall was dribbling flags at every spout. A bevy of reporters turned their backs on it.

'And what have you to say about Insomnia?' a wistful scribe asked the alighting Mr Stung.

Mr Stung thought it over.

'I slept well,' he said cautiously. . . .

* * * * *

At the banquet Quill found he had not been laid for. This rankled.

After all he had gone through to get the blasted Gardenium the least he felt his grateful country might do for him was to stand him a lunch.

'Never mind,' said a Stomach consolingly. 'Come and have lunch with me.'

Quill turned. It was Sergeant Banner.

'Thought I'd find you here,' said Sergeant Banner. 'You're wanted at the Ministry of Elimination. Urgent.'

'What about?' asked Quill.

'I wouldn't know,' said Banner virtuously. 'But he says he's an old friend of yours.'

'And what about my Envoy?' demanded Quill.

'Leave him to the Cabinet,' said Banner. 'They're kinda keen on him.'

They hailed a taxi.

Taken at a slower pace Quill had time to look about the streets. London had altered a bit. The tenseness of those early days of the war had gone. Taxis could rev up without passers-by looking into the sky for enemy planes. Wooden casings had neatened the sandbags. The bright arrows pointing encouragingly to the nearest air-raid shelter had become little more than tattered spear heads. If there was any apprehension it was confined to what was going to happen to Sweden. Nobody, excepting Quill, was carrying a gas mask.

In the vestibule of the Ministry of Elimination a little man was pacing anxiously up and down.

He was Kurt Carruthers.

He bounded forward as Quill entered, and embraced him.

'Good God,' said Quill. 'How did you escape from the Brigand?'

'But it was easy,' said Kurt, pumping Quill up and down by the hand. 'I won my ransom with the three-card trick.'

'Skinned him?' asked Quill.

'No,' said Kurt. 'I teach it to him.'

He pumped Quill's hand again. 'Ah, my friend,' he said, 'I cannot tell you how pleased I am that your mission has reached England in safety.'

Quill looked at him.

'I know what you are thinking,' said Kurt cleverly. 'But prepare yourself for a big surprise!'

Quill touched wood.

'Since yesterday,' said Kurt, 'I am now on your side.'

'Oh, you are?' said Quill.

'Yes, yes,' Kurt reassured him, 'it is true. The Greater Reich,' he said reproachfully, 'is not a man of honour. I have served them faithfully. I have sent them enough information to blow up the whole of London. Not only do they not do this,' he said severely, 'but also, not once have they remembered to pay me.'

'Too bad,' said Quill.

'So I walk out on them,' said Kurt. 'I resign and I listen to no entreaties.'

'Did they plead very hard?' asked Quill.

'They will do so,' said Kurt confidently. 'But I am immovable. From now on I sell my talents to England.' He put his hands in his waistcoat pockets and wriggled them contentedly.

'I hate to depress you,' said Quill, 'but they shoot spies in wartime.'

'That is the point on which I wish to consult you,' said Kurt, taking his hands out of his waistcoat pockets. 'It is against me that I worked for Germany. I realize this. But it would be all right,' said Kurt, 'if you would vouch for me.'

'Me!' said Quill.

'They have confidence in you here in England,' said Kurt. 'They trust you,' he pointed out.

'Quite,' said Quill.

Kurt looked at him beseechingly. 'We are old friends,' he pleaded. 'And I give you my word that I will be quite the man of honour.'

'No confidence tricks?' asked Quill.

Kurt pondered. He decided to make a concession.

'Only on the Cabinet,' he promised. . . .

* * * * *

The lift-gates opened. Sir Humphrey shot out. He had dark hollows under his eyes, his cigar had gone out and he was definitely shaken.

'Ah, Quill,' he said. 'Can't stop. Lord Beaverbrook—blast him.'

'What's wrong?' asked Quill.

Sir Humphrey looked at him like a hurt child.

'They're going to eliminate us,' he said whitely.

* * * * *

Canterbury Brindle shifted in his chair, stubbed out his cigar, and failed to look Quill in the eye.

'I'm ashamed,' he said. 'Terribly ashamed.'

They were sitting in the canteen. If Quill had not by now been shockproof he might have wasted time wondering how Brindle had got there.

'Terrible,' said Brindle, 'for me to overlook a thing like that. It isn't even in my book,' he said bitterly.

'What isn't?' asked Quill.

'Clause 347/e,' said Brindle.

Quill blinked. 'What's that?'

'Insomnian Constitution,' said Brindle blushing. 'And I never knew it,' he admitted sadly. 'So I had to sit there and take it while Tabouis put me right.'

Poor old boy, thought Quill. He seemed to be taking Clause 347/e very much to heart, but thank Heaven that was his trouble.

'I'm losing my grip,' moaned Brindle, 'she even had to tell me who sent Hannibal his journey-money.'

'And who was that?' asked Quill idly.

'Al Schenk,' said Canterbury Brindle.

Quill sat up. Maybe this was going to be his trouble as well.

'What is Clause 347/e?' he asked.

'I'll tell you,' said Brindle, stubbing him dramatically in the waistcoat. 'Should the monarch absent himself from the country for more than seven days his authority automatically passes to a Council of State until such time as he returns.'

Quill gasped.

'It was passed,' said Brindle, 'in the reign of Queen Nana the Nymphomaniac. Very necessary.'

'How long has King Hannibal been away?' cut in Quill.

'Seven days,' said Brindle with melancholy satisfaction. 'The Council took over this morning.'

'Then we're sunk,' said Quill.

'Not necessarily,' said Brindle. 'They've still got to wait for Von Papen.'

Hope dawned.

'Then,' said Quill, 'if we can get King Hannibal away from Cartier. . . .'

'Exactly,' said Canterbury Brindle.

Quill leapt to his feet.

'Come on,' he said. 'Let's break the news to the Cabinet.'

* * * * *

The Cabinet were doing a gloat. Here they were, all together. And here was the Envoy from Insomnia, a little crusty but definitely alive. And here, stretched on the table, beautifully engrossed on paper of pre-war quality, like two contracts about to be exchanged, lay the treaties.

With a practised flourish the Prime Minister picked up his fountain pen and made a few preliminary passes in the air before embarking on the flowing signature. His wrist was in perfect shape.

'Don't sign!'

A hatless Quill and a breathless Brindle burst simultaneously into the room.

The new commissionaire, a fatalist, resigned himself to his destiny.

'What is all this?' said the First Lord of the Admiralty peevishly. 'Is the Cabinet never to be allowed to meet in peace. First it's a little man in a bowler hat and now it's a detective in,' he paused, 'a most distinctive suit.'

'He got it abroad,' said Canterbury Brindle standing up for his friend.

Quill led the Prime Minister to one side and explained the situation.

'I don't believe it,' said the P.M. He turned to one of his trusted secretaries. 'Ring up the Insomnian Embassy.'

'They've been ringing us all afternoon,' said the trusted secretary. 'Something about Clause 347/e.'

The Prime Minister took the First Lord of the Admiralty aside.

'I don't believe it,' said the First Lord of the Admiralty. He snatched a telephone.

The Insomnian Embassy read Clause 347/e across the wire. They read it over and over again while the Cabinet took it in turns to listen.

Finally they were convinced.

Encouraged, the Insomnian Embassy now informed them that the Council's first action had been to revoke the powers of the envoy.

'Give him the air,' they counselled tersely.

But Sasha Podushkin refused to take the air.

'You may do as you like,' he told the P.M., 'but for my part I shall sign.'

There was a shocked silence.

'But you've got no powers,' pointed out the P.M. with his world-famous patience.

'*Je m'en fou*,' said Sasha. 'To get to England I have endured much discomfort. You throw me into prison. You put me in a procession. And also,' he remembered, 'you make me ride a bicycle.'

'A bicycle,' said the P.M. faintly. The narrative seemed to have lost its way.

The Cabinet tut-tutted. They looked round for a scapegoat. They saw Brindle.

'You shouldn't have done that,' they said as one man.

* * * * *

'I don't know, I'm sure,' said the P.M. rubbing his chin.

'It's your only chance, laddies,' said Canterbury Brindle.

Night was falling. The crowd outside Downing Street, fearing that in the black-out they might cheer the wrong minister, had taken no chances and gone home. In the famous study, stretched on a sofa, Sasha Podushkin had fallen asleep. But the Cabinet were still arguing the delicate point of who should be sent to prise King Hannibal from Paris and deliver him to Insomnia to kick out the Council of State.

As a further complication there was the time factor. King Hannibal must be got back to take over the reins before Germany could nip in and sign up with the newly-formed Council.

One by one the illustrious names that lit up the Downing Street address book of British Diplomacy had been turned up by the Cabinet, only to be turned down by Canterbury Brindle.

By what right he was present none of the Cabinet knew. Yet here he was, ensconced in the largest armchair, turning down all their suggestions out of hand. He didn't want Halifax, he opposed Henderson, and he wouldn't even consider Horace Wilson. All he wanted was Quill.

They argued with him. They reasoned with him. They pointed out that never in the history of Protocol had a policeman been sent to repatriate a monarch on the sole grounds that they had got drunk together. But Bulldog Brindle would not budge an inch.

An embarrassed flunkey appeared for the third time to tell the P.M. that dinner was now quite uneatable and that in five minutes Madame would be on her way to the Savoy Grill.

But this made no difference.

'What you won't understand,' said Brindle, 'is that King Hannibal likes Quill.'

The Minister for Home Defence smiled condescendingly. 'Great Britain,' he pointed out, 'is not in the habit of sending abroad diplomats who make themselves liked.'

'Quite,' said Brindle.

'Still,' said the P.M., 'it mightn't hurt.' He rubbed his chin again. He was remembering Munich.

CHAPTER

32

IT was Gala Night at the *Pantoufle Tricorne*.

There were garlands of paper roses and the wine cost double.

From the miniature stage a bunch of pink tulle, perched bewitchingly on roller-skates, blew kisses to the champagne tables, twirled a bit and blew some more.

'Enchanting,' said King Hannibal the Hothead. From his pocket he pulled a string of pearls and beckoned a waiter.

'For Mademoiselle,' he said, 'with my compliments.'

The blonde in black sitting beside him looked bitter.

'Come back,' said King Hannibal to the waiter.

He picked up the pearls, detached a ticket marked forty-five francs, and restored the necklace to the tray.

The blonde in black felt better.

'Jealous one,' said King Hannibal fondly.

There was a roll of drums.

A pair of adagio dancers in tinsel knickers bowed promisingly at the audience.

King Hannibal clapped.

The girl wore rosebuds. They were round the knickers.

King Hannibal clapped some more.

Breathing heavily the adagio dancers achieved a graceful pose.

'Plastique,' explained King Hannibal to the very bored blonde.

The adagio dancers flung each other about.

'Clever,' said King Hannibal, impressed.

He plunged into his pocket and pulled out a sapphire necklace.

'For Mademoiselle,' he said.

The waiter bowed.

'Are you sure you love me?' asked the blonde in black doubtfully.

'Madly,' said King Hannibal, his eyes glued to the stage.

The next turn was a *diseuse*. It wasn't the way she said it, it was what she said.

'An artist,' said King Hannibal. His French was excellent.

'Waiter,' he called.

A pair of ruby clips wended their way to the *diseuse*.

The blonde in black looked at her diamond bracelets. Doubt was beginning to dawn.

The lights went up. The Hawaiian band went into action. Recalled gigolos (so much more youthful than their younger colleagues now in the army) bowed invitingly to the dieting wives of fat husbands.

Soon the floor was crowded.

There was no doubt about it, the *Pantoufle Tricorne* was a great success. They could even afford to be particular who they let in.

'*Non*,' said the *maître d'hôtel* violently. '*Pas dans cette costume.*'

But Quill who had already had to cope with twenty-seven other *maîtres d'hôtels* had found the technique. He slipped a pound note into the trembling palm and, followed by an agog Sergeant Banner, strode in.

It was easy to spot King Hannibal. He was the only cavalier dancing cheek to cheek.

Relieved, Quill sat down at the monarch's table.

The music changed to a rhumba. King Hannibal was not so good at this. After a few out-of-time bottom-waggles he gave up and returned to his table.

He was delighted to see Quill in spite of his suit. The blonde in black was delighted to see Sergeant Banner. Profiles might set off a grande toilette but it was the watch-chained stomachs who wrote the cheques.

'*Il est gentil ton pappa*,' she told Quill while she beamed at Banner. '*Viens, mon Koko—dansons un peu.*' She stretched out her hands invitingly.

Sergeant Banner backed.

'Allay Koko,' said Quill. 'You heard.'

He wanted to get King Hannibal to himself.

'Enchanting little woman,' said King Hannibal, beaming fondly at the capering pair.

'Too bad you've got to leave her,' said Quill.

But King Hannibal was not attending. For the full import of Quill's visit had just dawned on him.

'By King Konrad the Continuous,' he cried. 'You've brought me the cheque!'

'No cheque,' said Quill sadly.

'Oh, well,' said King Hannibal luxuriously. 'As long as it's on the way . . . Waiter,' he beckoned. 'Another magnum.'

'You've done wonders,' said King Hannibal, pouring lavishly. 'You deserve a decoration.'

Quill wished King Hannibal wouldn't take so much for granted. Telling him about Clause 347/e was going to be like disappointing a small boy. Besides, he had an uneasy feeling that the monarch was about due to run out of ready cash and that he would be forced to foot the bill.

'Tell you what,' said King Hannibal, lost in gratitude. 'You shall have a decoration. I'll see to it myself.'

'Sire,' said Quill. 'I've got some bad news.'

'Impossible,' said King Hannibal waving it aside. 'Now what is it to be,' he mused.

'The order of the fatted calf,' suggested Quill, fed up.

'No, no,' said King Hannibal. 'That's got a bad colour scheme.' He brooded again.

There was a commotion in the bar. The dancers stopped and crowded round the entrance. A figure flew through the air, was caught by the commissionaire, and flung into the night.

King Hannibal beckoned a *maître d'hôtel*.

'*Qu'est-ce-qui-se-passe?*' he enquired.

The *maître d'hôtel* rushed over to find out. He came back swathed in reassuring smiles.

'It is nothing,' he said. 'One client has hit another—that is all.'

'But why?' pursued King Hannibal.

The *maître d'hôtel* smoothed the air with apologetic palms.

'*Comprends rien,*' he complained. '*Mais paraît qu'il n'était pas M'sieur Kalliputsky.*'

* * * * *

The blonde in black and Sergeant Banner came back. The blonde's orchids had come adrift but Sergeant Banner was just loosening up.

'Dansay,' said Sergeant Banner invitingly and cuddled up again.

'*Tu est riche?*' murmured the blonde. She was too exhausted to be subtle.

'Dansay,' repeated Sergeant Banner fondly.

At last he had found a bit of skirt who loved him for himself alone.

King Hannibal turned to Quill.

'You were saying,' he said politely.

Quill sweated in every pore. He swallowed. He took a deep breath. 'It's like this,' he said. . . .

* * * * *

The *maître d'hôtel* was in a black rage. Majesty had left the *Pantoufle Tricorne* in a hurry and his eccentrically dressed attaché had worked out the regulation ten per cent to a centime.

The Blonde was in a black rage too. That Profile had taken her poppa away and the bar-tender who knew everything had just been explaining her diamond bracelet.

The night clerk at King Hannibal's hotel was seriously alarmed. Never before had Majesty come home so early. Was Paris beginning to pall?

In the Royal Suite King Hannibal looked sadly at his silk pyjamas. He had exchanged the coils of a scented blonde for the toils of Adam Quill.

But Quill was right. He had to get to Insomnia quickly or he might never get to Paris again.

There were three telephones in the Royal Suite. The over-plugged telephone girl was attending to all of them.

'Get me the aerodrome,' snapped Quill.
'Get me a taxi,' urged Sergeant Banner.
'Get me Bauldstok!' roared King Hannibal.

CHAPTER

33

'WATERLOO Station,' said Herr Hitler, pointing with an inspired finger to a small black dot on a large map, 'shall retain its name. It is good to remind the French of their defeats.'

The Architect bowed. For the past three weeks he had been rebuilding London after Germany had won the war—on paper.

But the Fuehrer was frowning.

'Why,' he demanded, 'have you razed the National Theatre to the ground?'

'It was never completed,' explained the Architect.

'But of course,' said the Fuehrer. 'They feared we would bomb it.'

'Silly,' said the Architect.

'Prepare the plans at once,' ordered the Fuehrer hurriedly. 'They shall include a revolving stage, standing room for ten thousand, and a bomb-proof box. We will open,' he said, blushing slightly, 'with *The Merry Widow.*'

'A wonderful idea,' said the Architect grimly.

Himmler came into the room and mooched himself into a chair. The boys were getting out of hand.

'What is it this time?' asked the Fuehrer.

'Franzi,' said Himmler. 'He's lost his bloody aeroplane.'

'Send him another,' said the Fuehrer with a fine disregard for future war needs.

'Oh, no,' said Himmler. 'This time I'm going to collect him myself. Just called in,' he explained, 'to borrow your bullet-proof flying helmet.'

'Help yourself,' said the Fuehrer generously. 'I'm not stirring out for a few days.' He remembered something. 'And bring the man Schenk back with you.'

'H'm,' said Himmler dubiously.

'He is a bungler,' declared the Fuehrer, 'and he must answer for it to me. I will see him,' he promised ominously, 'at Berchtesgarten.'

'But will he come?' asked Himmler.

'I don't suppose so,' said the Architect and ran.

* * * * *

In an aeroplane speeding to Insomnia an exhausted Quill leant back in his seat.

He had been explaining the Insomnian Constitution to King Hannibal the Hothead.

* * * * *

At Downing Street the Cabinet was meeting again. Washington had just sent in another note of protest. The U.S.A., they pointed out, was resigned to having its mails opened, but they weren't going to stand for having their spelling Anglicized by the censors.

A corps of commissionaires guarded the door while a detective guarded the commissionaires.

'Now,' said the First Lord of the Admiralty rubbing his hands, 'let's get down to a good morning's work.'

A window broke.

A little man in a bowler hat crawled through it.

'You've got to listen to me,' he said from the window-sill.

'Go away,' said the Prime Minister annoyed. 'Shoo-shoo!'

But the First Lord of the Admiralty made a strange suggestion.

'Why not hear what he has to say?'

The Cabinet looked at him.

'It would save time in the long run,' argued the First Lord of the Admiralty.

The little man hopped down from the window-sill.

'You've got to listen to me,' he said and ducked.

But no commissionaire appeared to fling him out. Instead a row of attentive faces were waiting.

The little man took courage. He began to speak. He told them he had been educated at Manchester University. The Cabinet did not doubt this for a moment. He was an analytical chemist. The Cabinet reminded themselves that this was a reserved occupation. He was a specialist in Gardenium. The Cabinet sat up.

Gathering momentum, the little man became technical about Gardenium. He talked for forty minutes, growing more and more incomprehensible as he went on. But from the plethora of years of research, millions of test-tubes and complicated chemical equations, one grim fact began to emerge. Presently there was no doubt about it.

The palooka who bought Gardenium was buying a pup.

'But are you sure?' said the Minister for War palely.

The little man explained why he was so sure. He was incomprehensible.

The anxious Cabinet escorted the little man to Imperial Chemicals. The little man said something incomprehensible to the Head Chemist. The Head Chemist went haggard. They disappeared together into a laboratory.

Very worried, the Cabinet paced up and down the waiting-room.

The Head Chemist came back. He looked twenty years older.

'He's right,' he said.

The Cabinet looked twenty years older.

They took the little man back to Downing Street. They sat him next to the P.M. They asked him what to do next.

The little man told them diffidently that he did not know much about politics, but that if he were in their shoes he would stop Quill from signing the treaty.

The Cabinet saw his point. No time must be lost.

'Get in touch with Stung,' snapped the Prime Minister.

'And tell him to hurry,' said the First Lord of the Admiralty.

It took six trusted secretaries and half Scotland Yard to get in touch with Stung. He was at the Dover quarantine visiting his Labrador.

They rushed down a plane.

The little man fidgeted with his bowler.

'Do you need me any more?' he asked. 'My wife gets cross if I'm late for dinner.'

The P.M. nodded understandingly.

'You've done a great service to your country,' he said.

The little man looked uncomfortable. He was heard to mutter something about only doing his duty.

The Prime Minister reflected. The well-known genial expression returned to his face.

'England shall honour her son,' he said. 'The birthday list. A baronetcy. Who,' he asked, 'was your father?'

The little man put on his bowler hat and twirled his cane.

'Strube,' he said and vanished.

CHAPTER

34

A HIGH wind blew across Central Europe. In the early morning sky the clouds billowed and streaked like hags' skirts and witches' broomsticks.

Hecate threw three counters into space. Three aeroplanes were racing towards Insomnia.

Quill. Stung. Von Papen.

Von Papen shouted with exhilaration as the plane cut through the wind. The world was a cauldron and he was on top of it.

Foreboding hung over Quill. His bones told him he would not get the Gardenium.

And as for Mr Stung, he sat in his plane fondling the Labrador. Soon he would be reunited with General Jodpur.

*   *   *   *   *

'Come on,' said Quill.

He took King Hannibal and hurled him into the waiting car.

Through the streets. Up the steps of the Palace. Into the Council Chamber.

A gloating Bauldstok was smoothing out the treaty for disposing of eighty per cent of the world's Gardenium.

'Welcome home, Your Majesty,' he said smugly. 'We are very pleased to have you back.'

'So!' said King Hannibal.

Bauldstok held out the parchment. 'We have just finished signing this treaty,' he said.

Quill sat down heavily.

'Germany,' said Bauldstok, 'gets the Gardenium.'

'And what do we get?' asked King Hannibal.

For just a fraction of a second Bauldstok hesitated. 'One hundred thousand tons of aspirin,' he announced.

King Hannibal sat down heavily.

'I shall need them,' he said.

Through the streets, up the steps of the Palace, and into the Council Chamber rushed the Labrador.

Mr Stung was only just behind.

'Don't sign,' he panted.

Quill looked up.

'Don't sign the treaty,' pleaded Mr Stung. 'Please tell me you haven't signed yet. . . .'

'I haven't,' said Quill, hardly daring to hope.

'Thank God,' said Mr Stung. He sat down heavily. 'The stuff's no good—'pon my soul, it isn't.'

'It stinks,' said the Labrador and vanished.